A Wizard Alone

Diane Duane
AR B.L.: 5.8
Points: 13.0   UG

A
Wizard
Alone

DIANE DUANE

A
Wizard
Alone

Harcourt, Inc.
San Diego   New York   London

Requests for permission to make copies of any part
of the work should be mailed to the following address:
Permissions Department, Harcourt, Inc.,
6277 Sea Harbor Drive, Orlando, Florida 32887-6777.

www.HarcourtBooks.com

Library of Congress Cataloging-in-Publication Data
Duane, Diane.
A wizard alone/Diane Duane.
p. cm.—(Young wizards series; 6)
Summary: While Nita mourns her mother's death, teenage wizard
Kit and his dog, Ponch, set out to find a young autistic boy who
vanished in the middle of his Ordeal, pursued by the Lone Power.
[1. Wizards—Fiction. 2. Autism—Fiction. 3. Fantasy.]
I. Title.
PZ7.D84915Wj 2002
[Fic]—dc21 2002007638
ISBN 0-15-204562-7

Text set in Stempel Garamond
Design by Trina Stahl

First edition
A C E G H F D B

Printed in the United States of America

For all the friends from Payne Whitney

Contents

Life
more than just being alive
(and worth the pain)

but hurts:
        fix it
grows:
        keep it growing

wants to stop:
        remind
        check / don't hurt
        be sure!

One's watching:
get it right!
        later it all works out,
        honest

meantime,
make it work
now
(because now
is all you ever get:
now *is*)

—The Wizard's Oath,
        excerpt from a private recension

Footsteps in the snow
suggest where you have been,
point where you were going:
  but where they suddenly vanish,
  never dismiss the possibility
  of flight. . . .

—*Book of Night with Moon, xi, v.3*

A
Wizard
Alone

Consultations

IN A LIVING ROOM of a suburban house on Long Island, a wizard sat with a TV remote control in his hand, and an annoyed expression on his face. "Come on," he said to the remote. "Don't give me grief."

The TV showed him a blue screen and nothing more.

Kit Rodriguez sighed. "All right," he said, "we're on the record now. You made me do this." He reached for his wizard's manual on the sofa next to him, paged through it to its hardware section—which had been getting thicker by the minute this afternoon—found one page in particular, and keyed into the remote a series of characters that the designers of both the remote and the TV would have found unusual.

The screen stayed mostly blue, but the nature of the white characters on it changed. Until now they had been words in the Roman alphabet. Now they changed to characters in a graceful and curly cursive, the written form of the wizardly Speech. At the top of the screen they showed the local time and the date expressed as a Julian day, that being the Earth-based system most closely akin to what the manual's managers used to express time. In the middle of the blue screen appeared a single word:

WON'T.

Kit let out a long breath of exasperation. "Oh, come on," he said in the Speech. "Why not?"

The screen remained blue, staring at him mulishly. Kit wondered what he'd done to deserve this. "It can't be that bad," he said. "You two even have the same version number."

VERSIONS AREN'T EVERYTHING!

Kit rubbed his eyes.

"I thought a six-year-old child was supposed to be able to program one of these things," said a voice from the next room.

"*I* sure feel like a six-year-old at the moment," Kit muttered. "It would work out about the same."

Kit's father wandered in and stood there staring at the TV. Not being a wizard himself, he couldn't see the Speech written there, and wouldn't have been able to make sense of it if he had, but he could see the blue screen well enough. "So what's the problem?"

"It looks like they hate each other," Kit said.

His father made a rueful face. "Software issues," he said. He was a pressman for one of the bigger newspapers on the Island, and in the process of the company converting from hot lead to electronic and laser printing, he had learned more than most people cared to know about the problems of converting from truly hard "hardware" to the computer kind.

"Nope," Kit said. "I wish it were that simple."

"What is it, then?"

Kit shook his head. Once upon a time, not so long ago, getting mechanical things to see things his way had been Kit's daily stock-in-trade. Now everything seemed to be getting more complex by the day. "*Issues* they've got, all right," he said. "I'm not sure they make sense to me yet."

His father squeezed his shoulder. "Give it time, son," he said. "You're a *brujo;* nothing can withstand your power."

"Nothing that's not made of silicon, anyway," Kit said.

His father rolled his eyes. "Tell me all about it," he said, and went away.

Kit sat there staring at the blue screen, trying to sort through the different strategies he'd tried so far, determining which ones hadn't worked, which ones had worked a little bit, and which ones had seemed to be working just fine until without warning they crashed and burned. The manual for the new remote said that the new DVD player was supposed to look for channels on the TV once they were plugged into each other, but the remote and the DVD player didn't even want to acknowledge each other's existence so far, let alone exchange information. Neither the DVD's manual nor the remote's was any help. The two pieces of equipment both came from the same company, they were both made in the same year and, as far as Kit could tell, in the same place. But when he listened to them with a wizard's ear, he heard them singing two different songs—in ferocious rivalry—and making rude noises at each other during the pauses, when they thought no one was listening.

"Come on, you guys," he said in the Speech. "All I'm asking for here is a little cooperation—"

"No surrender!" shouted the remote.

"Death before dishonor!" shouted the DVD player.

Kit covered his eyes and let out a long, frustrated breath.

From the kitchen came a sudden silence, something that was as arresting to Kit as a sudden noise, and that made him look up in alarm. His mother had been cooking. Indeed, she was making her *arroz con pollo,* a dinner that visiting heads of state would consider themselves lucky to eat. When without warning it got quiet in the kitchen in the middle of that process, Kit reacted as he would have if he'd heard someone say, "Oops!" during the countdown toward a space shuttle launch: with held breath and intense attention.

"Honey?" Kit's mom said.

"What, Mama?"

"The dog says he wants to know what's the meaning of life."

Kit rubbed his forehead, finding himself tempted to hide his eyes. "Give him a dog biscuit and tell him it's an allegory," Kit said.

"What, *life*?"

"No, the biscuit!"

"Oh, good. You had me worried there for a moment."

Kit's mother's sense of humor tended toward the dry, and the dryness sounded like it was set at about medium at the moment, which was just as well. His mother was still in the process of getting used to his wizardry. Kit went back to trying to talk sense into the remote and the DVD player. The DVD player blued the TV's screen out again, pointedly turning its attention elsewhere.

"Come on, just give each other a chance."

"Talk to *that* thing? You must have a chip loose."

"Like I would listen!"

"Hah! You're a tool, nothing but a tool! *I* entertain!"

"Oh yeah? Let's see how well you entertain when *I* turn you off like a light!"

Kit rolled his eyes. "Listen to me, you two! You can't get hung up on the active-role-passive-role thing. They're both just fine, and there's more to life—"

"Like what?!"

Kit's mama came drifting in and looked over Kit's shoulder as he continued to speak passionately to the remote and the DVD player about the importance of cooperation and teamwork, the need not to feel diminished by acting, however briefly, as part of a whole. But the remote refused to do anything further, and the screen stayed blue. Kit started to think he must be turning that color in the face.

"It sounds like escargot," his mother said, leaning her short, round self over him to look at the TV.

"What?"

"Sorry. Esperanto. I don't know why the word for snails always comes out first."

Kit looked at his mother with some interest. "You can hear it?" he said. It was moderately unusual for nonwizards to hear the Speech at all. When they did, they tended to hear it as the language they spoke themselves—but because the Speech contained and informed all languages, being the seed from which they grew, this was to be expected.

"I hear it a little," his mother said. "Like someone talking in the next room. Which it was . . ."

"I wonder if the wizardry comes from your side of the family," Kit said.

His mother's broad and pretty face suddenly acquired a nervous quality. "Uh-oh, the chicken broth," she said, and took herself back to the kitchen.

"What about Ponch?" Kit said.

"He ate the dog biscuit," his mother said after a moment.

"And he didn't ask you any more philosophical stuff?"

"He went out. I think he had a date with a biological function."

Kit smirked, though he turned his face so she wouldn't see it if she came back in. His mother's work as a nurse expressed itself at home in two ways: either detailed and concrete descriptions of things you'd never thought about before and (afterward) desperately never wanted to think about again, or shy evasions regarding very basic physical operations that you'd think wouldn't upset a six-year-old. Ponch's business seemed mostly to elicit the second response in Kit's mama, an effect that usually made Kit laugh.

At the moment he just felt too tired. Kit paused in his cheerleading and went rummaging through the paperwork on the floor for the DVD's and remote's manuals. *We're in trouble when even a remote control has its own manual,* he thought. But if a wizard with a bent toward mechanical things couldn't get this kind of very basic problem sorted out, then there really *would* be trouble.

He spent a few moments with the manuals, ignoring the catcalls and jeers that the recalcitrant pieces of equipment were trading. Then abruptly Kit realized, listening, that the DVD *did* have a slightly different accent than the remote and the TV. *Now, I wonder,* he thought, and went carefully through the DVD's manual to see whether the manufacturer actually had made all the main parts itself.

The manual said nothing about this, being written in a broken English that assumed the system was, indeed, being assembled by the proverbial six-year-old. Resigned, Kit picked up the remote again, which immediately began shouting abuse at him. At first he was relieved that this was inaudible to everybody else, but the DVD chose that moment to take control of the entertainment system's speakers and start shouting back.

"Oooh, what a nasty mouth," said his sister Carmela as she walked through the living room, wearing her usual uniform of floppy jeans and huge floppy T-shirt, and holding a wireless phone in her hand. She had been studying Japanese for some months, mostly via watching anime, and had now graduated to an actual language course—though what she chiefly seemed interested in were what their father wryly called "the scurrilities." *"Bakka aho kikai, bakka-bakka!"*

Kit was inclined to agree. He spent an annoying couple of moments searching for the volume control on the DVD—the remote was too busy doing its own shouting to be of any use. Finally he got the DVD to shut up, then once again punched a series of characters into the remote to get a look at the details on the DVD's core processor.

"Aha," Kit said to himself. The processor wasn't made by the company that owned the brand. He had a look at the same information for the remote. It also used the same processor, but it had been resold to the brand-name company by still another company.

"Now look at that!" Kit said. "You have the same processors. You aren't really from different companies at all. You're long-lost brothers. Isn't that nice? And look at you, fighting over nothing! She's right, you *are* idiots. Now I want you guys to handshake and make up."

There was first a shocked silence, then some muttering and grumbling about unbearable insults and who owed whom an apology. "You both do," Kit said. "You were very disrespectful to each other. Now get on with it, and then settle down to work. You'll have a great time. The new cable package has all these great channels."

Reluctantly, they did it. About ten minutes later the DVD began sorting through and classifying the channels it found on the TV. "Thank you, guys," Kit said, taking a few moments to tidy up the paperwork scattered all over the floor, while thinking longingly of the oncoming generation of wireless electronics that would all communicate seamlessly and effortlessly with one another. "See, that wasn't so bad. But someday all this will be so much simpler," Kit said, patting the top of the DVD player.

"No, it won't," the remote control said darkly.

Kit rolled his eyes and decided to let the distant unborn future of electronics fend for itself. "*You* just behave," he said to the remote, "or you're gonna wind up in the Cuisinart."

He walked out of the living room, ignoring the indignant shrieks of wounded ego from the remote. This had been only the latest episode in a series of almost constant excitements lately, which had begun when his dad broke down after years of resistance and decided to get a full-size entertainment center. It was going to be wonderful when everything was installed and everything worked. But in the meantime, Kit had become resigned to having a lot of learning experiences.

From the back door at the far side of the kitchen came a scratching noise: his dog letting the world know he wanted to come back in. The scratching stopped as the door opened. Kit turned to his pop, who had just come into the dining room again, and handed him the remote. "I think it's fixed now," he said. "Just do this from now on: Instead of using this button to bring the system up, the one the manual tells you to, press this, and then this." He showed his pop how to do it.

"Okay. But why?"

"They may not remember the little talking-to I just gave them—it depends on how the system resets when you turn it off. This should remind them... I hard-wired it in."

"What was the problem?"

"Something cultural."

"Between the remote and the DVD player?! But they're both Japanese."

"Looks like it's more complicated than that." There seemed to be no point in suggesting to his pop that the universal remote and the DVD were both unsatisfied with their active or passive modes. Apparently doing what you had been built to do was a prospect no more popular among machines than it was among living things. Everything had its own ideas about what it really should be doing in the world, and the more memory you installed in the hardware, the more ideas it seemed to get.

Kit realized how thirsty all this talking to machinery had made him. He went to the fridge and rummaged around to see if there was some of his mom's iced tea in there. There wasn't, only a can of the lemon soft drink that Nita particularly liked and that his mom kept for her.

The sight of it made Kit briefly uncomfortable. But neither wizardry nor friendship was exclusively about comfort. He took the lemon fizz out, popped the can's top, and took a long swig. *Neets?* he said silently.

Yeah, she said in his mind.

There wasn't much enthusiasm there, but there hadn't been much enthusiasm in her about anything for some weeks. At least it wasn't as bad for her now as it had been right after her mother's funeral. But clearly Kit wondered whether the bitter pain she'd been in then was, in its way, healthier than her current gray, dull tone of mind, like an overcast that showed no signs of lifting. Then he immediately felt guilty for even being tempted to play psychiatrist. She had a right to grieve at whatever speed was right for her.

Busy today?

Not really.

Kit waited. Normally Nita would now come forth with at least some explanation of what "not really" involved. But she wasn't anything like normal right now, and no explanation came—just that sense of weariness, the same tired *why-bother* feeling that kept rearing up at the back of Kit's mind. Whether he was catching it directly from her via their private channels of communication, or whether it was something of his own, he wasn't sure. It wasn't as if *he* didn't miss Nita's mother, too.

I finished fixing the TV, Kit said, determined to keep the conversation going, no matter how uncomfortable it made him. Someone around here had to try to keep at least the appearance of normalcy going. *Now I'm bored again . . . and I want to stay that way for a while. Wanna go to the moon?*

There was a pause. *No,* Nita said. *Thanks. I just don't feel up to it today.* And there it was, the sudden hot feeling of eyes filling with tears, without warning; and Nita frowning, clenching her eyes shut, rather helplessly, unable to stop it, determined to stop it. *You go ahead. Thanks, though.*

She turned away in thought, breaking off the silent communication between them. Kit found that he, too, was scowling against the pain, and he let out a long breath of aggravation at his own helplessness. *Why is it so embarrassing to be sad?* he thought, annoyed. *And not just for me.* Nita's overwhelming pain embarrassed her as badly as it did him, so Kit had to be careful not to "notice" it. Yet there wasn't anything he seemed able to do for her at the moment. He felt like an idiot—unable to think of anything useful to say, and just as idiotic when he was tempted to keep saying the same things over and over: "It'll pass," "You'll come out of it eventually." They all sounded heartless and stupid. *And besides, how quick would* I *come out of it if it were* my *mama who died?*

Kit let out a long breath. There was nothing to do but keep letting Nita know that he was there, one day at a time. So he'd taken care of today's responsibility.

The phone rang, mercifully relieving Kit of his guilt for thinking that doing the right thing for his best friend was some kind of awful burden.

"*IgotitIgotitIgotit!*" Carmela shrieked from upstairs. "*HolaMiguelque*—" A pause. "Oh. Sorry. *Kit!!*"

"What?"

"*Tomás El Jefe.*"

"Oh." Kit went to the extension phone in the kitchen. His mother, deep in the business of deboning a chicken, glanced at him as he passed and said nothing, but her smile had a little edge of ruefulness about it. She was still getting her head around the concept that a man she routinely saw at hospital fund-raisers, a successful writer for commercial television and a pillar of the community, was also one of two Senior wizards for the New York metropolitan area. Ponch, Kit's big black Labrador-cum-Border-collie-cum-whatever, was now lying on the floor with his head down on his paws, carefully watching every move Kit's mother made that had anything to do with the chicken. As Kit stepped over him, the dog spared him no more than an upward glance, then turned his attention straight back to the food.

Kit smiled slightly and picked up the phone. His sister was saying, "And so then I told him— Oh, *finally*! Kit, don't hog the line; I'm expecting a call. Why can't you two just do the magic telepathy thing like you do with Nita? It'd be cheaper!"

"*Vamos,*" Kit said, trying not to sound too severe.

"Bye, sweetie," Tom Swale said on the other end.

"Bye-bye, Mr. Tom," Carmela said, and hung up the upstairs phone.

Kit grinned. " 'Magic telepathy,' " he said. "Like she cares that much about the phone bill."

Tom laughed. "Explaining the differences of communications between you and me and you and Nita might make more trouble than it's worth," he said. "Better let her get away with it just this once. Am I interrupting anything?"

"I just finished dealing with a hardware conflict," Kit said, "but it's handled now, I think. What's up?"

"I wouldn't mind a consultation, if you have the time."

He wants a consultation from me? *That's a new one.* "Sure," Kit said. "No problem. I'll be right over."

"Thanks."

Kit hung up, and saw the look his mother was giving him. "When's it going to be ready, Mama?" he said. "I won't be late. Not too late, anyway."

"About six. It doesn't matter if you're a little late... It'll keep." She gave him a warning look. "You're not going anywhere sudden, are you?" This had become her code phrase for Kit leaving on wizardly business.

"Nope," Kit said. "Tom just needs some advice, it looks like."

His father wandered back into the kitchen. "The TV working okay now?" Kit said.

"Working?" his pop said. "Well, yeah. But possibly not the way the manufacturer intended."

Kit looked at his pop, uncomprehending. His father went back into the living room. Kit followed.

Where the TV normally would have shown a channel number, the screen was now displaying the number 0000566478. The picture seemed to be of a piece of furniture that looked rather like a set of chrome parallel bars. From the bars hung a creature with quite a few tentacles and many stalky eyes, which were *not* in the usual places. The creature was talking fast and loud in a voice like a fire engine's siren, while waving around a large, shiny object that might have been an eggbeater, except that, in Kit's experience, eggbeaters didn't usually have pulse lasers built into them. Characters flashed on the screen, both in the Speech and in other languages. Kit stood and looked at this with complete astonishment. His father, next to him, was doing the same.

"You didn't hack into that new pay-per-view system, did you?" his father said. "I don't want the cops in here."

"No way," Kit said, picking up the remote and looking at it accusingly. The remote sat there in his hand as undemonstratively as any genuinely inanimate object might...except that Kit was less certain than ever that there really *were* any such things as inanimate objects.

He shook the remote to see if anything rattled. Nothing did. "I told you to behave," he said in the Speech.

"But not like *what*," the remote said in a sanctimonious tone.

His father was still watching the creature on the parallel bars, which pointed the laser eggbeater at what looked like a nearby abstract sculpture. This vanished in a flare of actinic green light, leaving Kit uneasily wondering what kind of sculpture screamed. "Nice special effects," Kit's father said, though he sounded a little dubious. "Almost too realistic."

"It's not special effects, Pop," Kit said. "It's some other planet's cable." He hit the reveal control on the remote, but nothing was revealed except, at the bottom of the screen, many more strings of characters flashing on and off in various colors. "Shopping channel, looks like." Kit handed the remote back to his father.

"This is a *shopping* channel?" his pop said.

Kit headed for the coat hooks by the kitchen door and pulled his parka off one of them. "Popi, I've got to get to Tom's. I'll be back pretty soon. It's all right to look at it, but if any phone numbers that you can read appear—do me a big favor, okay? *Don't order anything!*"

Kit opened the back door. Ponch threw one last longing look at what Kit's mama was doing with the chicken, then threw himself past Kit, hitting the screen door with a *bang!* and flying out into the driveway.

Kit followed him. At the driveway's end, he paused, looking up briefly. It was almost dark already; the bare branches of the maples were showing black against an indigo sky. January was too new for any lengthening of days to be perceptible yet, and the shortness of the daylight hours was depressing. But at least the holidays were over. Kit could hardly remember a year when he'd been less interested in them. For his own family's sake, he'd done his best to act as if he was, but his heart hadn't been in the celebrations, or the presents. He hadn't been able to stop thinking about the one present Nita most desperately wanted, one that not even the Powers That Be could give her.

Kit sighed and looked down the street. Ponch was down there near curbside in the rapidly falling dark, saluting one of the neighbor's trees. "Back this way, please?" he said, and waited until Ponch was finished and came galloping back up the street toward him.

Kit made his way into the backyard again, with

Ponch bouncing along beside him, wagging his tail. "Where did the 'meaning of life' thing come from all of a sudden?" Kit said.

I heard you ask about it, Ponch said.

The question had, indeed, come up once or twice recently in the course of business, around the time Ponch started talking regularly. "So?" Kit said, as they made their way past the beat-up birdbath into the tangle of sassafras at the back of the yard, where they were out of sight of the houses on either side. "Come to any conclusions?"

Just that your mama's easy to shake down for dog biscuits.

Kit grinned. "You didn't need to start talking to her to find that out," he said. He reached into his pocket, felt around for the "zipper" in it that facilitated access to the alternate space where he kept some of his spells ready, and pulled one out—a long chain of strung-together words in the Speech that glowed a very faint blue in the swiftly falling darkness. "I'd keep it in the family, though," Kit said to Ponch. "Don't start asking strangers complicated philosophical questions...It'll confuse them."

It may be too late, Ponch said.

Kit wondered what that was supposed to mean, then shrugged. He dropped the spell-chain to the ground around them in a circle. The transit wizardry knotted itself together at the ends in the figure-eight wizard's knot, and from it a brief shimmering curtain of light went up and blanked the night away as displaced air went *thump!* and Kit's ears popped. A moment later he and Ponch were standing together in Tom's backyard, behind the high privet hedge blocking the view from Tom's neighbors' houses. Across the patio, lights were on in the house, and banging noises were coming from the kitchen.

Kit and Ponch made their way past the stucco koi pond toward the sliding porch doors, Ponch shaking his head emphatically. "Are your ears bothering you?" Kit said, as the sound of barking came from further inside the house.

Only lately, Ponch said.

"Sorry. I'll have a look at the spell later." Kit pushed the patio door to one side and went into Tom's dining room. That space flowed into the living room area, where Tom's desk sat in a corner, past the sofas and the entertainment center. But at the moment all the action was in the kitchen, off to the left, where big, dark-haired Carl, his fellow Advisory wizard, was doing something to the strip lighting that ran below the upper kitchen cupboards. Tom was leaning against the refrigerator, holding a cup of coffee, with the expression of a man who wants nothing to do with whatever's happening.

"Hi, Kit," he said, as Ponch ran through the kitchen and out the other side, heading toward the bedrooms, where the sheepdogs Annie and Monty were barking at something. "Coke?"

"Yeah, thanks." Kit sat down at the table and watched Carl, who was bent over sideways under the upper cupboards and making faces.

"I told him to call an expert," Tom said as he fished a can of Coke out of the refrigerator and sat down with Kit at the dining room table, where a number of volumes of the Senior version of the wizard's manual were piled up.

"We're expert enough to change the laws of physics temporarily," Carl muttered. "How hard can wiring be?"

With a *clunk!* all the lights in the house went out.

Carl moaned. Kit could just see Tom make a flicking motion with one finger at the circuit-breaker box near the kitchen door, and the lights came back on again. "You should stick to physics," Tom said.

"Just one more time," Carl said, and went down the stairs to the basement.

"This will be the sixth 'one more time' in the past two hours," Tom said. "I'm hoping he'll see sense before he blows up the transformer at the end of the street. Or maybe the local power station."

"I *heard* that!" said the voice from the basement.

Kit snickered, but not too loudly.

"Anyway," Tom said, "thanks for coming over. Briefly, one of our wizards is missing, and I'd like you to look into it."

This was a new one on Kit. "Missing? Anybody I know?"

"Hard for me to tell. Here's the listing." Tom pulled down the topmost manual and opened it; the pages riffled themselves to a spot he had bookmarked. It was a page in the master wizards' address listing for the New

York area, and one block of information glowed a soft rose. Kit leaned over to look at it. In the Speech, it said:

McALLISTER, Darryl
18355 Hempstead Turnpike
Baldwin, NY 11568
(516) 555-7384
power rating: 5.6 +/− .3
status: on Ordeal
initiation: 4777598.3
completion:
duration to present date: 90.3
resolution: nil

Kit stared at the duration figure for a moment: There was something wrong with it. "That doesn't look right," he said at last. "Did a decimal point get misplaced or something? That looks like months."

"It *is* months," Tom said. "Just a whisker over three, which is why it came up for attention today. The manual normally flags such extended Ordeals to be audited by a Senior."

"I thought nobody was allowed to interfere with a wizard's Ordeal," Kit said. "It's what determines whether you ought to be a wizard in the first place. Whether you can run into the Lone Power and survive…"

"Normally that's true," Tom said. "But Ordeals aren't always so clear-cut; they do sometimes go wrong. A resolution can get delayed somehow, or there can be local interference that keeps the resolution from happening. An area's Seniors are allowed a certain amount of information about Ordeals among probationary wizards who'd be in their catchment area if things went right, especially if something goes wrong in a specific sort of way—a stuck Ordeal, or a contaminated one. We have some latitude to step in and try to kick that Ordeal back into operation again. While interfering as little as possible."

Kit nodded, glancing to one side as Carl came up from the basement with a very large roll of duct tape. "Ah," Tom said. "The substance that binds the universe together."

"We'll see," Carl said, and bent himself over sideways again.

"It's a brute force solution," Tom said. "Inelegant. The phone's right there!"

Carl ignored him and started doing something with the duct tape.

"So now we come to this kid," Tom said, indicating the highlighted listing again.

Clunk! went the circuit breaker, and the house went dark again; only the text on the page in front of them continued to glow, while in the back bedroom the dogs paused, then went on barking. Tom gestured once more at the breaker box, and the lights came on. "It's not like he's been physically absent from the area for all this time, as far as I can tell," Tom said. "If he were, certainly there would have been something about it in the news, and there's been nothing. But at the same time, this is not a normal duration for a human Ordeal. We need to find out what's going on, but quietly. Do you or Nita know him well enough to look in on him and see what's happening? Or do you know anyone who does?"

Kit shook his head. "I can check with Neets, but she's sure never mentioned him to me," Kit said. "Why bring me in on this, though? You're a Senior; you'd probably be able to tell a lot better than I can what's going on with him."

"Well," Tom said, "let's put it this way. How come you chose to do a direct transit here rather than just walk over and knock on the front door?"

Kit was briefly surprised that Tom would bother asking so obvious a question. "It's not exactly like you've got any kids of your own," he said. "And if the neighbors keep seeing kids wandering in and out of here every five minutes—"

"Say no more," Tom said. "We're on the same wave-length. It's just another facet of the way wizards have to behave in our culture. Attracting attention to your-self is usually unwise. In this particular situation, if people start noticing *you* in the neighborhood around the object of our mutual interest, they won't think too much about it—it's not far enough from your own stamping grounds to provoke suspicion. Whereas if Carl or I went to investigate personally, notice might be taken. This kind of initial fact-finding is better suited to a wizard of your age."

"Besides," Carl said, peering up at the bottom of the cupboard, "lately you've been evincing a certain talent for finding things."

"Well, Ponch has," Kit said.

"I'm not sure he'd be producing these results with-out you as part of the team," Carl said, as he applied duct tape liberally to the cupboard's underside. "Let's not get overly tangled up in details at the moment."

"From a man in your position, that has a hollow ring," Tom said.

"Sure, go ahead, mock me in my torment."

"Anyway, are you willing?" Tom said. "To go over there during the next couple of days? See what the kid's doing, physically, talk to him if you can, try to get a sense of what his state of mind is."

"Sure," Kit said. "Am I allowed to tell him I'm a wizard, if he asks?"

"I'll leave that up to you," Tom said. "Normally I would suggest that you try to avoid it if possible. You don't want to take the chance of altering his perception of his Ordeal, maybe even making him think you're supposed to be involved in it somehow. But if you can come by any sense of why his Ordeal's taking him so long, I'd be glad to hear it."

Carl straightened up. "Okay," he said. The strip lights under the cupboards were now actually on. He looked at the light they cast on the counter with some satisfaction. "At least now I'm going to be able to see what I'm cooking without getting blinded." He went over to the wall, turned the dimmer switch.

Clunk!

"I could stop by the supermarket on the way home and get you some candles," Kit said as he got up. "Fire still works."

"Very funny," Carl said. "I hope that someday, when duct tape is sticking to *your* gray hairs—"

"Kit," Tom said, "ignore the whimpering from the sidelines for the moment...Be careful not to get sucked in. This youngster may seem very, very stuck when you meet him, and you've got to resist the temptation to give him help he doesn't need. You could end up endangering yourself, not to mention altering the focus of his Ordeal...which could make him fail it. Or worse."

"I'll watch out."

"Okay. Go see what you can find out. You may want to leave your manual on record when you're talking to him; it may pick up some nuance that you miss at first." He paused. "Listen to that," he said.

Kit listened, puzzled. "I don't hear anything."

"What the master of sarcasm over there means is that the dogs have stopped barking," Carl said. "They've been having some kind of metaphysical discussion for days now. And they're loud about it."

"Have they been asking you about the meaning of life?" Kit said.

Both Tom and Carl gave Kit a look. "Uh, yes," Tom said.

Kit covered his face. "It's my fault," he said. "A new kind of blackmail, and I know where they got it. They probably want dog biscuits."

"New tactic," Tom said wearily, getting up. "Old problem. I'll bear it in mind."

Ponch came lolloping back into the dining room. Kit got up, too. "I'll get in touch as soon as I find anything out," Kit said, opening the patio door to let Ponch out.

"Thanks, fella," Tom said. *Dai stihó.*

"Yeah, you go well, too. Well enough not to electrocute somebody, anyway!"

They headed back the way they'd come, Kit pausing briefly in Tom's backyard with the spell-chain in his hands to adjust the variable that determined how much and how fast the air displaced around their transiting mass when they "came out of nowhere." Ponch was bouncing up and down around him, making it difficult for Kit to remember where in the structure of the spell the variable actually was. "Would you sit *down*?" he said under his breath to Ponch, while passing the softly glowing chain of words through his hands until the little barbed bit sticking out from the variable scratched his skin. Kit held the word up in front of his eyes, squinting at it like someone threading a needle, and managed to catch the delicate outward-hooked tail of the spell character between finger and thumb.

Chicken! Ponch was shouting in his head. *Hurry up! It's chicken!*

"And philosophy goes right out the window, huh?" Kit said as he twiddled the mass-displacement variable; it shaded down from a bright blue to a darker one. "You're a bad influence on those guys, you know that?"

Me? Never. Chicken!

"Right," Kit said, folding the variable's tail back in and shaking the spell through a quick sine wave to unkink it. It fell smoothly to the ground and knotted itself. "Now sit down or you're gonna wind up in two different places, and not in one piece!"

Ponch sat down but still managed to bounce a little.

The spell flared up, its blue a little darker this time. A second later they were standing in Kit's backyard again, without the ear-popping effect this time, and the light faded out of the spell.

"Better?" Kit said, winding the spell-chain up and sticking it back in his "pocket."

It's fine. I'm hungry! Ponch shouted, and ran for the house.

Kit breathed out, feeling hungry, too, and tired. This, at least, had nothing to do with the emotional climate. No wizardry is without its price, and this was the normal reaction to a transit wizardry: a small but significant deduction from Kit's personal energy supply. It was one of the reasons why, as they got older, a lot of wizards spent as much time as they could making sure they were in decent physical shape.

Kit went after Ponch and was surprised not to see his mama and pop eating in the kitchen, as they usually did. He wandered into the living room and found them there on the sofa. Kit's pop was finishing the last of what must have been a second helping of *arroz con pollo*, watching the TV screen, while Kit's mama sat next to him, cross-legged, punching the scan button on the remote and looking at the TV with an expression of extreme bemusement.

His father looked up. "Five billion channels and nothing on," he said in a kind of horrified astonishment.

"The story of modern life," Kit said, resigned, and headed to the kitchen to get himself a plate. "Just because a species is more scientifically advanced than us doesn't mean its TV is any better, believe me."

His father absorbed this assessment with a thoughtful look. "Maybe that should make me feel better. I'll let you know. What did Tom have to say?"

"It's complicated," Kit said. "A missing persons case."

"And are *you* likely to go missing?" his pop said.

"Not right away," Kit said. "I have to do some detective work here first."

"Oh, my god," Kit's mama said, "what are they *doing*?"

Anything that could so seriously gross out Kit's mama, the nurse, was worth a look. Kit grabbed a plate and ducked back into the living room, looked at the writhing, thrashing, stridently colored image for a moment, then took the remote away from his mama and punched it for subtitles. "Oh, that's what I thought," he said, after spending about ten seconds reading them. "It's a soap."

"Not of any brand *I* recognize," his mother said. She looked scandalized.

"It's real basic, Mama," Kit said. "Boy meets girl meets thing meets other thing. Boy loses girl loses other thing finds thing. Boy loses thing gets girl loses thing. Happily ever after..." He tossed the remote back to his mother.

She fielded it badly as she studied the screen for any signs of boys or girls, and looked like she was having trouble finding any, though there were plenty of "things." " 'Basic,' you said?"

"Old, old story, Mama. You should see some of these guys' literature. Shakespeare would have loved it." Kit considered that briefly: His lit class had been doing the late Shakespeare comedies, and suddenly a whole set of opportunities opened out before him. "Just imagine *A Midsummer Night's Dream* with ten or twelve extra genders..."

His mother raised her eyebrows, gave up on the soap, and started changing channels again. "Doesn't this thing have an online channel guide?" she said.

"I'll have a look at it later and let you know," Kit said.

He saw the look she threw at his pop. "Are there cooking channels?"

"Oh, yeah." Then Kit paused, having a horrible thought. "On second thought, it might be smarter to avoid those. Some of them feature humans...and not as the cooks."

The look on his mother's face made Kit wish he'd kept quiet. She began changing channels with unusual speed. Kit raised his eyebrows and went back into the kitchen with the plate.

He was spooning out rice when his dad came back in and began rooting around in the silverware drawer in an aimless way that didn't fool Kit for a moment. "Son," he said, very quietly, "is there *really* a cooking channel, uh, 'about' us?"

"Pop, there's lots of them."

His father looked shocked. "But how is something like that *permitted*?!"

Kit shrugged. "You go where you shouldn't go," Kit said, and couldn't help grinning, "you find out stuff you shouldn't find out. Like how you taste in a sweet-and-sour sauce with galingale. The universe is full of little surprises."

"I always have the feeling that there's a lot about this wizardry you're not telling me," his father said. "Sometimes it worries me. Then come times like this when I'm horribly glad about my ignorance. Just don't go places where you shouldn't go, okay?"

"I try to avoid it," Kit said. "Is it okay with you if I go to Baldwin in the next couple of days, though?"

His pop looked surprised. "Baldwin? No problem with that."

"Thanks."

Kit brought his plate into the living room, where he sat down on the floor and watched his mother change channels one more time. "Well, *that's* pretty," she said, sounding relieved.

Kit glanced up at the screen, chewing. "Uh, Mama," he said, "I'm probably too young to be watching anything that explicit."

Her eyes widened. "But, honey, it's just a big cloud of gas, or smoke, or . . ." She stopped, her eyes widening even more, then changed the channel six times in a row without stopping.

Kit grinned and turned his attention back to the chicken.

Investigations

CIRCUSES—EVEN JUST the thought of them—had always scared Nita when she was little. Later on, she had felt that the fear was ridiculous. Circuses were supposed to be so much fun for small children—all the sparkle, glitter, and noise, the processions of elephants parading along trunk-by-tail, the blare of brass music, the daring acrobats and tumblers, the goofy clowns.

Yet it hadn't worked that way for Nita the first time she actually went to one. Where the other kids in the audience had laughed and clapped, she sat amid all the raucous noise feeling terribly unnerved. It wasn't so much being afraid that an acrobat would fall, that a lion would eat the lion tamer...nothing so concrete or obvious. But the darkness, the gradually strengthening smells of sawdust, animal sweat, greasepaint, and canvas, the spotlighting that left too many other things purposely obscure while half-seen forms moved in those shadows, themselves concealed by the light—all these slowly combined to suggest that something unexpected, something unavoidable, was going to happen. And that looming unknown frightened Nita badly. At intermission she'd begged her parents to take her home. Dairine had cried at the thought of leaving, and so their mom had stayed with Dari while her father drove Nita back to the house.

That her dad had never pressed her for details about this was still one of the things Nita thought about when counting up the reasons she loved him. But even his silent support couldn't do anything about the nightmares that followed, nightmares full of leering clown faces and the musky smell of big cats. Finally the nightmares faded away and left Nita wondering what in the world had been the matter with her. Yet she never went to another circus. And even now, sometimes the mere sight of a spotlight aimed at an empty floor, with darkness lying silent beyond it, was enough to induce in her a feeling of tremendous foreboding that would darken her soul for hours.

Sometimes she tried to work out in more detail why she'd been so scared. She kept coming back to the clowns. To Nita, there was a fake quality about them, nothing genuinely humorous. It was strange to think that someone seriously thought that makeup could make you funny. But there was no question in Nita's mind that makeup *could* make you scary. The stylized clown face, too generic, too cartoony: That really bothered her. The baggy, motley costume, disguising the real body shape so that it could have been a bare steel skeleton underneath instead of flesh and bone. The slapstick jokes, endlessly repeated, which were supposed to be amusing *because* of the repetition—all these left Nita cold. There was something mechanical about clowns, something automatic, a kind of robot humor; and it gave her the creeps.

It was doing so again, right now, because here in the darkness, followed around by one of those sinister spotlights, was a typical clown act—the clown riding around and around in circles on a ridiculously small bicycle, in ever decreasing circles. There was nothing funny about it to Nita. It was pitiful. Around and around and around, in jerky, wobbling movements, around and around went the clown. It had a painted black tear running down its face. The red-painted mouth was turned down. But the face under the white greasepaint mask was as immobile as a marble statue's, expressionless, plastered in place. Only the eyes were alive. They shouted, *I can't get off! I can't get off!* And, just this once, the clown didn't think it was funny, either.

The drumroll went on and on, as if for a hanging rather than a circus stunt. The chain of the bicycle rattled relentlessly in the silence inside the light. Beyond the light, in the darkness, the heartless crowd laughed and clapped and cheered. And through the sound of their applause, low, but building, came the growl of the tiger, pacing behind the bars, waiting its turn.

The drumroll never stopped. The clown rode in tighter and tighter circles, faster and faster. The wheels of the bike began to scream. The crowd shouted for more. "Stop it," Nita yelled. "Stop it! Can't you see it's killing him?"

"As often as possible," growled the tiger. "And never often enough."

The crowd roared louder. "Stop it!" Nita shouted back, but now they were drowning her out, too. "Stop it!"

"STOP!"

She was sitting up in the dark, alone. It took her a ragged three or four breaths to realize she was in her own room, in bed, and that her own shout had awakened her.

Nita sat still for a few moments, praying that she wouldn't hear anyone coming to find out if she was okay. She wasn't, but she still hoped no one would respond. There wasn't anyone in the house who'd been sleeping well for a while now.

She stayed still for a long time. Mercifully, no one showed up, and Nita began to relax, realizing that she might have expected this outcome if she'd really thought about it. Dairine, when she slept these days, slept hard, in utter exhaustion. Their dad lately had been doing much the same, a change from the previous month, when he had hardly slept at all. It didn't take a wizard to figure out that he'd been *afraid* to fall asleep, because of who he would, again and again, *not* find beside him when he woke up. Finally his body had overruled that kind of behavior and now was trying to sleep too much, to not wake up at all, if possible. The reasons were the same, and just thinking of them made Nita want to cry all over again.

She lay back against the pillows and let her breath out at the thought of the dream. *It's just me,* she thought. She hated to describe it any further, for the next line of explanation would have been, *Since Mom—* And she refused to blame her mother for it; her mom now had nothing further to do with pain. It was Nita's own pain that made her nights so awful. The shrink at school, the counselor at the hospital, both told her the same thing: "Grief takes time. The pain discharges in a lot of different ways, in old repeated patterns, weird symbolic images, mental unrest. Try to stop it, and it just takes longer. Let it take its own time; let it go at its own speed."

Like I have a choice, Nita thought bitterly. She could have used wizardry to combat the sleep disturbances, but the manual had told her plainly that this would be counterproductive. Easing others' pain is one thing; willfully trying to avoid experiencing one's own is another, and has its own price, too high for the intelligent wizard to pay. It was smarter to let the hurt discharge naturally, without interfering.

But these commonsense counsels were still no comfort in the middle of the night, when she was alone in the dark. All Nita could do was wipe her face repeatedly, dry her eyes on the pillow, and hope to fall asleep eventually. Lacking that, she'd lie there and wait for dawn.

Nita lay there, almost seeing the eyes hidden in the exaggerated colors and shadows of the painted face, and squeezed her own eyes shut. *It's just my pain in disguise,* she thought. *Pain expressed as a symbol, one step away from the reality.*

I wish this were over with. I wish life were normal again... But she knew that the old kind of normal was never going to come back. Somehow she was just going to have to make a new one.

Nita turned over to try to go back to sleep, but it took a long while: From the shadows of dream, those eyes kept watching her....

The next day was Tuesday. Kit went through his early classes more or less mechanically. The problem of Tom's "lost wizard" was on his mind. Tracking him down and identifying him wouldn't be a problem—the manual would be able to localize him and point him out when Kit was close enough. *But what then?* he thought as the bell rang for fourth period. He picked up his backpack and walked out of his math class on his way to history. *Do I just walk up to him, say, "Hi, there. I'm on errantry and I greet you. What's the problem?" Is it better to just take a good look at him from a distance, maybe?*

"Hey, KF, don't say hi or anything!"

Kit glanced around and found Raoul Eschemeling walking along next to him. Or rather, he glanced over and then up, because Raoul went up a good ways. He was a skinny, pale blond guy, tall enough to be a basketball player—the kind of person for whom the word *gangly* originally could have been coined. Friendly and gregarious, Raoul was constantly inventing bizarre nicknames for the other kids in the advanced history class, a motley crew of crazies of various ages, all fast-tracked together into a single advanced unit. "KF" was short for "kit fox," and this nickname had stuck longer than any of the others Raoul had hung on Kit at one point or another.

"Hey, Pirate," Kit said. "Sorry, I was daydreaming."

"Saw that. You almost walked into a locker there. You ready for Machiavelli's quiz?"

"Oh, god, no," Kit said as they turned the corner and headed down the corridor toward their classroom. "Machiavelli" was Mr. Mack, their history teacher, and, in his case at least, the nickname was justifiable: He had a twisty, calculating mind that made learning history from him a pleasure. "I forgot. Well, I did the reading. Maybe I'll survive."

Raoul looked at him closely. "You got stuff on your mind?"

"Yeah, I guess."

"She doing okay? I haven't seen her around a lot lately."

"Huh? Oh, Nita." They went into the classroom together and took seats near the back wall. There was no assigned seating in Mack's class, which meant there was always a rush for the rearmost seats, everybody's desperate attempt to be somewhere that would make Machiavelli less likely to call on them...not that sitting in the back ever seemed to work. "She's okay, pretty much." Kit paused, watching the room fill up hurriedly—no surprise since Mack made the lives of latecomers a question-filled hell. "I mean, as okay as she can be under the circumstances."

Raoul looked at Kit with interest. "So if you weren't going all vague about her just now, then what's on your mind?"

"Oh, just home stuff…"

The bell rang. *Saved!* Kit thought. With the bell came Machiavelli, moving fast, as always, five feet tall and balding, in a blue suit and wearing a red tie ornamented with the images of many tiny yellow rubber duckies. The suit never changed, but the tie changed every day, and in the few seconds of fascination it produced, Mr. Mack would always pick the unfortunate student who looked most off guard and start peppering him or her with questions. "Rodriguez," he said, and Kit's heart sank. "You ready for our little quiz today?"

Wizards do not lie; too much depends on the words they use seriously for them to play fast and loose with the less serious ones. "I don't know, Mr. M., but I think I'm about to find out."

Machiavelli grinned at him. Kit restrained the urge to groan out loud, and once again wished it wasn't unethical for a wizard to use his powers to read the closed textbook in his backpack. All he could do now was pray for the bloodshed to be over with quickly.

Forty-five minutes later, Kit and the rest of the class walked out, mostly looking like they had been run over repeatedly by the same steamroller. "Remind me never to go to sub-Saharan Africa in the eighteen hundreds," Raoul muttered. "After today, just seeing it would make me come down with post-traumatic stress disorder."

Kit theoretically *could* have gone to that time and place if he wanted to and was willing to pay the price, but right now he felt about the same as Raoul did. "Still, it could have been worse. At least we passed."

"Yeah. Not sure I have any appetite left for lunch... I guess we can go look, though."

Kit grinned, privately thinking that it would take a nuclear war to ruin Raoul's appetite. "Let me know how it was. I have to go home for lunch."

"God, I wish I lived as close to school as you do," Raoul said. "When I think of all the cafeteria food I wouldn't have to eat...!"

"Go on, Pirate," Kit said. "Suffer a little. I'll see you later."

He made his way back to his locker, chucked his backpack into it, locked it up again, and headed out the school's back door, jogging across the parking lot, through the gate, and around the corner onto Conlon Road.

Ponch was bouncing around in the backyard, jumping almost to the top of the chain-link fence, as Kit came down the driveway. "Okay, okay, give me a minute," Kit said. He pulled the screen door open and poked the lock with one finger. "Hey, Chubbo..."

The lock obligingly threw its bolt back for him. Kit patted the lock, opened the door, loped into the kitchen, very hastily threw together a ham sandwich on rye with some mustard, and ate it. For his mother, who was still asleep because she had been working night shifts at the hospital over the past week, he left a note scribbled on the pad on the refrigerator: "I had lunch. See you later." He thought of adding the code phrase "Out on business now" to let his mama know that there was wizardly work afoot, but then he changed his mind. He'd have no more than his lunch period minus the time to eat the sandwich before he would have to be back at school again, anyway.

Kit cleaned up the crumbs from his sandwich and went out, pulling the door softly closed behind him so as not to wake his mama. "See you, big guy," Kit said to the lock. "Keep her safe."

I'm on it!

He went around the back, opened the gate softly, and closed it again, grabbing Ponch by the collar and roughing him up a little by way of saying hello. "And you weren't even barking," Kit said. "Good for you."

She's asleep, Ponch said. *I don't want her to yell at me.*

"Neither do I. Good for you for thinking of it."

Are we going out?! Ponch began chasing his tail in delight.

"Just for a quick look at our guy. I want to see if he's okay before I come barging in on him. We're going to have to be stealthy, though."

Ponch finished his running around and sat down, his tail sweeping the sparse grass while Kit reached into his "pocket" and came out with the long chain of his transit spell, and another spell, more complex, that he had prepared earlier. There were several different ways for wizards to be invisible, and this one was probably the most comprehensive of them: Even if someone bumped up against Kit, he would feel nothing, and the spell would incline him to think he'd just stumbled somehow. Building the spell had required half an hour's careful reading from the manual at a time of morning when Kit would rather still have been in bed, followed by fifteen or twenty minutes on his back, as exhausted as if he'd run around the school track about ten times. But now, as he shook the cloaking spell out onto the air in a cloudy web of woven Speech, he had to admire his handiwork. The basic spellweb would last a good while, as long as he remembered to recharge it at intervals.

"Okay," he said to Ponch. "You ready?"

Yeahyeahyeahyeah!

"Good. Stay close to me. This thing only has about a six-foot radius." He draped the invisibility spell over his shoulder for a moment, stuck the chain of the transit spell into the belt of his parka, and reached down into the "pocket" for his wizard's manual. "Now then," he said. He flipped it open, and the pages riffled to the spot he'd bookmarked. He ran a finger down the listing of functions on that page. "Location and detection... cross-reference to personnel listings... Right." The locator spell blocked out on the page rearranged itself to include Darryl's listing, and the listing itself pulsed to indicate that it was "in circuit" with the rest of the spell and ready to go.

"This is a temporal-spatial locator routine with sync to an existing transit nexus now balanced for two," Kit said in the Speech. "Purpose: Locate and identify the wizard in the listing. Additional info: Linkage to stealth routine referenced on page..." He stopped and had to check his other bookmark, on the cloaking spell's page, because the manual's pagination was constantly changing, depending on Kit's needs (and sometimes its own). "Three-eighty-nine. Ready?"

The whole spell pulsed bright on the page as he turned back to it. Slowly Kit started reading, making sure of his pronunciation, and that his and Ponch's names were correctly entered. The usual waiting silence—of the universe leaning in around them to hear the Speech spoken and implement it—now started to build. Ponch sat there with his big eyes glinting and his tail thumping as the power of the spell built all around them. Kit felt a brief pang because of the absence of the other voice that usually would have been there, reading her half of the work, but there was no time for the feeling right now. Kit finished the spell, snapped the manual shut, and in the moment before the spell worked, flipped the cloaking routine over himself and Ponch.

The power washed up over and around them, blotting out the backyard. A moment later, Kit and Ponch were standing in a parking lot two towns away, looking at another school building.

It was considerably smaller than Kit's junior high, though this place shared the same kind of late-seventies institutional architecture: a lot of plate glass, a lot of brick. Kit looked around them through the slight heat-haze shimmer of the invisibility spell, keeping Ponch with him for the moment simply by holding on to his collar. The school was surrounded by suburban housing and, off to one side, what looked like the back of a strip mall; maybe about fifty cars were parked around the school. It had a small playing field, but nobody was out there.

Kit wasn't overly concerned—even if anyone had been out there, they wouldn't have been able to see Ponch and him. Now the point was to find Darryl. The structure of the locator spell mandated that Darryl was somewhere within a two-hundred-meter radius: All Kit had to do was look around.

Two hundred meters, Kit thought, *could definitely include at least part of the school building.* He walked toward it, looking for any sign of the characteristic aura that would surround the object of his search once he got within visual range. Beside him, Ponch paced along, looking at everything, his nose working.

From around the side of the school, a white van drove toward the front entrance and pulled up. Kit gave the van a wide berth, having no desire to be run over by something that couldn't see him. A moment later, the driver got out and went in through the front doors. Kit looked through the front windows of the school, found himself looking at office space, not classrooms. "Okay," he said, "so we'll go in. Don't start barking at anything, whatever you do!"

Please, Ponch said in a somewhat offended tone. Kit smiled in slight amusement as they headed for the doors. Once upon a time, his dog wouldn't have been quite so focused during a wizardry, but lately, since Ponch had started actively finding things—like other universes—this had changed.

They went up to the doors together. They were all closed—no surprise, in this weather—and Kit was unwilling just to pull one of them open: Someone might be watching. *Never mind. We can just walk through the glass,* he thought. But then, through the glass of the door, Kit saw the van driver coming back toward them. "Okay," Kit said softly to Ponch, "he can let us in. Just step back and don't let him bump into you. We'll slip past before the door closes behind him."

Fine.

The van driver, a small, slender man in a big parka, pushed the door open right in front of Kit's nose, and then reached up to the closing mechanism to pull down the little toggle that would hold the door open. *Convenient,* Kit thought, and slipped through the door with Ponch close behind him.

In the main tile-and-terrazzo corridor of the school, a number of people were moving around; some of them were coming toward the doors—some students, Kit thought, heading for the van with a few teachers. *Field trip?* he wondered. Then Kit paused, for the locator spell said in his head, *Proximity alert—subject of search within fifty meters. Forty meters—*

That's them, Kit thought. "Ponch, come on," Kit whispered. "Over here—" Together they moved off to one side of the hallway as the group approached. Kit started examining them for signs of that faint, glowing halo.

There were five kids in the group. Three of them were girls of different ages, one quite short and round, the other two taller and thinner; they went by Kit in silence, not speaking to each other, though one of them was smiling a placid smile. Two teachers followed close behind, then came the two boys and a third teacher.

One was a thin, small, blond guy, who went past

with a very uneven gait. But Kit's attention was on the boy behind him. Visible only to Kit and Ponch, the locator halo clung to him. He was, perhaps, eleven years old, an African American kid with a handsome, sharp little face. He was slender, and was dressed in jeans and a bright T-shirt and beat-up sneakers. Handsome his face was, but also expressionless, flat and as still as a mask, his eyes looking only at the ground. He held his body tilted slightly forward, and he went past Kit fast, breaking almost into a run as he headed through the doors out into the cold, gray day.

Kit turned and followed him back outside. The teachers helped the other kids into the van: Darryl was the last one in. One of the teachers was helping him with his seat belt. This took some moments. And while the teachers were sitting down, while the van driver came back to let the school door close again, Darryl began, very slowly and steadily, to bang his head against the window of the van.

Kit's heart seized. Next to him, Ponch stood looking. The driver started up the van, and slowly drove away.

That was him, Ponch said.

"That was him," Kit said softly. *But what's the matter with him?* Though he thought perhaps he had a clue. The manual would be able to confirm it . . . now that Kit knew what kinds of questions he needed to ask.

"Did you get a scent on him?" Kit said.

Yes. I can find him again, wherever he goes. Even when he's not here, like a few moments ago, Ponch added.

Kit gave his dog a look. "What? He was right in front of us."

Some of him. Not all.

Ponch wasn't given to making cryptic statements without reason: He was still developing the language skills to tell Kit what he was perceiving, and there were sometimes misunderstandings as a result. "Okay," Kit said. "We'll figure out what that means later. For the moment, at least we know what he looks like...and we can start making a plan to find a way to talk to him."

If he can talk at all...

He glanced at the timekeeper inside the front cover of the manual. "Come on," Kit said. "I have to get back to school."

And you have to feed me.

Normally Kit would have laughed at this, yet another of Ponch's stratagems to get an extra meal. But the laughter had been knocked out of him by the unexpectedness of what he'd just seen. *Since when do the Powers That Be dump an autistic kid into an Ordeal?*

"Come on," Kit said to Ponch. They went home.

After school Kit went straight to Tom and Carl's, the discreet way, to tell him what he'd found.

"Physically, he's there all right...mostly," Kit said, sitting at the table with Tom again. "Or so Ponch says. I'm still working on what he meant by that conditional description he gave me. But Darryl's problem...Why didn't anything about it turn up in the manual before?"

"Need-to-know restrictions, possibly," Tom said. "And often enough the manual'll let you find out something for yourself, rather than just tell you about it. That approach can keep you from prejudging a situation." He paged through his own manual to Darryl's entry. "Certainly it confirms that he has an individualized type of autistic disorder. The manual says it's a fairly recent development. He hasn't been autistic from a very young age: It seems to have come on him suddenly, shortly after he turned eight."

"So the Ordeal itself didn't have anything to do with it?"

"I don't know that for sure. It wouldn't *seem* to be connected... but we could be wrong there. At any rate, because the manual doesn't say anything further, it suggests that the Powers That Be don't think we need any more detail on that particular facet of the situation. Or that what you discover during investigation may be more valuable than what They already know."

"It doesn't seem fair somehow," Kit said after a moment, trying to find words for what was making him so uncomfortable. "You'd think he has enough problems. Why's he been stuck in the middle of an Ordeal, on top of everything else?"

Tom shook his head. "If he's been offered wizardry, that means that there's some problem to which *he* is the solution. But he can't merely have been offered wizardry; he also has to have been able to agree to the offer. He found the Wizard's Oath, in some form or another, and he accepted it. Now we have to find out how we can assist... without removing the basic challenge."

Kit nodded. "It makes you wonder, though," he said. "If *he's* the answer, what's the question?"

"I think I know what you mean," Tom said. "He does seem an unlikely candidate. But even in what we laughably refer to as 'normal' life, all too often the unlikely people turn out to be the ones who have the answers; the objects you would have thrown away are the ones you find you can't do without. 'The stone rejected by the builder becomes the cornerstone.'" Tom got a wry look then. "It happens too often to be accidental. Is the universe trying to tell us something important about the way it works—that sometimes even what we call fate has an element of unpredictability?"

Kit nodded. "Or maybe the One's just saying, 'Don't be so sure you know it all.'"

Tom stretched and leaned back in his chair. "Could be. There are people in our world who've made a tremendous difference but who would have died in another time. In this time, people every day are making choices of who should live and die on the basis of criteria like whether you're going to be the 'right' sex, or whether your whole body is going to work perfectly. Who knows how we may damage ourselves if we insist too hard on what, this week, looks like perfection."

He stopped, a somewhat rueful expression coming over his face. "Sorry," Tom said. "But being a wizard makes philosophers out of most of us eventually. As long as that's not *all* it makes of you, you're okay ... Anyway, now you have to plan how to approach him." Tom chewed one lip briefly. "You may have to go to his home, secretly. But maybe you'd have better luck at his school."

"I'm not wild about sneaking around in his house,"

Kit said. "School, yeah. I'd thought about that, too. But there are still too many ways to be noticed. I was considering another option."

"Oh?"

"Ponch has been able to treat someone's interior landscape like an exterior universe before," Kit said. "He can go into Darryl's head and take me with him... and maybe Darryl will find it easier to talk to me that way."

Tom brooded over that for a moment. "My initial reaction," he said, "is to say no. We're uncertain enough about how the heck Ponch does what he does. Add that set of imponderables to whatever's going on inside Darryl's head..." He shook his head. "It starts getting uncomfortably complex."

"We're wizards," Kit said. "We're supposed to learn how to get comfortable with the uncomfortably complex."

Tom gave Kit a look that would have seemed annoyed if there hadn't been a resigned quality to it as well. "In theory," he said, "of course, you're right. But turning theory into practice without taking due care and attention can screw things up big-time."

Kit sat quietly, knowing better than to argue his case too hard with a Senior: That was a sure way to make it seem like he had some kind of ulterior motive.

Tom looked off into the middle distance, pondering. "Yet here's this very atypical Ordeal," he said, "and we can't just let the kid go on suffering unnecessarily for the sake of caution and correctness. Some more information gathering, at least, seems prudent. But I want you to be very, *very* cautious, and watch yourself at least as carefully as you're watching him. Even normal Ordeals are subjective, and getting another entity's subjectivity involved with one, even temporarily, brings considerable dangers with it. *This* Ordeal, where the candidate is autistic—" He shook his head. "It might be an attempt to resolve the autism, which is likely to be incredibly traumatic for Darryl whether it works or not...or it might simply be about some mode of wizardry we haven't seen before, one that involves Darryl *staying* autistic. What looks like our idea of 'normal' function may not, in the One's eyes, be the best function. Judgment calls in these cases can get dangerous."

"If you don't judge, though," Kit said, "or at least decide to do *something*, nothing gets done!"

Tom sat still and looked out the window, where a cold wind was rattling some brown, unfallen beech leaves in the hedge beside his house. "There you're right," he said. "Not that that makes me any happier. But judgment calls are one of the other things we're here for: The One has better things to do than micromanage us."

He looked back at Kit. "So go do what you can," Tom said. "Let me know how it comes out. But I want to really emphasize that you need to stay in the observer's role. This Ordeal is strange enough to get extremely dangerous, especially if you stray out of your appropriate role."

"I'll be careful."

Tom's expression got slightly less severe. "I've heard

that one before," he said. "From myself, among many others. But, particularly, I want you to watch yourself when you're inside his head. Talking to Darryl is a good idea...but getting too synced to his worldview may make that more difficult, not less. Talking is something you do to *other* people; if he has trouble with that concept, you could get in trouble, too. And when you're inside someone else's head and using wizardry, no matter how careful you are, there's always the danger of rewriting his name in the Speech. Do that in such a way that Darryl buys into the rewrite, and you take the risk of excising something that makes the difference between him passing his Ordeal and him never coming out of it. Walk real softly, Kit."

"We will."

Kit left Tom's by use of another transit spell, one that let him out in a sheltered spot by the town library. He spent a while there Web surfing, printing out what he'd found, and then located a few books and checked them out. His mother was up when he got home, showering; by the time she came out, wearing her bathrobe and drying her hair, Kit was lying on the living room floor with papers and books all around him. His mama paused, looking over his shoulder at one of the printouts he was reading. "Autism?" she said.

"Yeah."

She headed past him into the kitchen to find her big mug, filled it with the coffee that Kit's pop had left in the pot for her, sugared it, and came back in to sit down on the sofa behind him. "Big subject, son," she said.

"You know much about it?"

"Enough to get by." She drank some coffee. "There are a lot of different kinds, and we're still feeling our way around to the causes. Once they thought autism was caused by being raised wrong, by having parents who were cold or abusive. That theory got thrown out a long time ago. But there are still a lot of possible causes, and some of them seem to include each other. Some autism may be too little of one chemical or another in the brain. Or it may be caused by an enzyme that's missing, so that certain chemicals build up in the nervous system and damage it, or make it behave erratically. It may be caused by something wrong with the immune system, or rogue antibodies that attack brain and neural tissue, or even a virus, or pollution, or vitamin A deficiency..." She raised one hand in a "who knows" gesture, then let it fall. "There're a hundred answers, maybe all of them right sometimes... Is this for school?"

"No. It's what Tom wanted to see me about."

His mama's eyes went wide. "Your missing person? He's autistic? Oh, honey, that's *terrible*! His parents must be heartbroken. Do you think you're going to be able to find him?"

"I already have," Kit said, sitting down at the table and tilting his chair back to rock on its rear legs. "He's at school. Centennial, over in Baldwin."

"What? Well, that's a relief! I thought you'd meant he'd vanished. So how is he missing?"

"It was just a figure of speech, Mama." Kit had been wondering for a while how much detail he should give his parents about his wizardry. Now it occurred to him that he should have been giving them a lot more, if only to keep them from worrying. "When the wizardry first comes to you, it doesn't come all at once. You get a test first: your Ordeal. If you pass, you're a wizard. If you don't..."

Immediately, the look on his mother's face suggested to him that he might have misstepped. "You *die*?" his mother said.

"Not always," Kit said. "Sometimes you just lose the power that was given you to take the test with." His mama was looking at him rather narrowly now, and Kit realized that she would immediately detect any attempt to soften this. "But it's true that some kids don't come back," Kit said. "Some disappearances are failed Ordeals. Maybe a few percent."

His mother sat, quietly digesting that, and had another drink of her coffee. "So this Ordeal," she said. "He's having some kind of problem with it?"

"He's been in the middle of it for a long time," Kit said. "He may need help. And I can't help thinking the autism has something to do with it." He sighed. "I've been doing a lot of reading, but I don't know anything about what's going on in his head yet. And he may not be able to tell me. I think I'm going to have to get in there and take a look myself."

"In his *head*?" His mother looked alarmed. "Kit, my love, I don't claim to understand the details of what you're doing...but wouldn't that be a violation of his privacy?"

"Maybe," Kit said. "But couldn't you make a case that CPR is, too? Still, you do it."

"To save a life, yes."

"That's what this might be," Kit said. "Ordeals are crucial by definition, Mama. I had some help on mine. Maybe now I get to pay those favors forward."

"So you get inside his head how, exactly?" his mama said. "Is this what Carmela keeps describing as 'magic telepathy'?"

Kit shook his head. "It's more complicated," he said. "I'm still working out how to describe it. Ponch sees it as making a new world to go to...or finding that world ready-made. Once you make it, or find it, you go there."

"*Ponch* sees it..." His mother shook her head, sloshed the coffee around in her cup, drank some, and made a face: It was going cold.

"We'll go there and look around," Kit said. "We'll see what his world looks like to him. Assuming we can get in all right. If that doesn't work...I'll have to think of something else. But at least this is a place to start."

His mother put the cup down and pushed it away. "If you do actually get to talk to him," she said, looking thoughtful, "there's possibly something you should keep in mind. Autistic people have trouble, sometimes, predicting what other human beings' minds are going to do. It's a skill they have to develop with practice, whereas we take it almost completely for granted, that prediction inside: 'If I do this, then she'll do that,' and so on. So you have to be prepared for the things you say to really upset him, more than would seem reasonable. He may even have trouble believing in you."

Kit looked at her, wondering what she meant. "It's not that he'd think he was hallucinating you, exactly," his mama said. "This isn't that kind of perceptual problem. But some autistic people have trouble conceiving of anything existing outside the workings of their own minds. The concept of 'the other' seems to take a long time forming. That's part of why so many of them can't make or keep eye contact with other people. Yet for the same reason, a lot of them seem not to know what fear is."

"Weird," Kit said.

"Not as such," said his mother. "Different, yes. You may not scare him, but you may upset him…so be ready for that."

"Okay," Kit said.

His mother sat back and looked sad. "The problem is that there are probably as many kinds of autism as there are people who have it," she said. "And not enough of them come back from that side of things to tell us how what's happened to them looks or feels." She shook her head. "Some of the few who have say that the world just got too overwhelming to be borne. They felt like they were surrounded by sounds that were too intense, sights they couldn't bear to see. So they had to withdraw inside themselves to get away, or even hurt themselves over and over again as a way to blot out the pain outside. It's the only way they can control it. Others tell about feeling so sealed away from the world and the things and people in it that they hurt themselves just to be *able* to feel something. You get kids who are autistic from age two, and others who're perfectly normal until suddenly they turn ten or twelve and something just goes wrong...and they turn inward and don't come out again for years. If ever." Kit's mama looked haunted.

Kit nodded slowly. "I didn't know it was this complicated."

"It is."

"You know anything that would be good for me to read?"

"There are lots of books," his mother said. "Some of the ones in the hospital library are going to be too technical for you." She looked over Kit's shoulder at the books spread out on the floor. "But some won't be, and they're more recent than these. Let me see what I can bring you."

"Great. One thing, though. I really need to take tomorrow off to work on this. Can you call school and get me off?"

She scowled at him. "You don't have a test or anything tomorrow?"

"Huh? No."

"I'm not going to make a habit of this..."

"I'm not asking you to, Mama! But it's going to take more than just lunch hour to make a start on this, and I don't want to have to run off all of a sudden in the middle of something that's going to make a difference."

His mother sat thinking. "All right," she said. "I'll take care of it. You can have a stomach bug or something."

"No, Mama! Don't lie to them. Just tell them I need a personal day."

She gave him a slightly approving look. "Okay."

"Thanks, Mama. You're the best." He got up and kissed her, and took her coffee cup. "You want some more?"

"Yes." His mother leaned back on the sofa. "Two sugars. And then I want you to explain to me why I can hear the DVD player and the remote yelling at each other in Japanese in the middle of the night."

Kit shut his eyes briefly in horror, and went to get the coffee.

Pursuits

QUITE EARLY THE NEXT morning, Kit came downstairs to find his sister sitting in front of the TV with a
plate of half-finished toast, and a most peculiar expression on her face. "Brother dear...," Carmela said.

This tone of voice usually meant that something bad
was going to happen. *And I haven't even had my cornflakes yet,* Kit thought. "What?"

"I need to talk to you about the TV."

"Uh...what about it?" He went into the kitchen to
make a start at least on the cornflakes, before she really
got rolling.

"Why did Pop tell me not to watch it?"

"Uh," Kit said, "maybe I should ask you first—if
Pop told you not to watch it, then what're you doing?"

If he hoped that taking the offensive with his sister
would help him even a little, the hope was misplaced.
"Why do what they say until you can figure out why?"

Carmela said from the living room. "And with Pop at work and Mama asleep, there's no way I'm going to find out the *why*s from *them* for hours. So I ask you, instead... while having a look myself."

Kit said nothing, just rummaged enthusiastically in the fridge for the milk.

"Most of the shows don't make much sense," Carmela said. "And a lot of others are in weird languages. This has to do with all the yelling in Japanese the other day, am I right?"

"To a certain extent," Kit said, getting a bowl out of the cupboard and then opening a drawer for a spoon.

His sister sighed. "You know," she said, "you're bad at covering your tracks when you've busted something. Hey, that's a local phone number!"

Kit's eyes widened with shock. He hurried in to find his sister goggling at a screen full of billowing white smoke and a number with a 516 area code... both of which, to his vast relief, then dissolved into whangy guitar music and an offer for cut-rate Elvis CDs.

Carmela looked up at Kit, registering his reaction, and shook her head. "I can't believe you're into this retro stuff," she said, changing channels to her more usual morning fare, the channel with all the cartoons. "It's a good thing you've got Nita, because it's gonna be a long time before anybody else wants to date you, the taste you've got."

"I have not 'got' Nita," Kit said through gritted teeth. "And as for taste, you shouldn't be talking. Tom and Jerry cartoons? Give me a break."

"I'm waiting for the Road Runner," Carmela said,

managing to sound both pitying and incredibly stuck-up. "A symbol of innocence endlessly pursued by the banality of evil."

Kit went back to his cornflakes. "I wish the evil *I* keep running into was a little more banal," he muttered as he picked up his bowl and started eating. The Lone Power's favorite tool, entropy, had already struck locally: His cornflakes had gone soggy.

Resigned, he sat down and ate them anyway. Shortly Carmela came wandering into the kitchen and stuck her head in the refrigerator. "You got today off, huh?"

"Yeah. 'Business' stuff." He ate the last spoonful of cornflakes and went to rinse the bowl. "And I didn't 'bust' the TV, either."

"Well, it has a gigabillion new channels, looks like," his sister said. "The one before this one looked pretty neat. They were selling some kind of eternal-youth potion." She paused to primp herself unnecessarily in the dark glass of the microwave. "Might come in handy."

"You have to grow up first before the fountain of youth's going to do you any good," Kit said, putting the bowl and spoon in the dishwasher, "and anyway, what *you* need is the fountain of brains."

Kit spent the next few minutes running around the house while his sister, in pursuit, whacked him as often as possible with a rolled-up boy-band fan magazine. He could have teleported straight out of there, but it was more fun to let her chase him, and it would keep her in a good mood. Finally eight-thirty rolled around, the latest time when she could leave and still get to homeroom on time, and Carmela got her book bag and headed out. "Bye-bye," she said as she went out the back door. "Don't get eaten by monsters or anything."

"I'll try to avoid it."

The door closed. Kit went off to get his manual, reflecting that things could be a lot worse for him. A resident sister who found wizardry freaky or annoying could cause endless trouble, forcing him to live like a fugitive in his own house, hiding what he was. *But so many human wizards have to do that, anyway,* he thought, going into his room to get the manual off his desk, and carefully walking around Ponch, who lay on the braided oval rag rug beside his bed, still asleep. *They have families they can't trust, or who can't cope...* The thought of telling someone you loved that you were a wizard, and then discovering that he or she couldn't handle it and would have to have the memory removed, made Kit shudder. *I was lucky. Not that it wasn't a little traumatic at first, with Mama and Pop. But they got past it. And so did Helena, sort of.*

His older sister had been the cause of some worries for Kit when he'd told her he was a wizard. Helena had at first been dismissive, in an amused way: She hadn't believed him. But when Kit had started casually using wizardry around the house, Helena had actually gone through a short period when she'd thought he'd done some kind of deal with the devil. Finally she calmed down when she saw that Kit had no trouble participating at church along with the rest of the family, and when Kit got Helena to understand that the Lone Power, no matter which costume It was wearing, was never going to be any friend of his. But Helena's moral concerns had died down into a kind of strange embarrassment about Kit, which was as hard to bear, in its way, as the accusations of being a dupe of ultimate evil. When she went away to college and didn't have to see what Kit was doing from day to day, their relationship got back to normal, if a rather long-distance kind of normal. *What would it have been like if she'd stayed around, though?* Kit had found himself thinking, more than once. *How would I have coped?* It was a question he was glad not to have had to answer. *And if that makes me chicken, fine. I'm chicken.*

He glanced down at Ponch. He was still asleep, his muzzle and feet twitching gently as he dreamed. Kit sat down to wait until the dog finished the dream. The wizard's manual lay on his desk; he flipped it open to Darryl's page again and considered that for a few moments.

He's only eleven, Kit thought, looking over the slightly more detailed personal information that had added itself to Darryl's listing since Kit had become involved. Eleven wasn't incredibly young for a wizard — Dairine had been offered the Wizard's Oath at eleven — but it was still a little on the early side: a suggestion that the Powers That Be needed Darryl for something slightly more urgent than usual. *All we need to do is try to figure out what it is ... try to help him find his way around whatever's blocking him. Without getting in the way of whatever his Ordeal's supposed to do for him.*

That's likely to be a tall order ...

Ponch had stopped dreaming and was breathing quietly again. Kit hated to wake him, but free days like this weren't something he got often. He nudged his dog's tummy gently with one sneaker.

"Ponch," he said. "C'mon, big guy."

Ponch opened one eye and looked at Kit.

Breakfast!

His dog might be getting a little strange, as wizards' pets sometimes do, but in other regards Ponch was absolutely normal. Ponch got up, stretched fore and aft, shook himself all over, and then headed for the hallway. Kit grinned, picked up the manual, stuck it into the "pocket" of otherspace that he kept things in for his wizardly work, and went after him.

In the kitchen, Kit opened a can of dog food and emptied it into the bowl. Ponch went through it in about five minutes of single-minded chowing down, then looked up. *More?*

"You're only supposed to get one in the morning. You know that."

But today's a workday. Today we go hunting.

"So?"

I have to keep up my strength.

Kit rolled his eyes. "I'm being had here," he said.

Boss! Ponch looked pained.

"Oh, all right," Kit said after a moment. "But if all this food makes you want to lie down and have a big long sleep all of a sudden..."

It won't.

Kit sighed and opened the cupboard to get out another can of dog food. *Not that one. The chicken this time*, Ponch said.

Kit looked at his dog, then at the label on the can. "When did you learn to read?"

I don't have to read. I can hear you doing it, Ponch said. *Anyway, the color's different on the food with chicken in it.*

Kit grabbed a different can and popped the top, shaking his head, and emptied it into Ponch's bowl. "The *color*?" he said after a moment. "I thought dogs saw only in gray."

Ponch paused in his eating. *Maybe we do,* he said. *But important things look different.*

Kit shook his head. Whatever color his dog saw his food in, it didn't matter much, as it all swiftly went inside him, where theoretically everything was the same color, especially after it was digested.

When he was finished eating, Ponch circled around a couple of times and lay down to start washing his paws.

"You're not going to go to sleep, are you?" Kit said.

Ponch looked at him with some mild annoyance. *If you're going to hunt,* he said, *your feet have to be clean.* He went back to nibbling his paws again.

Kit sighed and sat down to wait. When Ponch was finished, he got up, shook himself again, and said, *I have to go out.*

"You'll be ready then?"

Yes.

Kit opened the door and let the dog out. He put on his jacket, picked up his house keys from the hook inside the back door, and got one more thing from the place where the coats hung—the wizardly "leash" that he'd made for Ponch when they were working together in other worlds. For those who could see it, it looked like a slender, smooth cord of blue light, a tight braid of words in the Speech that had to do with finding things, remembering where you found them, and not losing what had helped you find them in the first place—namely Ponch. Kit coiled up the leash and stuffed it in his parka pocket, then locked up the house and went up the driveway to the gate in the chain-link fence. There Ponch was dancing with impatience. Kit opened the gate, and Ponch shot through and into the yard, straight to the back where the trees and bushes grew thickest.

Kit paused for a moment in the frosty morning air. It was one of those cold gray days, but the wrong kind of gray for snow—the kind of day that made you wish that spring would hurry up, but also a day when going to another universe, any other universe, would be a relief from the gloominess of your own. He reached into his pocket for the transit spell he'd used the other day to get to Darryl's school, and ran the long glowing chain of it through his fingers while Ponch did his business back in the bushes. A moment later Ponch bounced out of the underbrush again, and ran back to Kit, bounding up and down around him.

You ready?

"Yeah. Here's your leash."

Kit managed with some difficulty to get Ponch to hold still long enough to slip the leash-spell around his neck. Should Ponch's search for Darryl take them into some space where there wasn't air, or something else humans and dogs needed to survive, the leash would make sure Kit's fail-safe spells temporarily covered Ponch, until Kit could improvise something else. It would also keep them from getting separated in any hostile environment.

Where to first?

"Darryl's school," Kit said. "Let me get us invisible first. I want a closer look at him when we get there."

Kit reached out to one side and traced his finger down the air, "unzipping" his claudication pocket, then reached in for the wizard's manual. When he bounced it in his hand, it fell open at the spot Kit had previously marked, the invisibility spell. The wizardry was as he'd left it, in a partly activated state, waiting for the last few syllables to be pronounced.

Kit said them, and felt the wizardry take, expanding to fold around him and Ponch and then snug in close. This was one of the simpler ways to be invisible; the wizardry "looked" at what was behind you and made anyone in front of you see that instead of you. This light-diversion type of invisibility wasn't good for use in large groups, because it tended to break down under the strain of servicing too many viewpoints, but Kit thought this would be good enough for this morning; he didn't think he and Ponch were likely to wind up in a crowd.

Ponch shook himself as the wizardry settled in around them, then sat down and scratched. *It itches!*

"I know," Kit said. "It has to fit tight to work. Try to bear with it—we won't need it for long."

Kit dropped the bright chain of the transit spell on the ground around them. It knotted itself closed, and the sound of the words and the power of the spell reared up around them in a roar of light. When the brilliance and the noise faded down again, they were standing where they'd been the previous day: in the parking lot, looking at the bland front of Centennial Avenue School.

Kit picked up the transit spell, tucked it away in his claudication pocket. *We'd better keep it silent from here on,* he said. *Have you got his scent?*

Sure. He's in a room over on the left side of the building. He's close.

Show me where.

Together they padded quietly onto the sidewalk outside the school doors, and up onto the lawn on the left side, making their way down the length of the one-story building. About half a minute later, they were standing outside the schoolroom where Darryl and his classmates were working. Kit peered in.

It didn't look much like the classrooms at Kit's school, but he wasn't expecting it to: These kids had special needs. The furniture was sofas and cushions and soft mats rather than the desk-chairs that Kit was used to, with a scattering of low tables suitable for working either from a chair or while sitting on the floor. Four teachers, men and women both, casually dressed, were working with the same group of kids Kit had seen getting into the van the day before. Some of the kids were sitting and working with books at one or another of the tables; one was lying on a mat doing exercises with the help of a special-ed teacher. Off to one side, Darryl sat, dressed in T-shirt and jeans and sneakers again, his dark head bent over a large soft-cover book. He was rocking slightly, while next to him a young male teacher sat and read to him from the book.

There he is.

But still not there, Ponch said.

Then where, exactly?

It's hard to tell from here. I need to get a better scent. We should go in.

Kit nodded. *No point in going all the way back to the doors,* he said, and flipped through the manual for yet another spell. This spell, too, Kit had prepared the night before, knitting both his and Ponch's names and descriptions into it. The wizardry included a variant of the Mason's Word, which involves a very detailed description, in wizardly terms, of the structure of stone. As both wizards and physicists know, even the densest stone—indeed, almost all kinds of matter perceived as solid—is mostly empty space. Now as Kit and Ponch walked toward the wall of the school, all the atoms in their bodies and the atoms of the wall engaged in a brief, complex, stately little dance, carefully avoiding one another in droves as wizard and dog passed through brick and mortar and reinforcing metal. A moment later, Kit and Ponch were standing inside the classroom.

The room was carpeted, which made it easy to walk softly. Kit and Ponch made their way carefully around the edge of the room, toward the side where Darryl sat on the floor, looking at the book. *Or is he really?* Kit thought, as his point of view changed and he could see more clearly that Darryl was looking in the general direction of the book, but not *at* it, more *through* it. His face was not quite expressionless: There was a shadow of a smile there, but it was hard to tell what he was smiling at.

They paused near him, behind him, while the teacher kept reading, something about the seven wonders of the ancient world. Ponch stood looking intently at Darryl, his nose working, while Kit looked over the boy's shoulder, trying to make something of that remote expression. *Definitely his body's here,* Kit said. *But as for the rest of him...*

Far away, Ponch said. *I can show you where now, though. The scent's strong.*

Okay—

In a moment. Ponch sat down and started scratching.

Unfortunately, in this small quiet space, a sound that Kit heard all the time, so often that he didn't pay attention to it anymore, suddenly made itself apparent. It was Ponch's dog-license tag and name tag, on his collar, jingling together. Just about everybody in the classroom, except for Darryl, looked up in surprise, trying to figure out where the sound was coming from.

Uh-oh, Kit thought. That *was dumb!* To Ponch he said hurriedly, and silently, *Now would be a good time!*

Right—

Ponch stepped forward, pulling the leash tight, and vanished, just as Darryl's teacher got up from the floor with a mystified look and headed toward them.

Kit stepped forward after Ponch and vanished, too, relieved—

The wind hit him then, so that Kit staggered, staring around him, half-blinded by the sudden blazing light after the soft fluorescents of the classroom.

"Where are we?"

Inside his mind. He's here somewhere, Ponch said.

Here was a landscape right out of the depths of the Sahara. Kit and Ponch were perched precariously on the crest of a dune so sharply wind-sculpted that its edge could have been used for a razor...except that every second, the wind stripped grains off it, eroding it, and whipping sand off the other dunes that stretched out all around them. A hard blue sky came down to the horizon on all sides, featureless; it held not a wisp of cloud, only the fierce sun...yet there was something mysteriously indistinct about that sun, as if, even in that sky, dust obscured it.

"Just *look* at all this," Kit said, gazing around him. "Did Darryl's autism make this? Or did he?"

I don't know.

Kit shook his head. "I've seen an interior landscape or two in my time," he said, "but this one...Look how empty it is." He scanned the horizon. "If this is the inside of Darryl's mind, then where is he?"

Maybe he's hiding?

Kit thought about that, and about what his mother had said about the autistic people who found life simply too intense to bear. "From himself, too?" Kit said.

I don't know. But he is here. Look! Ponch said. Kit looked where Ponch's nose pointed. Footsteps led down from the dune-crest, dug in deep where someone had had to dig his heels in to stop sliding, and then had kept on sliding anyway. Down at the bottom of the dune, in the space sheltered from the wind, the footsteps were better preserved, better defined. They reminded Kit of certain footsteps left in the moondust of Tranquillity Base, except that those were now being eroded by micrometeorites. These footsteps were still sharp, and they had a familiar sneaker company's logo scored across them, one that Armstrong's and Aldrin's boot soles had definitely been missing.

"Weird," Kit said softly. The footsteps led away across that blazing wilderness, up the next dune and into the unremitting day. "Where's he going?" Kit said.

Away from the Other One, Ponch said. *Can't you feel It? It's here, too. It's following him.* Ponch scented the air. *It's been following him for a long time.*

"Three months?" Kit said.

I think longer.

"How can that be?"

I don't know. But Its scent is strong in Darryl's neighborhood. I've smelled it often enough when It's been chasing after you. Ponch shook himself all over ... and this time it had nothing to do with feeling itchy; it was his version of a shudder. *He flees—It pursues.* Ponch's nose worked; he looked bemused. *And not just here.*

"Then where?"

I'm not sure. Come on.

The sand they slid down was more pink than golden. Kit looked at it and thought of the book that Darryl's teacher had been reading him. It had been open to a page about the pyramids. *Something of the world's getting through to him,* he thought. *The question is, what's he making of it?*

The heat from the sun was oppressive. Kit pulled off his parka, rolled it up, and stuck it into his otherspace pocket. Then he and Ponch reached the bottom of the dune and started the climb up the side of the next one. "We could airwalk it...," Kit said.

He didn't, Ponch said. *His trail's down here. We need to go the way he went, for now.*

Kit nodded, put his head down to try to keep the wind-whipped sand out of his eyes, and went up the next dune in Ponch's wake. *That way,* Ponch said as he came up to the top of the dune.

Kit looked across the sand, following Ponch's gaze. Maybe eight or ten miles away, almost obscured by the height of the farther dunes and the haze of sand and dust in the air, a low line of jagged stone rose against the horizon. "Are those hills?" Kit said.

I think so. He's there somewhere. Come on.

Ponch led, and Kit followed. Once or twice, Ponch was certain enough of the trail to let Kit use a transit spell to cover some distance, but more often he insisted on doing it on foot, so Kit simply had to slog after him, for the time being unwilling to use any spells to protect him from the wind and the sand, on the off chance that they would somehow interfere with Ponch's tracking sense. The sand seemed to get into everything—down

Kit's shirt and up his pants, into the bends of his knees and elbows. It rubbed him raw around the neck and even under his socks. *I can barely stand this,* Kit thought as he toiled up yet another dune after Ponch. *And if I can't, what's it doing to Darryl?*

Ponch reached the top of that dune and looked ahead of them. From here the low, jagged hills that had shown earlier near the horizon finally seemed within reach, no more than a few miles away. They looked taller than they had, harsher and more forbidding; they cast long, dark shadows at their feet, under that unforgiving sun, which hadn't moved in the sky the whole time they had been there. Kit glanced up toward it, then away. "It's almost like this is a real place," he said softly.

It's real to him. And therefore it's real to What's chasing him…

Kit shook his head at that. Tom's warning not to get caught up in Darryl's Ordeal had been straightforward enough. Yet was it going to be possible to stand to one side and let another wizard handle the Lone Power by himself? *And what if It doesn't want just to concentrate on him?* Kit thought. *What am I supposed to do if It decides to try to do something about me? Just cut and run, just leave him there?*

I wish Neets were here. I could really use some backup.

Ponch stood panting in the heat, gazing down. *That looks sort of like a building,* he said.

Kit squinted. Down among the rock-tumble at the foot of the steep, jagged hills, there did seem to be something that looked built, and in it was a vertical, oblong darkness that could have been a gigantic door. "Is that where he went?" Kit said.

I think so. Do you want to take us down there?

Kit looked at the dark patch in the long ominous shadows thrown by the hills. *Want to?* he thought. *Wow, I can't wait.* Nonetheless, he pulled out the transit spell. "Let's go," he said.

A few moments later, they stood at the foot of the biggest cliff. Kit looked up at it, and up, and up, and hardly knew what to think. The whole side of the cliff was a dark red stone, carved, deeply, for at least three hundred feet up. The red stone must have been the source of the pink tint in all the sand they'd been toiling through. Someone had carved the cliff into pillars and arches, galleries and balconies, reaching back into solid stone that looked as if it had been laboriously hollowed out, chip by chip, by truly obsessive artisans. Niches and pedestals were carved into the stone; in them and on them stood statues, of people and animals and creatures not native to Earth, some of them not native to any planet Kit knew. Some of the poses, some of the expressions, were very creepy, indeed; all the statues, human or not, were staring down at the space in front of the oblong opening with stony blind eyes— staring at Kit as if, stone or not, they could still see. And it all looked brand-new, as if whatever or whoever had done this work might still be here, somewhere inside the gigantic gateway that loomed, dark and empty, in front of Kit and Ponch right now.

It wasn't an idea that made Kit particularly happy. *What a great place to have a cozy chat with Darryl about what's bothering him,* Kit thought. "Can you smell anybody else here?" he said to Ponch. "Besides us, and Darryl, and you-know-who?"

No. Ponch stood there with his nose working. *But I'm not sure that means that nobody else* can *be here...*

I've got to stop asking him questions when I know the answers are going to make me more nervous than I already am, Kit thought. "In there?" he said, breaking his resolution immediately.

In there.

"Let's go, then."

Ponch stalked forward into the darkness. The way he was walking made Kit almost feel like laughing a little, even through his nervousness; it was the way Ponch stalked squirrels out in the backyard: stealthy, a little stiff-legged. *That's all we need in here,* he thought as he followed Ponch into the dimness. *To be attacked by millions of evil squirrels.*

As the darkness around them got deeper, Kit pushed that thought away as one it was probably smarter not to encourage. "Can you see all right?" he said very softly to Ponch.

I can smell all right. Seeing doesn't matter so much.

Kit swallowed as the darkness got deeper. *To you, maybe,* he thought. He reached into his "pocket," got out his manual, and riffled through it briefly for a spell that would produce a bit of light, no more than a pocket flashlight would produce. After a few whispered sentences in the Speech, he pointed one finger to test it out. No light source showed, but a soft white light nonetheless fell on what he pointed his finger at—in this case, another immense carving, set into the wall to their left. Kit took one look at it and immediately turned the light elsewhere, reminded much too clearly of the alien with the laser eggbeater. The carving could have been one of that alien's relatives in a very bad mood, and it seemed to be looking right at him—not only with all its eyes, but also with all its teeth.

Kit shook his head and turned his attention elsewhere, using the wizardly flashlight to look around as Ponch led him further into the hill. There was no dismissing this space as just a cave: It was a long hall, a vast corridor of a dwelling of some kind, as intricately carved inside as it had been outside—as if thousands of creatures with a passion for strange statuary had been working here for centuries. Where the walls were lacking actual statues, they were wrought in weird but wonderful bas-reliefs, vividly colored, touched here and there with the glint of gold or the glassy sheen of gems. Kit moved past them in a mixture of nervousness and admiration, his light flicking past stern creatures with vast, spread wings; tall, rigid humanoid shapes with arms held in positions ungainly but still somehow expressive; strange beast shapes whose expressions were peculiarly more human than those of the man shapes that alternated with them. The place made Kit think of the set of some kind of adventure movie about exploring ancient tombs, but realized in a hundred times more detail—every chisel mark accounted for, the backs of the statues as perfectly executed as their fronts, everything sharp and clear, down to the last grain of sand or dust.

Who'd have thought somebody autistic could notice *things this way,* Kit thought. But then he shook his head at himself. He'd hardly ever thought about autistic people except to feel vaguely sorry for them, and he'd never given any thought to what they might or might not be able to do. That was changing now. Whatever else might be going on inside of Darryl, he could *see* things—possibly more clearly than Kit had ever seen them, except under the most unusual circumstances. If that was any kind of hint to what Darryl's talents as a wizard might eventually become—

Ponch stopped, and growled.

Kit stopped, too, looking around, a little more nervously now. It had occurred to him that one of the other things Darryl had managed to include in this space, if he had, indeed, created it for himself, was a sense of it being haunted. And only now, alerted by Ponch's growl, did Kit start to see the dark shapes moving beyond where his little light could reach, beyond the statues, in the gloom through the archways that opened here and there off the great main hall. And— Kit looked up, unsure whether he had heard wings flapping way up above them, under the soaring shadows of the unseen ceiling.

What are they? he said silently to Ponch.

Ponch sniffed, let out a long whoosh of breath, as if smelling something bad. *Fears.*

Kit frowned, seeing more of the dark shapes gathering in the path he and Ponch had been taking toward the heart of the hill. Even when he tried to look straight at them, they stayed vague, like the things you see or half suspect you see out of the corner of your eye, the things that creep up on you from behind in the dark. Point the light at them, and they're gone, flitting to either side; but let the light slide away, and they gather there again, seen better by averted vision than straight on. The glint of eyes, of teeth, showed in the dark: the flailing, skittering motion of too many limbs—

Ponch growled again. It's *here. Ahead, to the right, then left again. In the center of it all.*

From ahead, further into the hill, came a low rumble of thunder. The sound of it went right up to that unseen ceiling, echoing, and went right through the floor; Kit could feel it through his feet.

The shadowy fears crowded closer. Ponch bared his teeth and growled more loudly, and the closest of the fears skittered away. Kit looked all around them, reaching out with a wizard's senses to try to tell if whatever avatar the Lone Power was using here was particularly close by. It seemed to him that It wasn't, that Its attention was elsewhere, closely centered on someone else. *Darryl...*

They came to the end of that immense hallway, a T-junction; the wall just ahead of them held another of the immense carvings, reaching up and out of sight into the gloom. It showed a tangle of human and alien bodies that seemed to struggle and push against one another, trying to go in one direction or another, but that seemed unable to get much of anywhere, like a stone rush hour in some otherworldly subway station. Kit shook his head at it as Ponch pulled him to the right. A faint mutter of sound was coming from that direction, and from far away, reflected on the endless carvings, a gleam of light.

The corridor through which they moved got narrower, the much-carved walls of it seeming to press slowly together, like another gimmick from a bad adventure movie. Kit tried to convince himself that the effect was just a trick of perspective, but no matter how he tried, he wasn't sure that when he wasn't looking, those walls didn't actually creep inward, just a little bit. And off to either side of him and Ponch, slightly more visible now that there was a little light up ahead, the fear-shadows paced them, flitting in and out among the carvings, skittering, chittering softly to themselves with, every now and then, the occasional little chattering laugh. In the way they moved, and in the way they avoided being seen, they began to remind Kit very unpleasantly of cockroaches... and he longed for the leisure to pause and stomp on some of them, just for the fun of it. But there wasn't time for that now. Ponch was intent, his head down, in full tracking mode, growling softly again. The sound ahead of them started getting louder, and louder still—a repetitive, thundering noise. *I don't think this place is going to be conducive to a relaxed conversation with Darryl,* Kit thought.

Ponch turned a corner to the left; Kit followed him. The light up ahead was cold and flickering, like something glimpsed through the doors of a movie theater while the feature was showing. But no theater on Earth would have had a sound system capable of producing the thunder-rumble that accompanied the light. They turned down yet another carved corridor, this one a tall, narrow slit that Kit soon realized was two doors, easily several stories tall, that weren't quite shut.

Kit stopped at another of those earthshaking, wall-shaking rumbles of noise, louder than ever, and the hair on the back of his neck stood up because he could sense the Lone Power nearby. If Darryl and the Lone One or Its minions were having it out up ahead, some kind of protection would probably be a good idea. *You stick close to me from here on,* he said to Ponch. *All we have to do now is figure out what's going on, and what to do about it.*

Let me know when you do that, Ponch said, *because right after that, I want to go home.* He sounded unusually definite.

You're not alone there, believe me. Kit wondered if Ponch was feeling what he himself had started to feel—a wearying pressure that made him too tired to look at things, too tired to pay attention to what was going on around him. *And just when I need to pay attention the most. If Darryl has to put up with this all the time, then, boy, do I sympathize with him...*

There was one other spell that Kit had been keeping ready in the back of his mind, twenty-six words of its twenty-seven already spoken. Now, under his breath, Kit said the last word of the spell. Nothing visible happened around him and Ponch, but the silent sizzle of a wizardly force field flicked into being there, a half sphere of protection against sudden violent force. The field wasn't anything that would hold off the Lone Power for very long if It decided to get really aggressive, but it would buy Kit and Ponch time enough to think of something else, or to get away.

Kit reached just above his head and felt the expected bump and slight shock of touching the field, like the shock you get from walking on carpet and then touching something metallic. *It's running,* he said. *You ready?*

No, but let's get it over with, Ponch said.

His dog's nervousness surprised Kit a little... but then he wasn't exactly calm himself. Kit slowly went forward toward the partway open doors, Ponch keeping close beside him. The increasingly bright light spilling out of the doors showed some of the carvings on them, another tangle of the strange half-man, half-beast creatures, all with their heads turned away from the viewer, or their faces hidden, as if afraid to be looked at directly. Kit began to wonder about that, but the crescendo of thunder coming from inside the doors distracted him. Light flared again and again from inside, blue-white, blinding.

Kit moved a little to one side, so that he and Ponch would be sheltered by the right-hand door, and wouldn't immediately be seen by whoever was inside. They crowded up against the writhing shapes carved into the great brazen doors, the force field complaining softly in the back of Kit's mind about having to press up against something solid. Kit ignored the complaint and had a good long look into the darkness, back the way he and Ponch had come, to make sure they weren't being followed by anything that might be capable of breaching the force field. Then he turned and peered, very carefully, around the edge of the door.

His view was somewhat limited, but he could see enough of what was going on to have to catch his breath in astonishment. Beyond the door was a huge open space—enclosed, Kit thought from the way the sound echoed in there, but with a ceiling so high up that he couldn't even see it. Well below that point, the awful blinding light contained in that space started to give way to gloom. For what looked like about half a mile in front of him, and off to either side, stretched a huge pit of the red stone, carved into endless rings of bleacherlike seats—an amphitheater, its upper walls crowded with more of the creepy blind-eyed statues, their gazes turned down toward the central stage, watching, though seeming not to. In the stands of the amphitheater were hundreds of the shadows that Kit had seen in the outer darkness, maybe even thousands of them, all as intent as the statues on what was happening down in the space in the middle.

The fury of light concentrated there should have washed all those shadows away to nothing. The center of the amphitheater was crowded with writhing whips of lightning, ropes and sheets of lightning, whole curtains of it, such as Kit hadn't seen since he was last deep in the atmosphere of Jupiter. All of the deadly fire was striking at one spot, washing over it again and again as if trying to obliterate the single small shape that stood alone in the middle of it all, arms up around his head, twisting from side to side. With every crack of lightning, the air was torn with a great havoc of thunder, a shattering drumroll that never stopped. Ponch, peering around the door and squinting into the lightning, crowded close to Kit, growling softly, and Kit hung on to him as together they peered down into the heart of that riot of fire and destruction, trying to make out what was happening.

For just a few moments, the lightning died back a little, and Kit was able to make out what stood on the far side of it, beyond the small shape that the lightning was tormenting. It was a tall form, dark, somewhat human at the moment, and wearing a deeper darkness around it like a cloak or a shroud—looking like an abyss into which everything must invariably fall and be devoured, a chilly, light-hating vacuum that would have made a black hole seem outgoing and generous by comparison. The Lone Power stood there, looking down on Its present handiwork, and finding it good.

The darkness around It rose up, and from it more lightning lashed down into the center of the arena at the little staggering boy shape that now turned and twisted and cried out, writhing and falling to its knees, clutching at its head, tearing at itself in a frenzy of trying to be somewhere else. Yet escape seemed impossible. The boy kneeling there was bent double now, impotent, rocking back and forth, rocking. Kit thought in pity and horror of the slight rocking motion that Darryl had been making in the classroom as he looked at the book.

The unfairness of all this, the cruelty of it, was making Kit furious, even as the crowding pressure of weariness in the air left him more and more uncomfortable and tired. Beside him, Ponch never stopped growling. *I wish I could do something,* Kit thought. *But I'm not sure what to do. This isn't my Ordeal . . . and right now, my job's to watch.*

And so he held still, and watched—though he got angrier all the time—while the Lone One whipped the little crouching shape with lightnings, and Its laughter, the earthquake, rumbled through all the stone around them. In the stands, the fear-shadows hissed and whispered and heaved with amusement, and Kit stood there and held his peace until he felt like he just couldn't keep quiet anymore. He started to stand up and shout, *He's not alone!*

But Ponch shouldered Kit to one side, behind the door again, and Kit sat down hard. Ponch put his nose up against Kit's ear, cold, his own style of wake-up call, and said, *He's not here!*

What?? Kit said.

Darryl. He's not here.

But you said he wasn't in school, either—

The scent's changed! Watch.

Kit shook his head, got up, looked around the door again. There was the small, dark shape, crouching in the center of that huge lightning-scarred space, rocking, rocking, hiding its head in its arms, while the Lone Power scourged it with lightnings and laughed, the hissing of the watching fears a soft, evil accompaniment. It went on for a long time, a little eternity . . . but Kit held still. The lightnings descended with more and more violence every moment, until even that last faint glimpse of Darryl was washed out in their fury.

Watch, Ponch said again, sounding perplexed but somehow also amused. The air stank of ozone, the stone of the floor began to run and go molten in places, and there was nothing at the center of things anymore but a ferocious knot of pale, blue-white fire, lightning that unnaturally endured for breath after breath, washing and burning through this one last stubborn spot that it had not been able to abolish—

—until it faded away, and all that huge amphitheater rustled with the satisfied hissing of a thousand fears.

But there was one sense of satisfaction that was missing. The greatest, deepest darkness—the tall one now moving down into the center, to where a young boy's body should have lain—was not at all satisfied. All the shadow-fears that looked on slowly stilled their hissing, becoming afraid themselves, as that master darkness towered over the place where Darryl should have been...and wasn't.

"Gone!" the Lone Power cried. "Gone again!

"Find him!!"

With a vast wind-rush rustling of terror, the shadows vanished. The Lone One, furious, swept Its darknesses about Itself. They writhed like an angry cloak, wrapped in close around their master. A second later, It was gone.

And Kit and Ponch stood there at the edge of it all, behind the door, in the dark, shaking.

It didn't even notice you, Ponch said, confused but relieved. *That's good.*

No argument. But what about Darryl? Kit was seriously confused. *How could he be there and* not *be there at the same time?*

I don't know, Ponch said. *But I want to go home now. And when we get home, I want a biscuit.*

Five biscuits, Kit said. *Maybe ten. Let's get out of here.*

They started making their way back through the carved corridors of the hill. "Where did he go?" Kit said after a while, when he started to get his breath back, for he'd held it again and again.

The Lone One? He didn't "go" anywhere. He's still where he always is: here. One side of Ponch's mouth curled again in a soft growl.

"No, I meant Darryl."

Oh. It may take me a little while to find out. Ponch's nose was working again. *But I don't think this is the first time he's done this maneuver; he did it too quickly. I can scent the change. I can find where he goes next.*

They came out of the dark, back into that pitiless day. "What I don't get is, *why's* he doing it?" Kit said, looking out across the endless, scorched, barren waste. "Why doesn't he get it over with? Not that he didn't look like he was having a bad time. But running away from the Lone One is no way to end an Ordeal. Sooner or later you have to tackle It head-on...before It catches you from behind, when you're not looking, and finishes you off."

I don't know. I'm not a wizard. But I know what it's like to be scared.

Kit heard the pity in his dog's voice, and was slightly surprised. Normally Ponch saved his concern for members of the family, or friends. "You're sure you can pick up the trail again?"

Any time. But not right now. Ponch trotted away from the bottom of the cliff, purposeful, not looking back. *I'm tired.*

But Ponch is sad, too, Kit thought. *And that makes it worse.* "Come on, big guy," he said. "Let's go."

Together, they vanished.

Conversations

NITA LOOKED UP out of darkness at the giant robot that was staring down at her.

At the time this seemed like the most natural thing in the world. There she stood, barefoot, in her long, pink-striped nightshirt, and there stood the robot, glittering in the single spotlight that shone down on the dark floor. The gleam of the downfalling light on the metal of the robot's skin was nearly blinding. *What kind of metal is that, I wonder?* Nita thought, for the skin sheened a number of colors, from a hot blue through magenta to a greenish yellow, depending on how the robot moved. Right now it was shifting idly from foot to foot, as if it was waiting for something to happen.

Titanium, Nita thought, recalling some jewelry she'd seen one of her classmates wearing to school recently; it had had the same hot-colored sheen as the robot's skin.

Or was it palladium? I forget. "Hello?" Nita called up to the robot.

There was no reply. But the robot did hold still, then, and incline its head a little to look down in Nita's general direction. There was no telling whether it was actually looking at her: Where eyes normally would have been, there was a horizontal slit, which probably had sensors behind it. The robot strongly resembled the kind of giant robot that kept turning up on Saturday morning television, and Nita found herself wondering whether this one might suddenly start breaking apart into jet fighters and tanks and other such paraphernalia. But for the moment, it just stood there.

Nita started to get a strange, repetitive, ticktock feeling in the back of her head—an emotion or thought recurring, again and again, as regular and inevitable as clockwork, but recurring at a distance, in a muffled kind of way. It wasn't a pleasant feeling, either—it was a kind of thought or emotion that you would suffer from, rather than experience with any particular pleasure. Fortunately, it wasn't so acute that Nita had to pay much attention to it, though she felt vaguely sorry for the robot, if this weary feeling did, indeed, belong to it.

"Is there anything I can do for you?" Nita called, more loudly this time. There was no question of speaking to the robot more conversationally: Its head was at least fifty feet above the ground. *This is like having a conversation with a flagpole*, Nita thought.

The robot took a clunky step toward her, then another, then suddenly hunkered down in front of her with a great groan and screech of complaining, over-stressed metal. Nita thought at first that it might fall over, it looked so unsteady, and it wobbled and leaned from left to right to left again. It was intent on her, though again Nita couldn't be sure how she knew that: The metal face was blank, and it had no way to change its expression even if one had been there.

"So what is it?" Nita said. "Give me a clue!"

It loomed over her, possibly considering what to say. As machine intelligences went, the robot already seemed pretty reticent: Nita's limited experience with mechanical life-forms suggested that they were big talkers, but this one didn't seem to be so inclined. It just leaned over her, the size of a small apartment building, and a tongue-tied one at that.

"Oh, wait a minute, *now* I know what it is," Nita said. "You want to talk to my sister, right? I'm really sorry, but she's asleep right now."

No response from the shining form. "Asleep?" Nita said. "Temporarily nonfunctional? Off-line?"

The robot suddenly began emitting what Nita thought at first were more metal-stress sounds, but after she got past how deafening they were, she found she could catch the occasional word through them, and the words were in the Speech. *Oh good,* Nita thought, for there were quite a few alien species scattered throughout the Local Group of galaxies who knew the Speech, using it as a convenient common tongue.

"*[Grind, groan, screech]* difficulty *[screech-moan-crash]* entropy *[moan, moan, clunk-crash]* communications," the robot said. And then said nothing more, but just wobbled back and forth amid a whine of gyros, trying to keep its balance.

Nita was getting confused. *Why can't I understand it?* "Uh, okay," she said in the Speech, "I think I got a little of that. Something's interfering with your communications. What exactly did you want to communicate about? Do you have some other kind of problem that needs to be solved?"

The robot just crouched there, wobbling, for several moments. Then it said, "Solve *[scream-of-metal, grind, ratchet]* problem *[moan, moan, much higher moan, crash]* cyclic-insoluble *[grind, grind]* time *[extremely long-duration whirly-noisemaker sound, crash, clunk]* no solution *[screeeeeeech, crash crash crash]* trap *[boom]*."

Nita revised her original opinion about having conversations with flagpoles. This was more like a dialogue with a garbage truck, that being the only other thing in her immediate experience that sounded anything like this. "I'm really sorry," she said, "but I'm having a lot of trouble understanding you. It's my fault, probably. Can you tell me more clearly how I can help you? Just what is it that you need?"

The huge shape crouched there for a few more moments, then, wobbling, it got up. For a long, long moment it stood over her, seeming to gaze down at her from that great height... but Nita still couldn't be sure. Then the robot turned, and slowly and clumsily went clanking off into the darkness, out of the spotlight where it and Nita had been standing.

Nita broke out in a sudden sweat, feeling that she'd missed something important. "Look," she called after it hurriedly, feeling incredibly inadequate and useless, "I really am sorry I can't help you! If you come back later, when my sister's awake, she should be able to figure out what it is you need. Please, come back later!"

But it was gone.

—and Nita found herself staring at the dark ceiling of her bedroom. The sun wasn't yet up outside, and she was still sweating, and feeling stupid, and wondering what on Earth to make of the experience she'd just had.

At least it wasn't a nightmare, like that other one, she thought.

But on second thought, considering how spectacularly dumb she felt right now, Nita wasn't so sure....

There was no chance of getting back to sleep, so Nita showered and got dressed for school, ate a cereal bowl's worth of breakfast that she didn't really feel like eating, and then dawdled over a cup of tea until it was time to wake her dad. This was an addition to Nita's morning routine that she heartily wished she didn't have to deal with, but her father really needed her to do it. Recently he'd been turning off his alarm clock and going back to sleep without even being aware of having done so.

She knocked at the bedroom door. "Daddy?"

No answer.

"Daddy...it's six-thirty."

After a few seconds came the sound Nita had been bracing herself for, the sound she didn't think her dad knew he made: a low, miserable moan, which spoke entirely too clearly of how he felt, deep down inside, all the time now. But this was the only time of day that sound got out, before he was completely awake. Nita controlled herself as strictly as she could, absolutely intent on not making things any worse for him by sounding miserable herself.

"Do you want me to make some coffee?" Nita said.

"Uh," her dad said. "Yes, sweetheart. Thanks."

Nita went down to the kitchen and did that. She had mixed feelings about making her dad's coffee: That had always been what her mother did, first thing. Nita also wasn't sure if she was making it strong enough—her mom had always joked that her dad didn't want any coffee that didn't actually start to dissolve the cup. Nita, being new at this, was still experimenting with slight changes to the package directions, a little more each morning, and secretly dreading the day when she would get it right, and it would most forcibly remind her dad of who had *not* made it.

She started the coffee machine and went quietly back up to her room. By then her dad was already in the shower. Nita sat down at her desk, picked up her book bag from beside it, and shoved in the textbooks she'd be needing today. She had a chemistry test that afternoon, so she picked up the relevant book from beside her bed and started reading.

It was hard to concentrate, even in the early morning stillness. In fact, it was hard to concentrate most times, but this was something that Nita had been pushing her way through by dint of sheer stubbornness. The rest of her life might be going to pieces, but at least her grades were still okay, and she was going to keep them that way. What Nita missed, though, was the sheer effortless enjoyment she had always gotten from science before. This stuff was harder than the science she'd loved as a kid. *That by itself isn't so much of a problem. I'm learning it. Though I'm not used to having to work at it.* But the shadow of pain that hung over everything was also interfering ... and about that, there wasn't anything she could do.

"Sweetie?"

Nita looked up. Her dad was standing in her bedroom doorway, looking at her with some concern. "Sorry, Dad, I didn't hear you."

He came over and gave her a hug and a kiss. "I didn't mean to distract you. I just wanted to make sure you'll see that Dairine gets out."

"Sure."

"Don't let her sweet-talk you."

Nita raised her eyebrows at the unlikeliness of this. "I won't."

"Okay. See you later."

He went out. Nita heard the back door lock shut behind him, heard the car start. She glanced out the window into the gray, early morning light, and saw the car backing out of the driveway, turning in the street, vanishing from sight. The engine noise faded down the street.

Nita sat there and thought of her dad's still, pale face as he spoke to her. Sad all the time; he was so sad. Nita longed to see him looking some other way ... yet for so long now she'd routinely felt sad herself, because she could understand his problem. *It's only been a month,* she thought, *and already I can't remember what it's like not to be sad.*

The school shrink had warned her about that. Mr. Millman, fortunately, had turned out to be very different from what Nita had expected, or dreaded, when she'd been sent to see him after her mom had died. The other kids at school tended to speak of "the shrink" in whispers that were half scorn, half fear. Having to go see him, in many of their minds, still meant one of three things: that you needed an IQ test—probably to prove that you needed to be put in a slower track than the one you were in; that you were crazy, or about to become so; or that you were some kind of closet boozer or druggie, or had some other kind of weird thing going on that was likely to make you a danger to yourself or others.

Nita had been surprised that the crueler mouths around school hadn't immediately started to spread one or another of these rumors about her. But it hadn't happened, apparently because her mother was well known and liked in town by a lot of people, and this attitude had spread down to at least some of their kids. It seemed that those kids at school who knew her at all thought that though Nita was a geek, it was a shame about her mother, and counseling after her mom died so young wouldn't count as a black mark against her.

So nice of them, Nita had thought when she first heard about this. But she had to admit to a certain amount of relief that mockery wasn't going to be added to the whispers of pity that she'd already had more than enough of. Not that she wasn't used to half the kids she knew making fun of her as an irredeemable nerdette. But having to deal with a new level of jeering, as well as the pain, was something she could do without right now.

She still had no energy to speak of. Sleep never came easily anymore, and she kept waking up too early. But once she was awake, she didn't really want to do anything. If Nita had had her way, she'd have stayed home from school half the time. But she *didn't* have her way, especially since Dairine was already in trouble with the principal at her school for all the time she'd been losing—so much so that their dad had to go see the principal about it this afternoon. Nita was completely unwilling to add to his problems, so she made sure she got to school on time—but she found it hard to care about anything that happened there.

Or anywhere else, she thought. Even though she was up before dawn half the time, the predawn sky, even with the new comet passing through, didn't attract her as it used to. Nita leaned on the sill of the window by her desk, looking out at the bare branches of the tree out in the middle of the backyard. She could see the slow words its branches inscribed against the brightening sky in the wind, but she couldn't bring herself to care much what they said. She felt as if there was some kind of thick skin between her and the world, muffling the way she knew she ought to feel about things... and she didn't know what to do to get rid of it. What really frightened Nita were the times when she clearly perceived that separation from the world as something unnatural for her, and *still* didn't care if the remoteness never got better—the times she was content to just sit and stare out at the world, and watch it go by.

She found herself doing that right now, staring vaguely at the clutter on her desk—pens and pencils, school notebooks, sticky pads, overdue library books, a few CDs belonging to the downstairs computer. And her manual, closed, sitting there looking like just one more of the library books. *Overdue,* she thought, glancing past it at the other books. *That's not like me, either. I'm so obsessive about getting them back on time, usually... I should take them back after school today.*

But taking them back just seemed like too much trouble. It could wait another day, or two, or three, for the little fine it would cost her. *Maybe I'll feel more like it over the weekend.*

Nita let out a long breath as she looked at her manual. It wasn't as if it was alive in any way, as if it had anything with which to look at her...

...but it *was* looking at her, and she wasn't sure what to make of its expression.

She flipped it idly open to the back section, where the status listings were. Turning a few pages brought her to Kit's listing, which she scanned with brief, weary interest. Then she paged along to her own.

CALLAHAN, Juanita L.
243 E. Clinton Avenue
Hempstead, NY 11575
(516) 555-6786
power rating: 6.76 +/− .5
assignment status: optional

Nita stared at that for a long moment, never having seen anything like it on her listing before.

"Optional"?

Since when am I "optional"?!

She sat there looking at the listing for a few seconds longer. *Jeez,* she thought, *that sounded more like Dairine than me...*

It was still a strange listing. And the longer she looked at it, the less she liked it.

But that brought her to her next order of business for the morning. Reluctantly, Nita got up and went across the hall to Dairine's room. "Dari...," she said, knocking on the door and knowing what was going to come next.

"*Ngggg,*" said a voice from inside.

"Get up."

"In a minute."

"Don't make me laugh, Dari. Say it in the Speech."

"*Ngggg.*"

Nita grimaced. Dairine was twisty and shifty in all kinds of ways, but even now, even angry and upset with life as she was, she would not dare say anything in the Speech that wasn't true. "Dairiiiiiiiiine..."

A pause. "Must you be so disgustingly responsible at this hour of the morning?"

"Yes," Nita said, unimpressed by either the volume or the sentiment. "Get up, Dairine. I have things to do besides deal with *you* all morning."

"Then go do them, and give them my regards."

"Not a chance. Get up."

"No."

And so it went for another fifteen minutes or so. Nita's temper started fraying. *I might have seen the daybreak,* she thought, *but I'm still going to be late for Millman, thanks to Dairine. Again.*

I've had about enough of this!

Nita held out her hand for her manual, which oblig-ingly picked itself up off her desk and came cruising along into the hall. She plucked it out of the air and began paging through it. *Okay, today's the day,* she thought. *Today I actually* use *that spell instead of just thinking about it. But I have to add something fast.* Nita spent a moment wondering under which category she would find the addition she was contemplating for the wizardry she had in mind. *Well, it's a teleport, but now it's complex rather than strictly inanimate...* "Dairine," Nita said. "This is just another cheap at-tempt not to go to school."

"It's not an attempt."

"Uh-huh." *We'll see about* that. *Okay, here we go. The shape of the wizardry's a little weird now, but if I constrain the feeder end of the spell like this—and this— Yeah. Quick and dirty, but it'll do the job.* "You really ought to think about the consequences of your actions," Nita said, "especially insofar as they affect what Dad's gonna have to say to you when school calls him at work to find out where you are."

"Nita, that's my problem, not yours, so why don't you just butt out for a change instead of trying to run everybody's life. You're no replacement for Mom, no matter what you may think you're doing, and—"

A tirade, Nita thought, already halfway through the spell. *Good.* She paused just long enough to admit to herself that the remark about their mom did, indeed, really hurt, and then went on with the spell. Dairine was meanwhile still in full flow. "... when you come to your senses again, some time in the next century, you may discover that— *OW!*"

From inside Dairine's bedroom came a loud thump, the sound of a body hitting the floor—or, more accurately, parts of a body hitting the floor, and parts of it coming down hard on some of the many and varied things that Dairine routinely shoved underneath her bed. One-handed, Nita snapped her manual shut with a feeling of profound satisfaction.

"Where's my bed?!" Dairine shrieked.

"It's on Pluto," Nita said. "On the winter side, somewhere nice and dark and quiet, where you won't find it if you look all day—which you're not going to have time to do, because you'll be in school."

"Hah! I'll sleep in *your* bed!"

"You *hate* my bed," Nita said. "My mattress is too hard for you. And what's more, my bed and every other piece of furniture in this house have been instructed that after I leave, they're to teleport any living creature they touch right into the part of school where you're scheduled to be at that particular moment in time. How you explain your appearance there is going to be *your* problem."

"I'll take the wizardry apart."

"I've password-locked it. If you want, you can spend all day trying to unlock it from outside the house... and then *still* have to explain to Dad why you weren't in school again. After he's just spent an hour discussing the same subject with your principal. Meanwhile, if you want to sleep anywhere, you can do it on Pluto, if you like—but you're not doing it in *this* house till after you get back from school."

The bedroom door was flung open, and Dairine stormed through it, past Nita and toward the bathroom, head down, in a fury, refusing to give her sister so much as a glance. The severity of the effect was somewhat lessened by the dust bunnies that parted company with Dairine's pajamas along the way, floating gently in the air behind her.

"I wish I knew what alien force has kidnapped my sister and left this vindictive thug of a pod person in her place," Dairine said to the air, slamming the bathroom door shut. "Because when I find out, I'm going to hunt it down and kick however many rear ends it has from here to Alphecca!"

Nita stood there for a moment, watching a final dust bunny float toward the floor. "Enjoy your day," she said sweetly, and went to get her book bag.

Her meetings with Mr. Millman were always about an hour before homeroom, so that they were finished ten or fifteen minutes before other students started to arrive for the day. The covert quality of the meetings was enhanced by the fact that Mr. Millman didn't even have his own office, because he traveled from school to school in the district every day. Neither he nor anyone else in school knew where he was going to be from one session to the next. Nita most often found him in a spare office down in the administrative wing of the school, a room furnished with a metal desk and a few wooden chairs and not much else. Today he was there, sitting behind the old beat-up desk with the office door open, and working intently on one of those metal-ring puzzles in which the five constituent rings have to be interlaced.

This kind of behavior was typical of Mr. Millman, and was one of the redeeming features of having to deal with him. Whatever you might imagine a school shrink as being like, or looking like, he wasn't that. He was young. He had a large, frizzy black beard that made him look more like an off-duty pirate or an escaped Renaissance artist than a psychologist, and his long lanky build and loose-limbed walk made him look like a refugee from a Cheech and Chong movie. Though he wore a suit, he did so as if it had an invisible sign on the back of it saying, THEY MADE ME WEAR THIS: DON'T TAKE IT SERIOUSLY. He looked up at Nita from the ring-puzzle with a resigned expression. "Morning, Nita. You any good at these?"

"Morning, Mr. M." She sat down in front of the desk and took the rings he offered her. Fortunately Nita knew how the puzzle worked, and she handed the rings back to him, braided together, in about fifteen seconds.

He looked at the puzzle with helpless amusement. "Halfway to a doctorate," he said, "and I still have no grasp of spatial relationships. Remind me not to go into rocket science. How've your last couple of days been?"

"Not the best," Nita said. "I had to throw my sister out of bed this morning. She didn't want to go to school again."

"That seems to be turning into a routine," Mr. Millman said. "And from your expression, I get the feeling she didn't appreciate it. She try the line about your mother again?"

Nita nodded.

"And you didn't punch her out?"

Nita allowed herself a slight smile. "The temptation was there..."

They talked for maybe twenty minutes. Millman's style wasn't so much that of a shrink as that of a coach, Nita had decided: no long silences, no *mmm-hmm*s that transparently tried to draw you out and get you to talk about things. You talked or not, as you pleased, and Mr. Millman did the same. You asked questions or answered them, or didn't answer them, also as you pleased. It was all very leisurely and casual, and Nita was sure that Mr. Millman was getting a lot more out of what she said than she suspected. But, possibly because of the way he handled their sessions, she found that this wasn't bothering her. "Any more of those nightmares?" Mr. Millman said at one point.

"Some weird dreams," Nita said.

"Scary?"

"Not the one this morning. I felt more useless than anything else." Nita wasn't going to go too far into the specifics.

"Goes along with the rest of the symptoms at this point," Mr. Millman said. "The loss of appetite, the sleep troubles, and the mood swings—"

"Depression," Nita said.

Mr. Millman nodded. "That feeling of weight," he said. "Or of being weighted down...of feeling like your face'll crack if you smile."

"I wish I could make it go away," Nita said.

"Fighting it probably won't make it go away faster. May prolong it, in fact. Let it be there, and do your best to work around it, or through it, and do what you usually do. Work on things you would normally enjoy." Mr. Millman leaned back in the chair and stretched. "I would say *play,* but no one wants to hear that word at a time like this: It makes them feel guilty, even if it's what they need. If you have projects you work on, hobbies, keep them alive. You'll be glad you did, later—the work you do at a time like this is likely to be worth keeping. You do have hobbies?"

"Astronomy," Nita said. "Gardening—I help my dad." And then she added, "Magic."

And instantly panicked. *Now why did I say that?*

Millman raised his eyebrows.

Oh, god, no. What have I done?! Nita thought. *I'm gonna have to wash his brains now! And that's a* bad *thing to do to your shrink—*

"Ah, legerdemain," Millman said. "An interesting field. Not enough women in it. Some kind of gender bar there; don't ask me why all the famous magicians have been men. Anyway, it has to be good for your hand-eye coordination. Show me some card tricks, someday." He looked at his watch. "Not now, though—someone else will be here shortly."

"Thanks, Mr. M.," Nita said, and escaped from his

office as quickly as she could, wondering if, despite all Mr. Millman's casual reassurances, she was actually going crazy.

Kit had spent most of the previous day recovering from the exertions of following Ponch into the otherworld where they'd found Darryl. It wasn't as if he'd actually done so much wizardry himself, but it seemed to Kit that Ponch drew on his own power somewhat. *And then there's the leash,* Kit thought, as he headed into the kitchen to snatch a hurried breakfast. He'd overslept, partly in reaction to maintaining the leashwizardry and the shield-spell, partly just because of physical tiredness from toiling up and down all those dunes. His calf muscles certainly ached badly enough. But just as wearying, in their own way, were the events he'd seen taking place.

And also tiring, in a different way, was the amount of time he'd had to spend comforting Ponch afterward. The dog had seemed all right when they first got back, and had gone through the promised dog biscuits as if he hadn't eaten anything for days. But as the afternoon passed, Ponch started to look unhappy. And just after dinner, when Kit was helping his mama clear the table, they were both startled by a sound coming from outside. Ponch was howling.

Kit's mama gave him a peculiar look. "What's the matter with him?" she said. "Did the fire siren go off or something? I didn't hear it."

Kit shook his head. "I'll go find out," he said.

By the gate to the backyard, near the garage, Ponch

was sitting in the grass of the yard, howling as if rehearsing for a part in *The Call of the Wild.* Kit opened the gate. "Ponch! What is it? You want to come in?"

No. Ponch kept on howling.

Kit was mystified. He went to sit down by his dog, who ignored him and howled on. "What's the matter?" Kit said in the Speech, after a few moments more.

Ponch finished that howl and sat looking at the ground for a moment. *How could It do that to him?* Ponch said then. *He couldn't even do anything! And he was* good.

Kit blinked at that. "It's the Lone Power," he said. "Unfortunately, It seems to like to hurt people...and to like to see them hurting. Which is why we keep running into It, since it's our job to stop It from doing that whenever we can."

It's not fair, Ponch said. And he put his head up and howled again.

Down the street, Kit could hear one of the neighbors' dogs start howling, too, in a little falsetto voice that would have made him laugh if he wasn't rather concerned about Ponch. Soon every dog in the street was howling, and shortly there were some human shouts to go along with the noise: cries of "Shut up!" "Would you please shut your dog up?" and "Oh yeah, well, you shut *yours* up!"

Kit had no idea what to make of it all, and couldn't think of anything to do but sit with Ponch. Eventually the dog stopped howling, and one after another, slowly, the other dogs in the neighborhood got quiet. Ponch got up, shook himself, and walked out the still-open gate into the driveway. He made his way to the back door, waited for Kit to open it, and then went in and trotted up the stairs to Kit's bedroom.

Kit's mother had looked at him curiously as he came back in and closed the door. "What was that about?"

"Ponch was upset about what we were doing this morning," Kit had said. "I'd try to explain it to you, but I'm not sure I understand it myself."

Now, the next morning, as he went looking for his cereal bowl, he wasn't any closer to an answer. Ponch had been asleep when Kit had gotten up to his room, and he was sleeping still. *I'll talk to him about it later,* he thought, opening the cupboard over the counter.

There were no cornflakes. There was one box of his pop's shredded wheat, which Kit detested—whenever circumstances forced him to eat it, it always made him think he was eating a scrubbing pad. The only other box contained one of the cereals his sister liked, some kind of frosted, fruit-flavored, multicolored, marshmallow-infested, hyperpuffed, vitamin-reinforced starch construct, which was utterly inedible due to its being ninety-eight percent sugar—even though the word appeared on the box only once, in letters small enough for anyone without a magnifying glass to miss. "Mama," Kit said, aggrieved, "we're out of cereal!"

"Your kind, anyway. I know," his mother said, coming into the kitchen for another cup of coffee, with the TV remote in her hand. "Take it up with your pop: He had a fit of wanting cornflakes late last night, and he finished the box. He said he'd get some more on his way home from work. Have some toast."

"It's not the same," Kit muttered, but all the same he closed the cupboard and went to get the bread out of the fridge.

"Is Ponch all right now?" his mother said as she poured more coffee and reached past Kit into the fridge for the milk.

"I think so. Still sleeping, anyway."

His mama shook her head, and then smiled slightly. "All that noise last night...it reminded me. Is it just me, or has down-the-street's dog been louder than usual the past week or so?"

"You mean Tinkerbell?" That was not the dog's real name in the dogs' own language, Cyene, and possibly reason enough for the down-the-street dog's incessant barking. "I dunno, Mama. I'm so used to hearing him bark all the time, I don't notice anymore."

"Do you think you could talk to him, sweetie? You know." She wiggled her fingers in what she imagined was a vaguely wizardly gesture.

Kit raised his eyebrows while he put the bread in the toaster. "I can try. But, Mama, just because I talk to him doesn't necessarily mean he's going to listen. The dog's a head case. He thinks I'm a crook. But then he thinks *everybody* who doesn't live in his house is a crook."

"Dogs get like their owners, they say..."

"Huh?"

"Nothing, sweetie," his mother said, looking suddenly guilty.

Kit kept the smile off his face while he waited for the toast to come up. It was going to be fun to be middle-aged, someday, and be told the things his mother was *really* thinking, with no more need for the kid-filter that parents routinely seemed to self-install.

"What about the youngster whose head you were going to get into?" his mother said. "Were you able to talk to him?"

Kit shook his head. "He was real busy," Kit said. "Ponch and I are going to have to try again, when things are quieter." *If they* get *any quieter,* he thought. *And what if they don't?*

Then something else occurred to him. "Mom, you have any more trouble with the TV?"

"What?" She looked at Kit as if she couldn't understand what he was talking about, and then blinked. "Oh. No, it's been all right."

"Good," Kit said, and started buttering the toast.

"Except now that you mention it..."

Kit braced himself.

"Your dad told me you weren't joking. About the cooking shows..."

Kit sat down with his toast and tried desperately not to look as if he was about to have a panic attack. "Yeah."

His mother sat down across from Kit, looking thoughtfully at her coffee cup. "Honey, none of these people have ever tried to eat *you,* have they?"

"Aliens? No." That, at least, was the truth. "They might have *thought* about it, though. But so far it's not a crime to think about it. At least, not most places."

His mother's expression relaxed a little. "No, I guess

I can see where it might not be. I just worry about you, that's all."

Kit finished one piece of toast. "Mama, in one way it's like crossing the street. You know you have to watch out for traffic. So you look both ways before you cross. In some parts of the universe, you know that the locals think of you as a potential snack food, and you're just careful when you visit them not to act like a snack. But mostly"—Kit grinned—"wizards are nobody's snack. Dealing with those species mostly isn't any more dangerous than crossing the street. Also, some of them owe us."

His mama looked surprised. "What, humans?"

"No, wizards." Kit took a bite of the next piece of toast. "One of those species, the—" He paused; he wasn't used to saying their name except in the Speech, since their own word for themselves was hard to say. "Let's call them the Spinies, because they've got a lot of spines. They had a problem a while back: Their sun was going to go nova. One of us went in there and kept that from happening. It's not like they don't have their own wizards—they do. But a wizard from another species was passing through, caught the problem before any of them did, and fixed it." He shook his head. The story ranked as a hero-tale even among wizards, who, because of their line of work, were more or less used to saving the world, or worlds. "It was real time-critical stuff. The one who saved them came from one of the species that they normally would have thought of as food: humanoid, like us. The wizardry was a big one, complex—messing with the carbon cycle inside a star isn't for beginners. Doing the wizardry killed her. And the word got out. Now all the Spinies have something else to think about. 'Be nice to your food; it might save your life.'"

Kit worked on the second piece of toast while his mother thought about that.

"She was how old?" his mother said suddenly.

Kit had been hoping this wouldn't come up. "If you did it in human years," he said, "she'd have been about my age."

His mother's gaze rested on him as if a suspicion had been confirmed. "Does this kind of thing happen often?" she said.

It was so tempting to lie...but no temptation was more fatal for a wizard. "Every day, Mama," Kit said. "There aren't enough of us to do the job. Probably there never will be. Lots of us die of old age, in our beds. But some of us..."

His mother looked at him, and her expression changed. It became less confused, but the look that replaced it troubled Kit more, for reasons he couldn't understand. "I don't know why this surprises me," she says. "I'm a nurse, after all. It looks like we're both in a service profession. I just keep thinking you should have been offered a choice when you were old enough to understand what you were choosing."

"I was," Kit said. He pushed the plate away. "You told me you decided to be a nurse when you were eight."

His mama's expression turned first shocked, then

annoyed: the look of someone who doesn't expect to have her own revelations turned against her. "Yes, but—"

"You're gonna say that you didn't know everything that'd be involved in being a nurse, when you were eight," Kit said. "And right then being a nurse mostly looked to you like a pink plastic kit with a toy stethoscope and a toy thermometer in it. But you decided, anyway, because you wanted to help people. So when you were old enough you went to nursing school, and look, now you're a nurse. And it's not so bad. Right?"

His mother looked at him.

"That's what it's like to be a wizard," Kit said. "I promise, I'll keep letting you know what it looks like as I get older. But when I 'signed up,' I knew this was what I wanted to do. I knew right away. Sure, it gets more complicated as you go on. But doesn't everything?"

His mama gave him a long look. Then she smiled again, very slowly, and just half a smile: the kind of expression she gave his pop when she was admitting he'd been right about something, but didn't want to admit it out loud. "You should finish up your last piece of toast," she said. "And don't forget to rinse the plate."

She went to get dressed. Kit smiled nearly the same slow half smile, pulled the plate back, finished his toast, and then left for school.

At lunchtime, after he'd finished eating, Kit headed out to the front of the school for a breath of fresh air, and was irrationally pleased to see Nita out there waiting for him, in the parking lot, not too far from the doors.

He walked over to her, and together they strolled off some distance through the parking lot, away from the crowd of kids who always seemed to be standing around the main doors, watching who came in and went out, and who seemed to be doing what with whom. It was a game that Kit found both boring and dumb, but a lot of his classmates seemed to spend most of their time at it, so Kit enjoyed frustrating it as much as he could.

"How're you doing?" he said.

Nita frowned. "Okay," she said, "but something weird's going on."

Kit couldn't recall Nita having said that she felt "okay" for weeks now, and the sound of it encouraged him, but at the same time he didn't dare get too excited about it. "Like what?"

They paused by the chain-link fence that defined the school's boundary on the north side of the parking lot. On the other side of the fence was a cypress hedge too thick to see through, thick enough that it put hopeful green fronds through the fence; Nita idly took hold of one of these and ran it through her fingers while she told Kit about the strange dream she'd had. "Everything's supposed to understand the Speech," she said at last, when she'd given him all the details. "At least in theory..."

"I don't think it's theory," Kit said. "Everything that was made, was made using the Speech. Not being understood when you speak it is about as likely as matter not understanding gravity. Or light not understanding light speed."

Nita shook her head and looked out into the day as if seeing something at a great distance. "I know," she said. "But knowing the Speech also usually helps you understand what's being said...and it's sure not doing the job for me at the moment."

"Really weird," Kit said. "You have any idea what's going on?"

Nita heaved a long sigh and bounced her shoulders idly against the fence a couple of times. "I think that dream at least, and maybe another one I had a few days ago, were alien intelligences trying to get hold of Dairine."

Kit had to blink. "That happen to her a lot?"

Nita nodded. "On and off," she said. "It's mostly to do with her relationship with the mechanical sort of wizards—the computer intelligences and so on. She keeps getting feelers from life-forms that are half machine and half organic, and from a lot of the silicon-based types...some that I can't make anything of. She told me she's been doing a lot of work mediating between organic and inorganic lifestyles, way out at the edge of the universe, and it's specialized stuff. It even gives *her* trouble sometimes, translating between the ways they see life and the way we see it." Nita sighed. "So it's no surprise that I don't understand contacts from these guys right off the bat—I mean, as a species, in terms of their feelings and motivations and so on. But I should at least be able to understand them when they communicate about very basic things. And until now, I've always been able to. This last one, though..."

Kit waved a hand to stop her. "Time out for a minute. Why didn't Dairine take this contact, if it was her they were trying to reach?"

"Dairine wasn't up for it last night," Nita said. She let out a long breath. "Or most nights lately. Kit, she and my mom were even closer than Mom and I were, in some ways. She's taking everything a lot harder than I am. She's been missing a lot of school, and my dad's really worried about it." Nita's expression was that of someone purposefully putting a painful subject to one side. "Anyway, she was asleep when the 'call' came, and she didn't wake up to take it, the way she usually would. She was too tired, or else she just didn't want to. So I got it, somehow or other. But I couldn't understand it."

Kit shook his head. "You mean, whoever was on the other end wasn't using the Speech?"

Nita shook her head. "No, it was. But not the usual way. It was almost like it didn't know it was speaking: There was something... I don't know... *accidental* about the communication. Like whoever it was hadn't actually meant to call. Except it also felt kind of urgent."

Kit shook his head. "Were you able to get a location, a place of origin?"

"Just a sense that it was somewhere way, way out at the edge. I didn't have time for a proper trace," Nita said. "It didn't last long enough. Besides, I was asleep myself at the time. Maybe the trouble was that the message got garbled with something I was dreaming. But normally I would have woken up when something like that came in."

"You were tired, too," Kit said.

Nita sighed. "I'm tired all the time," she said. "It's just part of the depression, the shrink says. It'll go away someday."

"What a big help," Kit muttered.

Nita laughed then, an oddly wistful sound that startled Kit. "No," she said. "Really, it is a help. Knowing that someday it *will* go away makes it a little easier now. Not a lot... but every little bit helps, at the moment."

"So you got a call from the outer limits," Kit said. "And you're not sure what it was about... But at least a little of its message got through."

"Not a whole lot," Nita said. "I'm just hoping it 'calls back' and either gets Dairine this time, or gets me when I'm awake and can make something out of what it's saying." She leaned against the fence. "If the first message was from the same person, or people, it didn't make sense, either. At least not beyond 'I can't get off.'"

"'I can't get off...'" Kit thought about it, then shook his head. "Maybe it's just one of those situations where your brain takes a really alien concept and makes the best translation it can until you have more information."

"I really don't know," Nita said. "I'm going to sit down with the manual later and see if I can find something that'll throw some light on why I'm not able to understand more clearly what's coming through."

"It couldn't have anything to do with— You know."

Nita shook her head. "I don't think so. I think this is just something different that I need to grow into learning how to do. It's not like even people who've been wizards for a long time know *every* word in the Speech. I may just need to do some vocabulary building." She shrugged, glanced absently at her watch: The lunch period would be over shortly. "More research... How about you, though?" She looked up again. "I saw your listing, and Tom's note on it. You found the kid you were looking for?"

"Yeah, but not so that I could make any real contact with him. Another weird situation."

He told Nita in words, and a few images shared mind to mind, about where he had found Darryl and lost him again. At the sight of the indistinct shape twisting in a halo of lightnings, and the Lone Power standing there watching in the shadows, Nita sucked in a soft, concerned breath, and shook her head. "Poor guy," she said.

"Poor him, yeah, and poor me, if our 'old friend' had decided to shift Its interest elsewhere," Kit said. "I could have used you there, if only for moral support."

Nita looked at the ground for a few moments. "Are you sure I'd do you much good at this point?" she said. "I'm not exactly ... stable right now. If I lost my grip in the middle of something important, I don't know what I'd do afterward."

Kit wasn't sure what to say to that. Nita was too good a wizard to understate or overstate the problem. If she wasn't confident enough to work actively at the moment, maybe she was wiser to sideline herself somewhat until she felt more sure of herself. That certainty of what to do and how to do it had saved them both more than once. If her certainty should fail at a crucial moment...

"Your call, Neets," Kit said. "I don't want to push you."

"If you really need me," Nita said, "all you have to do is yell. You know I'll be there in a second, if I can figure out how to get to where you are."

"Ponch can find you," Kit said. He grinned. "I'm beginning to think there's not much he *can't* find...if I can just figure out how to ask him for it."

Nita nodded. Over at the school building, the end-of-period bell rang. "Let me know when you're going to go looking for him again," Nita said. "At least I can keep the time free for you if you do need me for something."

"Right. And let me know what you find out about your mystery messages." The two of them started to walk back toward the school doors. "It'd be funny if it's some rogue intelligence trying to figure out whether it's okay to invade the Earth. Whatever you do, don't give them our address."

"The way things are going in my life at the moment," Nita said, "it's more likely to be some alien kid making crank calls, or trying to order a pizza." And she actually smiled slightly.

Kit punched her lightly in the arm, and went to his next class.

Nita walked home from school that afternoon with the "robot" problem still very much occupying her mind. She found Dairine sitting outside on the back steps, staring idly down the driveway.

"Dad didn't come back early?" Nita said.

Dairine shook her head as Nita got out her house key. "What're you doing out here?" Nita said.

Her sister gave her a look. "Didn't seem to be much point in going into the house when you've left a live teleport spell going."

Nita opened the door. "Dairine," she said, "maybe I'm cruel, but I'm not a sadist. Besides, why waste energy? The spell expired at the end of your school day."

They went in. Nita hung up her parka and went to the fridge to find something to eat. Dairine stood there looking out the back door as she took off her own coat. "Close the door. You're going to let all the heat out," Nita said. "So how did the meeting with the principal go?"

Dairine rolled her eyes. "I made an agreement with him and Dad to stop cutting, if that's what you're asking about," she said, closing the door. She went through the kitchen toward the living room.

"That's not exactly what I was asking about," Nita said. "What about Dad? How did he handle it?"

"He was okay," Dairine said from the living room.

There was something about her sister's tone of voice that made Nita forget about food for the moment. She went into the living room after her. "Was he upset?" Nita said.

"No," Dairine said.

"He should have been," Nita said.

"If things were normal, he probably would have been. But nothing *is* normal."

Dairine sat down very abruptly on a hassock in front of one of the easy chairs. "Neets," she said, so softly that Nita could barely hear her, "school sucks. It sucks so completely that even the Speech barely has words for it. It doesn't feel like any of it *matters* anymore. And everyone who looks at me is thinking either 'Poor little kid' or 'She's just trying to get sympathy by looking so sad; why doesn't she just get over it?' If I can't actually hear them thinking it, I can see it in their faces. Every day of this is like Chinese water torture. The seconds just fall on your head one after another, and every one is just like the last one. The minutes just crawl by, and nothing gets better. Everything just keeps hurting. And you have to sit there, in the middle of all this meaningless junk, and put up with it, and act like it matters. Like *anything* matters."

Nita found herself thinking of the weary, repetitive feeling she'd sensed in the robot when she'd been confronted with it. Moment following moment, all of them the same, and none of them a happy one.... She shook her head sadly. "Dair—"

"I've thought of leaving," Dairine said, barely above a whisper. "Running away."

Nita flushed first cold, then hot. "It would *kill* Dad," she said. "You know it would."

Dairine was quiet for a few moments. "I know," she said. "That's why I haven't done it. But it doesn't make it any easier, Neets. And just when I could actually use some help dealing with...with *stuff*, the woman they've got assigned as my counselor is a complete waste of time. She's some girl just out of college who's more nervous about the kids at school than they are about her. What kind of good can *she* do anybody? Least of all me. She doesn't even have a clear memory of what it's like to be a kid anymore. I *know* she doesn't: That part of her brain might just as well have a big sign on it saying, 'Your message here.' She's completely relieved not to remember what it was like to be one of us poor, powerless creatures." Dairine's expression went fierce with contempt. "Just having to look at her makes my brain hurt."

"I wonder if they could give you Millman, instead," Nita said. "He's good."

"I don't care," Dairine said. "I'll put up with her, with school, with whatever. For Dad's sake. And I will not let this break me. But I am going to hate every single water-torture-drop second of it, and I may just let you know about that every now and then."

She looked up at Nita in defiance.

"Come here and gimme a hug," Nita said.

Dairine gave her a look. "You're just saying that because Mom would say it."

"I'm saying it," Nita said, furious, "because right now *I* need a hug."

The nature of the look Dairine was giving Nita changed. She got up off the hassock, went over to Nita, and hugged her hard. Nita hung on to Dairine, not saying anything for a few moments, then let go of her and went back into the kitchen. She assembled a sandwich, hardly paying attention to what went into it, put it on a plate, and started to take it up to her room. "By the way," Nita said as she went, and Dairine went after her, "I think your machine buddies have been trying to reach you."

"Huh?"

"I got a call from one of them this morning. At least I think that's what it was."

Nita went into her room and sat down at the desk. Dairine followed her in and sat on the bed. "I haven't been expecting anything."

"Then what was this?" In her mind, Nita showed Dairine the image of the clown, going around and around. "And this?" She showed her the image of the robot.

Dairine looked at the two images carefully, especially the second one, and shook her head. "Not for me, Neets," she said. "Neither of those are any of my guys. These are organic in origin."

"How can you be sure?"

"The silicon life-forms and the machine intelligences have a specific kind of flavor," Dairine said. "A couple different flavors, actually, but they're similar. Like fudge ripple and rocky road."

Nita gave her sister an amused look. Only Dairine would think of classifying other life-forms' telepathic signatures in terms of ice cream. "Whatever got in touch with you is organic, all right," Dairine said. "But you're right about the distance. A long way off... And it's thinking—I don't know—more like an organ than an organism. It doesn't seem to have any plurals in its thoughts, any sense of existing in relationship to a larger world. It's all alone." She sat silent for a moment, pondering. "I wonder if it even understands the concept of communication, as such. It might be all by itself in its own pinched-off space. Yet now it's trying to reach out."

"Trying to get out, maybe?" Nita said.

Dairine shook her head again. "I don't know," she said. "If you don't know you're by yourself, in your own universe, how do you know there's anyone else to try to reach...anywhere to get out to? Really weird."

She got up, stretched a little listlessly. "Anyway, Neets, that call wasn't for me," Dairine said. "It's all yours."

"Great," Nita said. "All I have to do now is figure out what it wants."

Dairine wasn't even listening anymore, though. She was already wandering out the door. Nita watched her go, and let out one more of many quiet, worried breaths. Wandering anywhere wasn't her sister's style. Dairine, when she went somewhere, went full tilt, focused like a laser.

Until a month ago, Nita thought. *Until the world changed.*

She gulped, feeling the tears rise. *No,* Nita thought. *I am not going to do that right now. I am going to sit here with the manual, have a look at the tutorials in the Speech, and see if there's something obvious I'm missing. Which is entirely possible, because there's always more of the Speech to learn. But when whoever this is calls again, this time I'm going to understand it.*

"Oh," Dairine said. "By the way..."

Nita looked up to see Dairine standing in the door-way again. "I'm sorry about this morning," Dairine said.

"Uh, okay," Nita said.

"Really, Neets. Very sorry. I was being incredibly stupid."

"Uh, yeah," Nita said, unwilling to agree too force-fully with this sentiment, no matter how true it was. "Thanks."

"So would you kindly get off your butt and *bring my bed back from Pluto*?"

Nita smiled slightly and reached for her manual.

That night, when the call came again, while she was asleep, she was ready for it.

Nita had spent the better part of four rather frustrat-ing hours buried in her manual after her talk with Dairine, and had been forced to realize that no matter how she might cram, she wasn't going to be able to make a big difference in her vocabulary in the Speech in a single night, or for that matter, a single month. Like any other serious language study, it was going to take time. In the short term, it made more sense to concen-trate on being able to make as much sense as possible of the next dream, when it came. That meant being in con-trol of the dream, instead of just wandering around in it.

What people had come in recent years to call lucid dreaming had always been a tool for wizards. In some ways the mind was at its most flexible when uncon-scious, and therefore not insistently trying to make sense of everything. Human logic wasn't the only kind, and it could get in the way. The dream-state's ready acceptance of just about everything often was a useful tool for understanding and getting comfortable with the thought processes of a species you didn't know well.

The spell to induce lucid dreaming was very easy to construct—hardly more than an instruction in the Speech to one's own brain to handle some of its chemistry, but only some, as if it were still awake. It took Nita about ten minutes and about the same effort as running up and down stairs a few times to knit the appropriate words of the Speech into a loose, glowing chain about a foot and a half long. This she fastened around her throat, necklace style, though the actual fastening took her several minutes: It was hard to do the wizard's knot with both hands out of sight behind her neck. *Oh, the heck with this,* Nita finally thought, giving up. She pulled the loose ends of the spell out in front where she could see them, did the "knot" up that way to clasp the "necklace" shut, and got into bed.

After that, it was just a matter of getting to sleep.

This took longer than usual when she was expecting something to happen. But it was becoming so normal for it to take a long time, lately, that Nita was beginning to just accept this. Gradually, enough of the tension and anticipation slipped away to let the fatigue of the day do its job on Nita, dropping her over the edge of consciousness into sleep.

It was the nature of the spell not to activate until dreaming actually began. How long she actually spent in the preparatory space between falling asleep and dreaming, Nita had no idea. But the activation seemed to come very quickly.

She was standing in the dark again, in a place where light fell in one spot from some source she couldn't see. The darkness was not entirely quiet; from outside it came a faint sound, blurred and confused, like traffic noise outside a closed window, or voices in another room with the door closed—a hum, a mutter that both sounded and felt remote. Alone in that faintly humming darkness, under the single source of light, lay a big slab or dais of some kind—and there was some kind of figure on it.

Slowly, Nita made her way through the darkness toward the patch of light. The feeling of this dream was entirely different from that of the previous ones. She could still taste metal in the air, somehow, but it now seemed to her less mechanical, less impersonal a flavor. *Maybe I'm just getting used to it,* Nita thought, as she passed through the immense darkness pressing down all around, heading slowly for the light.

It *was* a dais there, under the white radiance that seemed to fall on it from nowhere; and the figure kneeling there, in the center of the stone, glittered blindingly silver in the light. It was a knight, kneeling there on the pure white stone, completely covered from head to foot in plate armor, and holding before him, with its point resting on the stone, a sword in a metal scabbard that gleamed even more brightly than the armor did.

Nita tried to remember in what book she had seen this image, a long time ago. Yet at the same time she also thought of the robot she'd seen the previous night, for the knight's helmet was the same in front—a perfectly smooth, blank surface, with just a single dark opening crossing it, for the eyes to look out through. *Assuming there really are eyes in there,* she thought.

Quietly she stepped around in front of—him? There was no telling.

"I'm on errantry," Nita said, "and I greet you."

There was a long silence.

"Greetings also," the answer came back. Though it was a human-sounding voice, it didn't come from inside the armor. It was omnidirectional, and seemed to come out of nothing, the way the light did. And the armor did not move in the slightest, as Nita would have expected it to, at least a little, if there was someone inside it.

Nita was relieved. At least the spell was working insofar as it was making communication possible, or a lot more possible than it had been the night before. "Were you trying to talk to me last night?" Nita said.

"Many times," the voice said.

"I couldn't understand a lot of what you were saying to me then, but I think that may be fixed now," Nita said. "What can I do for you?"

There was another long pause. "Nothing," the voice said. "This is the vigil. There's nothing to do but wait for the fight to begin again."

"What fight?" Nita said.

"With the Enemy," the knight said. "What else is there? Outside of the fighting, nothing exists but this."

Nita glanced around her. There was no sign of anything else but the two of them in this whole place, which seemed to stretch away into a dark infinity. "When will the fight start again?" she said.

"Soon."

"What happens when you win?"

"There's no winning this battle. But also no losing it, because for the Enemy, for the shadow that stalks this darkness, there's no winning the fight, either."

For the first time, the knight moved, lifting his head up into the light. There was no telling how she knew it, but Nita knew that inside the helmet, the knight was smiling. All the darkness sang with the force of his resolve, and with his amusement—a grim but good-natured cheerfulness that seemed very strange when taken together with what he'd just said.

That good cheer in the face of what sounded like a hopeless situation struck a chord somewhere in Nita, even in her sleep. The sense got stronger and stronger in the dark air around her of a great strength being hoarded in this place for the oncoming battle, of an unusual bravery. *Valor:* That was the word that described what she felt seeping into this space from the glittering form at its center. It made her feel like she had to do *something* to be of use. "Are you *sure* there's nothing I can do to help you?" Nita said.

The silence that followed stretched out much longer than the other two had.

"Tell what fights the Enemy that It will be held here," the knight said. "That It will have to fight here, again and again. But that It won't pass." And again Nita could feel the fierce, amused smile inside the armor.

"I can't stay," Nita said. That was one of the only drawbacks to lucid dreaming: Even when reinforced by wizardry, a dream's duration was very limited. "But I know where this place is now. I can come back if you need help, or I can bring someone else with me who can help you better—"

"No help will avail here," the knight said, kindly enough, but sternly, too. "This fight must happen only as it has happened, or it will be lost. And if it's lost, everything else will be—"

Without warning, darkness fell. Nita, uncertain where she was or what had happened, tried to see, but in that complete blackness, there was no way to see anything at all. Briefly, she heard the sound of laughter, challenging and cheerful, and the ringing scrape of a sword being drawn—

And then Nita was sitting up in her bed, open-eyed and startled in the less unnerving darkness of her own bedroom. She wasn't frightened, even though she'd caught a taste, in the dream's last moments, of what had been coming toward the knight out of the newly fallen blackness. She knew that Enemy too well to be shocked by Its appearance anymore. But the thought of leaving that glad, tough presence to fight all by itself irked her. And though she'd at least been able to make out what it was saying this time, that wasn't the same as *understanding* it.

She glanced over at the hands of her bedside clock glowing in the darkness. They said two-thirty. Nita sighed and lay down again, feeling more determined than ever to figure out what was going on. In fact, she felt more determined than she had about anything for weeks.

"Tell what fights the Enemy that It will be held here..."

Eventually Nita fell asleep again, and down the corridors of dream, she heard the sword come scraping out of its sheath again, and again, and again....

Quandaries

WHEN HER ALARM went off at about a quarter after six, Nita dragged herself out of bed, showered, and got ready for school with that fierce, small sword-sound still repeating itself in her memory. When she woke her dad up, it was still very much on her mind. She found him a little later in the kitchen, having the coffee she'd made for him when she'd finished dressing, and saw him looking thoughtfully at her manual, which Nita had carried into the kitchen with her earlier and had left open and facedown on the counter.

"I thought you seemed a little distracted this morning," he said, pouring milk into his coffee. "You look like you're working hard on something. Harder than usual."

He means, harder than usual lately, Nita thought. "Yeah," she said. "First-contact problem."

"As in first contact with an alien species?"

"I think so," Nita said. "We've been having some trouble communicating."

Her dad shook his head. "I should get you to talk to my cut-flower distributor," he said. "If you can get through to something from another planet, maybe you could even get through to him."

Nita had heard enough stories about her dad's troubles with this particular supplier in the past couple of years to make her uncertain. "I might need more power than I've got at the moment," she said.

"I wouldn't be too sure about that," her dad said. "What exactly did you do to your sister yesterday?"

Nita raised her eyebrows. "I got her to see sense," she said.

Nita's dad gave her a loving but skeptical look. "Using what kind of nuclear weapon?" he said. "Just so I know when the government calls."

Humor, she thought. *When was the last time I heard Daddy make a joke? Since... well. Since* then.

"I moved her bedroom furniture around," Nita said. "Did a couple of other things... nothing life-threatening." She looked at her dad over the rim of her mug of tea as she took a drink. "Not that I didn't think about it."

Her dad sighed. "You wouldn't have been the first one," he said, rinsing out his coffee cup. He got his coat off the hook by the door and shrugged into it. "Keep an eye on her, though, will you?"

"Sure, Daddy."

Her dad came over and gave her a hug that lingered for a moment. He put his chin down on the top of her head, something else he hadn't done for a while, and said, "You've been the one holding everything together.

And that's not fair to you. I feel like I haven't been doing everything I could..."

Nita shook her head. "I'm not sure I see it that way, Daddy," she said, and that was all she could get out.

He squeezed her, let her go. "The shop's open late tonight," he said. "I won't be home till nine. You have anything planned?"

Nita shook her head. "I need to do some research," she said. "If I have to go out, it won't be for long, and nowhere far."

"Okay. Bye..."

She leaned against the counter again, leafing through her manual, while the sound of her dad's car faded off down the road. She thought she knew how he felt: as if he was the weak link in the family. But she often felt that way herself, and she knew Dairine did, too—and they couldn't *all* be right. This was something that had come up in one of her earliest talks with Mr. Millman, a simple piece of logic that had completely eluded Nita until then—probably her first sign that Millman was not just some "good idea" wished on her by the school, but was someone genuinely worth listening to. Nita knew now that all you could do was try to let the sense of inadequacy pass over you, or the other person, and dissipate. Arguing too hard about it was likely to make the other person think you were trying to hide the truth from them.

She sighed and turned another page. The size of her manual's linguistics section had nearly tripled since she got up with the day's research in mind, and she was left now with the realization that her own knowledge of the Speech was even more basic than she'd thought it was. *I can't believe how dumb I've been about this,* she thought. The quick vocabulary test she'd taken before her dad came down for his coffee had suggested that Nita was readily familiar with about 650 terms in the Speech...out of a possible 750,000. And more words were being rediscovered or coined every day by wizards of every species. There were even regional dialects and variants, alternate recensions used by species whose physiologies or brain structure, or sometimes even the structure of their home universe, meant that the most basic forms of the Speech had to be altered to make sense. *I've been treating this like it was a dead language,* Nita thought. *But it's alive. It's the language of Life Itself: How could it* not *be?*

And then, no matter how many of the words you might know, there was always the question of context...the way a species used the Speech. Some species understood it clearly, but meant very different things by their usage of it than other species did. Some members of other species, too, whether wizards or not, might have only a beginner's acquaintance with the Speech, a most basic understanding of how to use it. *Like it looks like I have,* Nita thought, turning the manual's pages ruefully.

So the question is: Was I the one being incompetent the other day, or was the robot? Or the clown? Because of the way she felt lately, Nita thought the incompetence was a lot more likely to have been on her side. *And how come I got so little from the knight?* Nita remembered Dairine's line about the robot, about how the species contacting Nita seemed to have no plurals, possibly even no personal pronouns. What she'd heard last night seemed to confirm the idea. *He never said "we,"* she thought. *But then, he never said "I," either. There was something so...I don't know...so limited about the way he was expressing himself. Was that just because I was having trouble dealing with the way he used the Speech? Or was he hiding something?*

And why?

She leaned there on her folded arms for a while, looking rather glumly at the manual, and didn't even bother looking up when Dairine came padding in wearing one of their dad's T-shirts, hunting her breakfast. "Morning."

"Yeah," Nita said, turning over another page covered with necessary vocabulary that she didn't know.

Dairine stuck her head in the refrigerator. "My bed *creaks* now," she said.

"It's always creaked," Nita said as Dairine came out with the milk. "That's because you jump on it."

"I think it's because it just spent the better part of a day down a crevasse full of liquid nitrogen," Dairine said, getting a bowl for her cereal.

"If it spent any time in liquid nitrogen, it wouldn't just creak," Nita said. "It'd shatter."

"Yeah, well, I'm thinking your wizardry wasn't temperature-tight," Dairine said, pouring first cereal and then milk. "I think you dropped a variable."

"No, I didn't."

"I bet you did."

"Didn't."

Dairine gave Nita a look that said, *Yes, you did, you idiot*, and went out into the dining room with her cereal.

Nita smiled slightly as she turned another page. At least Dairine seemed to be back to normal for the moment. *Of course, it might be a ploy to lull me into a false sense of security.* But Nita thought her sister knew better than to bother trying to mislead her just now, when Nita's fuse was shorter than usual. Next time, it might not be just Dairine's bed that wound up down a crevasse...and Dairine's present power levels weren't what they had been a while ago. Nita's couple of years' more experience as a wizard might be enough temporarily to keep Dairine in line.

She raised her eyebrows and went back to the vocabulary list. *I really wish there were ways to just magically make all this information go into my head*, Nita thought. *Oh well...*

Dairine finished her cereal and went to get dressed, and Nita kept reading, turning page after page in the manual, looking for a hint as to what she might have been missing. It was at least an hour later when Dairine came by again, dressed, with the backpack she used as a book bag over her shoulder; Nita glanced up just long enough to see Dairine putting her coat on, and to notice the small, glowing, rose-colored eye looking at her from inside the bag.

"Have you been upgrading Spot again?" Nita said.

"He's been upgrading himself," Dairine said. "Wireless, optical...some other stuff." She looked affectionately at the bag as she shouldered it, and the little eye on its silvery stalk disappeared back down between the backpack and its flap.

"I wouldn't let anybody see him, if I were you," Nita said.

"They can't. But he can see them. Gotta go, Neets."

"See you..."

Dairine left. Nita spent some moments more reading the manual in the quiet, until suddenly she realized that if she didn't get out of there, *she* was the one who was going to be in trouble for being late. She ran off to get her own backpack, and her manual went floating after her.

The rest of the day went by fairly quickly, partly because Nita's concerns about the communications between her and "her aliens" kept bringing Nita back to the manual in every free moment that wasn't taken up with class work. She hardly thought seriously about anything else until just before her lunch period, when Nita suddenly remembered that today was when the time and day for her next session with Mr. Millman would be posted.

When the bell rang, she made her way down into the corridor in the south wing of the school, where the administrative offices were, and from there into the main office, where the bulletin board for the special services messages was located. Nita found the pinned-up folded message that said N. CALLAHAN, pulled it off the board, and headed out into the corridor, opening it.

The message said, "Dear Nita: 7:30 A.M., Monday. Hope the magic's going okay. Don't forget to bring some cards. I want to find out how to keep them from falling out of my sleeve. R. Millman."

Nita looked at this and was tempted to shred the note right down to its component atoms. *What in the worlds made me say that to him,* she thought, shoving the note into the pocket of her jeans and stalking off down the hall.

By the time she got to the cafeteria, though, she'd shrugged off the annoyance and was once again worrying at the clown-robot-knight problem. Nita got herself a sandwich and a fruit juice, sat down by herself off to one side, and spent another half hour studying how species that didn't understand plurals handled the Speech. It was complex. Mostly they wound up repeating singular forms with a redactive or "virtual" plural, which—

It's sounding a little dry in there, Neets...

Nita smiled. *You have no idea,* she said, and shut the manual. Nita disposed of her lunch tray and went out of the cafeteria, into the small side parking lot. Kit was leaning against the chain-link fence on the far side, hugging himself a little against the cold, watching a boys' gym class out in the athletic field running easy laps to cool down after soccer practice.

Nita went to lean against the fence beside him. "You know any card tricks?" she said under her breath.

He looked at her oddly. "No. Why?"

"I did something incredibly stupid. I mentioned magic to Millman at our last meeting. He thought I meant magician stuff, though, the sawing-people-in-half kind of magic. Now he wants me to show him some."

Kit stared at Nita, then burst out laughing. "You should do some wizardry, and let him think it's magic. I bet you can do all kinds of fancy card tricks when you can *really* make them vanish."

"I hadn't thought of it that way." Nita frowned. "I'm not sure I like the idea, though. Making the real thing look like something fake...It's too much like lying."

Kit nodded. "What made you mention magic to him at all, though?"

"I wish I could remember. It was an impulse, and I felt like such a dork afterward." She sighed. "Never mind. Now I have to learn card tricks in my endless free time."

Kit raised his eyebrows. "You make any headway with your aliens?"

"Yeah. Or rather, I'm not sure."

"Not sure they're aliens?"

"Not sure they're aliens, plural. Then again, let's not get into the plural thing. I'm having enough trouble with it." Nita rubbed her face. "I seem to have been talking to the same one at least twice. I'm not sure if I was talking to him, or it, the first time, the time with the clown on the bike."

"But you understood him this time, anyway."

"I'm not sure of that, either. I think I did...but I keep thinking he was holding something back, or having trouble saying something. And it could have been important." She sighed. "I'm just going to have to keep trying. What about you? Did you have time to go after your Ordeal kid again?"

"Not yet. Ponch is still worn-out from the last time. I'm going to try to get in touch with Darryl again tonight, maybe tomorrow. You sure you don't want to come along?"

He sounded almost wistful. Nita gave it a moment's thought, but then shook her head: She might *feel* more like working today, but she still wasn't sure of her ability to be of use in a crisis situation. "Give me a little more time," she said. "I want to work on this Speech problem for the moment. I think if I bear down on it hard enough, I may make a breakthrough."

"I wouldn't want to derail you," Kit said. "But keep me posted."

"You okay?" Nita said.

Kit looked at her a little strangely. "Why?"

"You look kinda worn-out yourself."

He looked surprised at that, then shrugged. "What Ponch does," he said, "it takes a lot out of me, too, maybe more than I realize. I do feel a little run-down. It's okay: I'll get a good night's sleep tonight and be fine tomorrow."

"What *is* going on with Ponch?" Nita said. "You were still looking for answers to that..."

Kit shook his head. "I think I'm going to be looking for answers for a while. Trouble is, every time I try to settle down to work it out with the manual, something new goes wrong with the TV. Or something else interrupts me."

The bell rang. "See that? The story of my life," Kit said.

"Not just yours," Nita said. "Look, call me later.

You ought to take a look at what I'm working on from the 'inside'; maybe you can make some sense of it."

"Right," Kit said.

They parted company and went off to their classes. Nita more or less sleepwalked through her afternoon algebra and statistics class, grateful not to be called on. Her mind was still tangled up in virtual plurals, non-pronominal pronouns, and the question of what could be *that* wrong with Kit's TV that it would prove a distraction to him. The second-to-last period that afternoon was a study hall, and Nita got no more than three sentences into an essay on the abandonment of the gold standard before ditching the essay to return to the manual again; the gold standard made even virtual plurals look good by comparison.

Toward the end of that period, though, and during the next one—a music appreciation class full of jangly, early twentieth-century twelve-tone music, which Nita found impossible for *anyone* to appreciate—she started wondering exactly what was going on with her. Sure, she might occasionally detest her homework—more than occasionally, especially in the case of her present social studies class: Her teacher had a great love of saddling her students with essays on apparently useless subjects. But detesting the homework didn't mean Nita didn't get it done.

Oh, come on. It's not like the universe is going to come apart because I'm less than excited about the gold standard and feel more like working on wizardry.

Yet the excuse sounded hollow. More to the point, it sounded like an excuse. When the bell rang for the last time that day, at two-forty-five, Nita walked out through the exuberant Friday afternoon rush to the lockers in a somber mood. She looked for Kit in the parking lot, didn't see him, and wasn't surprised: He had quicker, quieter ways of getting home than the other kids here.

She could have taken that same way home, but didn't. She walked home slowly, thinking. Nita paused only long enough in her house to dump her books and change out of her school clothes into something more comfortable—looser jeans, a floppier sweatshirt—and to check on Dairine. Her sister was lying on her stomach, on her bed, with Spot lying on the bed next to her; the little computer had put out a couple of stalky eyes to look at a book Dairine was reading.

"School okay?" Nita said.

Dairine gave Nita the kind of look that someone in the Middle Ages might have given a relative who asked if the black plague was okay. Her only other answer was to bounce herself up and down on the mattress a little. The bed creaked loudly.

"Did *not*," Nita said, and went downstairs again to get her parka.

"Where you going?" came the voice from upstairs.

"Tom's."

Tom and Carl's backyard was already going twilit, this time of year, even so soon after school. Nita paused there a moment, looking up at the sky, which was clear for a change after several days' worth of cloudy weather, and wished that spring would hurry up—she hated these short days. She meandered over to the koi pond and glanced down into it. The pond wasn't heated, but it didn't freeze, either; into the pond and the ground beneath it, Carl had set a small utility wizardry that acted on the same general principle as a heat pump, keeping the water at an even sixty degrees Fahrenheit. All the same, at this time of the year the koi were naturally a little sluggish. Right now they were mostly gathered together under the weeds and water lilies down at one end of the pond. Nita peered down, able to see nothing but the occasional flick of tail or fin, and once a coppery eye glancing back up at her.

"Hey," she said. "Got any words of wisdom?"

The single koi that had looked back, a white one with an orange patch on its head, drifted up to just beneath the surface and regarded her. Then it stuck its mouth up into the air.

> *"Seen in plain daylight*
> *the firefly's just one more bug;*
> *but night restores it—"*

Nita raised her eyebrows. The koi gave her a look that suggested she was a waste of its time, and drifted straight back under the lily pads again.

"If you listen to them for too long," Tom said as he pushed open the patio door, "you won't be able to say anything that takes more than seventeen syllables."

"I should send Dairine over," Nita said.

"Even *their* powers have limits," Tom said, as Nita came in. "I just made some tea. Can I interest you?"

"Yeah. It's cold." Nita slipped out of her parka, draped it over one of Tom's dining room chairs.

"They're predicting snow," Tom said, pouring each of them a mug of tea and bringing them over to the table.

"That's funny. It's clear."

"For the moment. There's a storm working its way up the coast, though. Four to six inches, they said."

Nita gave him a wry look. "Why couldn't this happen on Monday and get us a day off from school?" she said.

"There are about thirty different answers to that, from the strictly meteorological mode down to the ethical," Tom said, looking equally wry, "but they all factor down more or less to mean, 'Just because. So cope with it.'"

Nita nodded and smiled a little, but the smile fell off almost immediately. "I need to ask you something."

"That's what I'm here for," Tom said, "though Annie and Monty doubtless have a different opinion. Anyway, what's up?"

She looked at him across the table. "Am I using wizardry to avoid life?" Nita said.

Tom raised his eyebrows. "Wizardry *is* Life," he said. "Or, at the very least, in service of Life. By definition. So, equally by definition, the answer to that question is no. Want to try rephrasing?"

Nita sat for a moment and thought. "I've been spending a lot of time with the manual."

"So do we all."

"No, I mean a *lot* of time. For me, anyway."

"And this means—?"

Nita paused, wondering how to phrase this. "My last really big wizardry," she said, "didn't work."

"Uh, there we'd have to disagree."

"I don't mean in terms of wizardry," Nita said. "I mean in terms of what the pissed-off places in the back of my brain think about it. My mom still died."

"Mmm," Tom said. His expression was noncommittal.

"What I want to know is—is it possible to use research as a way to put off doing other stuff you should be doing?"

"Again, anything's possible. What is it you think you should be doing?"

Nita shook her head, pushed her teacup back and forth on the table mat. "I don't know. Something more...active."

"You think research is passive?"

"Compared to what I've been doing up until now, yeah."

Nita reached sideways into the air for her manual, came out with it, opened it to the listings area, and pushed it over to Tom, tapping on her listing. "'Optional,'" Nita said. "I'm not real wild about that."

"I'm not sure I read that construct the same way," Tom said. "I'd translate it more as meaning your options are open: that you're not concretely assigned to anything at the moment. Maybe a better rendering would be 'freelance.'" He glanced at her manual. "But then you seem to be taking a look at the vocabulary end of things at the moment."

"Please," Nita said. "I feel so ignorant. Me with my whole six hundred and fifty words."

"Maybe it'll be some consolation to you that the average English-speaking person's day-to-day vocabulary is only a thousand or fifteen hundred words," Tom said. "But I understand how you feel. And the Speech is so much more complex than English in terms of specialized vocabulary. It has to be, if you're going to name things properly. And so that means doing vocabulary-building all the time."

He knocked one knuckle on the tabletop a couple of times. Immediately his version of the manual appeared on the table—seven or eight thick volumes like phone books. "This one," Tom said, pulling a single volume out of the stack—while the ones above it considerately remained hovering in place over where the middle one had been—"this one is *my* vocabulary work for this year."

Nita looked at it in horror as Tom dropped it to the table and flipped it open. "Remind me never to become a Senior," she said.

"As if you can avoid it when it happens," Tom said, sounding resigned. "Nita, you wouldn't be the first wizard to get confused about the apparent differences between active and passive work in wizardry. But the Powers That Be don't see the distinction—or They see it as largely illusory." He paged through the book, stopping about halfway through to glance at something.

"If you go through this, you'll see often enough where it says that wizards are told only what they need to know 'for the work at hand.' Which leaves you with the question: What do they find in it when there *is* no work at hand—no official assignment? You'd be surprised. But it's never anything that goes to waste. Sooner or later, every wizard's work, however minor, does someone, somewhere, some good. It's an extension of the 'all is done for each' principle."

"So what I'm doing isn't like...withdrawal or anything?" Nita said. "Not...unhealthy?"

"Oh, no. Don't forget, there are wizards who do nothing *but* read the manual." Tom looked thoughtful. "I wouldn't be that far down the road. My job tends more toward focused research. But I still spend maybe seventy percent of my theoretically 'inactive' time reading these things. It's a big universe out there. Just this planet, for example: Think how much you can discover about it just by going to the library, or rummaging around on the Web. Then imagine you have access to a book that contains most of the salient facts about your *universe*. Wouldn't *you* spend a lot of time between the covers?"

"Uh," Nita said. "Well, I guess I have been."

"So, at the very least, even if you didn't have a goal you were working toward, which I think you have, I wouldn't consider your time wasted," Tom said. "As for you not being on active assignment, that's between you and the Powers. They value the work we do sufficiently to avoid pushing us to function when it wouldn't be appropriate to the wizard's own best interests.

Emergencies do come up; but *routinely,* if being on duty would impair your own status, you're not called up." He eyed Nita. "If you're starting to feel the need to get back into the saddle, of course, that's not necessarily a bad thing. You'd be the one to tell me."

Nita examined the floor in some detail for a few moments before she said anything. "It's not like I actually feel all that much better," she said, hardly above a whisper. She was watching herself with great care to see if she was going to start crying again; she couldn't have borne it right this minute. "Every now and then I forget to hurt...but the rest of the time...I keep seeing those last few hours with my mom, over and over." Then she frowned. "But I can't just sit around. It's not bringing my mother back. And I keep getting the feeling she'd be annoyed with me for, I don't know, for indulging myself in just sitting around and feeling bad when I should be busy with something important. Because this is important."

Tom nodded. "I don't think I can argue with that," he said. "Meanwhile, tell me what you've been up to."

Nita spent a few minutes describing the contacts she'd been having from the aliens, especially the last one—the knight—and the cryptic message he, or it, had left her.

When she was finished, Tom shook his head. "'What fights the Enemy...,'" he said. "You're right, the phrasing's interesting."

"You think this alien's a wizard?"

"Hard to tell," Tom said. "There are lots of creatures all over the universe who both use the Speech and work to oppose the Lone Power without being wizards." He shrugged. "For the time being, I'd keep trying to get through, I suppose, and see if you can work inward to a mode where there's more clarity."

"Yeah. I'm going to try the lucid dreaming again tonight, I think. So far, that's where I've had the best results." Nita frowned. "I guess that's the other thing that's worried me. The possibility of getting stuck in a dreamworld..."

"I'm not sure I see that as a danger for you," Tom said. "I'd almost suggest the danger would lie in too much hardheaded practicality...in being too tough on yourself. For the time being, you seem to be okay. Let me know how you progress with your 'alien,' anyway."

"Yeah."

Nita got up and slipped into her parka, glancing at Tom's stack of manuals again. "You have to learn that whole *thing* this year?"

"*And* keep Carl from blowing up the house," Tom said. "Even wizardry may be insufficient to the task. See you later."

"Kit, *querido,*" Kit's mama said, "if you feed that dog so many dog biscuits, you'll spoil his appetite for dinner."

In the kitchen, adding a last few seasonings to what would shortly be a pot of minestrone soup, Kit's father laughed out loud. "Impossible."

Kit was sitting on the dining room sofa, trying to read one of the books on autism his mom had brought home for him. The language was pretty technical some-times, but he was more than willing to struggle through it; the analysis of autism in this book was making some sense to him in terms of what he'd been getting from Darryl. There were apparently autistic people who found the complications of life and emotion so threat-ening, the book said, that when they did artwork, it often featured landscapes that looked sterile and empty to a casual viewer—but the artists' intent was to express a desire for a little peace, for relief from the assault on their senses that caused them such pain. Since coming across this idea in the book, Kit had been doing his best to get the whole thing read, mining it for ways to make sure that he actually got some good out of his conversation with Darryl, when it finally happened.

Unfortunately the reading was being made difficult, if not impossible, by the large black muzzle that kept insinuating itself between Kit and the open pages, and the big brown eyes that looked beseechingly up into Kit's. *Just one more,* Ponch said.

"You're gonna turn into a blimp," Kit said.

I'll be a happy *blimp,* Ponch said. *What's a blimp?*

Kit's mama laughed. Kit glanced up at her.

"He's loud sometimes, honey," his mama said, handing Kit's papa the pepper shaker as he held his hand out for it. "I don't know why *you* can't hear it."

Kit's pop shook his head as he looked down into the pot, grinding pepper in. "From what Kit says, I don't know why *you* can hear it at all. None of us should be able to."

"Maybe it's because I usually feed him in the mornings," Kit's mama said. "I'm used to hearing him complain that he's not getting enough." She made a kind of *rrrgh* noise that went up into a whine at the end, a fair imitation of Ponch's reaction to an empty dish when there was someone around who could give him the rest of the can of dog food.

Ponch's eyes moved at that, a sideways glance. *Her accent's not bad. I could teach her Cyene.*

"Let's not deal with this right now," Kit said. He could just see his mom going down the street to try to talk sense to Tinkerbell.

One more! Ponch said.

"One," Kit said. He gave Ponch the last dog biscuit in the box, put the book aside, and got up to throw the box away.

"The onions done yet?" his mama said.

"Nearly," said Kit's pop, as Kit stomped the box flat to make it go in the trash can. Behind Kit, the emphatic crunching noises by the sofa came to an end, and Ponch ran into the kitchen. *Out?*

"Sure," Kit said, opening the door. A fierce cold wind came in as Ponch shot out.

"Shut that, sweetie. It's freezing!" Kit's mama said.

"Gonna snow tonight, they said on the TV," said Kit's pop, picking up the frying pan in which the onions had been sizzling, and scraping them out into the soup as Kit shut the door.

"A lot?" Kit said.

"Six to eight inches."

Kit sighed. It wouldn't be anything like enough to

make them keep school closed on Monday. That would take at least a few feet. Not for the first time he wished that it wasn't unethical to talk a snowstorm into dumping three feet of snow onto his immediate neighborhood. It was fun to think about, but the trouble he would have gotten into with Tom and Carl, not to mention the Powers That Be, would have made the pleasure short-lived.

Still, if I told the snowstorm to dump, say, twelve feet of snow just on the school, and then only enough everywhere else so that everybody could have fun for a day; say six inches or so...

Kit sighed again. Though such a course of action would be less trouble to the snowplow crews, the emergency services, and everybody else who wanted to go on about their lives, something like that would cause a whole lot of talk, and still get him in trouble. But the image of his school completely buried under a giant snowdrift made him smile. "By the way, Pop," Kit said, "is the TV still okay?"

"Seems fine," his pop said. "Every now and then the thing insists on showing me a news program from some other planet, but..." He shrugged. "As long as nothing happens to interfere with the basketball games over the weekend, I don't mind seeing who's grown a new head or whatever. Darlin', you know what I need?"

"Less time on the couch watching basketball?" Kit's mama suggested.

"Dream on. Celery seed."

"We're out of it."

"You're just saying that because you hate celery."

"I know celery seed is different from celery, or celery salt. But we're still out of it. Look for yourself."

Kit's pop went to the cupboard to look. Kit, looking at his mama, thought that her expression was far too innocent. She caught him looking at her, and said, "Isn't Ponch a long time out, Kit? He hates being out this long when it's cold. But he hasn't scratched."

She had a point there, though Kit thought she was more intent on him not saying anything incriminating about celery seed. Kit grinned. "I'll go see what he's doing," he said, and got his winter jacket off the hook.

He went out, shutting the door hurriedly behind him, and looked up and down the driveway for Ponch. To his surprise, Ponch was sitting at the street end of the driveway, looking up at the sky.

Kit walked down to him, looking up, too. The clouds were, indeed, coming in low and fast from the south on that wind. Past and above the houses across the street, only a few streaks and scraps of the low sunset remained in the west, a bleak, bleached peach color against the encroaching stripes of dark gray. Westward, the reddish spark of Mars could just be seen through the filmy front edges of one of the incoming banks of cloud.

Ponch looked over his shoulder at Kit as Kit came to stand next to him. "You okay?" Kit said to him in the Speech.

Pretty much.

Kit wondered about that. "I mean, about what happened the other day." He reached down to scratch the dog's head.

I think so.

The clouds drew together in the west, blanking Mars out, slowly shutting down the last embers of the sunset. "What *did* happen?"

I saw something.

"Yeah? What was it?"

Not that way, Ponch said. *I mean, I noticed something. I never really noticed it before.*

Kit waited.

You get hurt sometimes, Ponch said. *That makes me sad.*

"Yeah, well, I get sad when you're hurt, too."

That's right. And your dam and your sire and your littermates, they hurt sometimes, too. So does Nita. I noticed that. But it didn't seem to matter as much as you hurting.

Ponch paused for a long time. *But then I saw him: Darryl. And what That One was doing to him, and how it hurt him. And he didn't do anything to deserve that. It was* awful, *the way he was hurting. And that started to hurt me. And then I thought, Why doesn't the others' hurt make me feel like this? And then I felt bad about myself.*

Kit hardly knew what to say. It wasn't that it was a bad thing for his dog to learn about compassion, but that the lesson would come all at once, like this, came as a surprise.

And the others didn't deserve to be hurt, either, Ponch said, looking up at Kit. *Nita didn't do anything bad, for her mother to die. Why should she be hurt like that? Why should Dairine? Or your sire or dam?*

They're good. Why do they have to suffer when they haven't been bad? It's not fair!

Kit bowed his head. This line of reasoning all too closely reflected some of his own late-night thoughts over the past couple of months. And all the easy answers—about the Powers That Be and the Lone Power, and all the other additional theories or answers that might be suggested by either religion or science—suddenly sounded hollow and pathetic.

"I don't know," Kit said. "I really don't know."

I felt sad for them all, Ponch said. *Sad for everything, because it shouldn't have to be that way. All of a sudden I had to howl, that's all.* He looked embarrassed.

Kit couldn't think of anything to do but get down on one knee and hug Ponch, and ruffle his fur. After a moment Ponch said, *I'm not going to howl now. It's all right.*

"I know," Kit said. But he wasn't sure that it was "all right."

Ponch looked at him again. *So what do we do?* he said. *To make it right?*

That answer, at least, Kit was sure of. "Just get on with work," he said. "That's what wizards do."

And their dogs.

"And their dogs," Kit said. "After dinner tonight, huh? We'll go looking for Darryl again. We'll see if we can't get a word with him...find out what's going on. Then he can get himself out of there, and we can get back to doing what we usually do."

Right.

They walked back up the driveway together, and Kit let Ponch into the house, hurriedly shutting the door. The wind outside was beginning to rise. He ditched his coat in a hurry, because his pop had already carried the soup pot to the table, setting it on a trivet, and his mama was putting out bowls and spoons. "No Carmela tonight?" Kit said, because there were only three bowls.

"No, she's over at Miguel's with some of the other kids. A homework thing." His mama sat down, took her spoon, and tasted the soup as Kit's pop sat down.

"Oh, honey, that's so good!" his mama said. "Even without the celery seed. Who'd believe most of it came out of a can? What else did you put in there?"

"Genius," Kit's father said, and grinned.

Kit was inclined to agree. He finished his first bowl in record time, and reached for the ladle to serve himself some more.

"Another satisfied customer," his pop said.

Kit nodded, already working on the second bowl.

"You've got that fueling-up look," his pop said, as he chased the last few spoonfuls of soup around his own bowl. "You going out on business tonight, son?"

"Yup."

"How long?"

"Not late," Kit said. "I don't think, anyway. Back by bedtime."

"Yours, or mine?"

"Mine, Pop."

"Good," his dad said. "What you're doing is important...and so is getting your rest." His father gave him what Kit usually thought of as "the eye," a faintly warning look. "You're looking a little pooped, this past day or so. Try to relax a little over the weekend, okay?"

"If I can," Kit said.

His pop looked like he was going to say something, then changed his mind, and reached for the ladle himself. "Hey, who took all the beans?"

"That would be me," Kit's mama said.

"Now I'm going to have to make another pot of this!"

"How terrible for us all," she said.

Kit finished his own bowlful and, smiling, got up and put his bowl in the sink. Then he went to get his parka and Ponch's "leash."

They stood out in the backyard a little while later, in the near darkness, and Kit looked down at Ponch. "Ready?" he said.

All ready.

"You've got Darryl's scent?"

It's faint, Ponch said. *We're going to have to walk for a while.*

Kit checked the force-field spell, which he had integrated into the leash-wizardry, and saw that it was charged, up and running; it would keep hostile environments out for a good while, and protect the two of them from deadly force for at least long enough to come up with a better, more focused defense. "Okay. Let's go."

Ponch pulled the bright leash of wizardry taut, stepped forward, and vanished into a darkness deeper than anything in Kit's backyard. Kit stepped after him; the blackness folded in all around.

They did, indeed, have to walk for some time. Kit kept a careful eye on the line of wizardry stretching between him and Ponch, watching to make sure that it was drawing power correctly, and that the faint "diagnostic" glow of light running up and down it was doing so regularly. Beyond that, there wasn't much for Kit to do for a long while except keep walking through the dark, watching the ever-so-faintly illuminated shape of his dog as Ponch led the way.

A whispering sound—very faint, seemingly very far away—was the first thing that Kit started to notice as differing from the darkness and silence surrounding them. It was incessant, a soft white-noise hiss at a high frequency, but every now and then Kit thought he heard words in it. *Am I just imagining that?* he thought as the hiss got louder around them. "You hear that?" he said to Ponch.

The wind? Ponch said. *Yes. It's up ahead, where Darryl is. We'll be there soon.*

"I mean, do you hear something besides the wind? The voices?"

Ponch paused a moment, cocked his head to one side. *No,* he said. *Not right now, anyway. Let's get there and see if I hear it then.*

They started walking again. Quite suddenly, as if they'd walked through a curtain, Kit and Ponch were surrounded by blue-white light. Kit stopped, looking around him, blinking. After the darkness, this brilliance was dazzling.

At least there was gravity, though it felt lighter than Earth's; and he knew there was an atmosphere, because Kit could hear sound from outside his force field: the hiss of the wind. But he wasn't convinced that the atmosphere was breathable, especially because he could feel the cold outside, even through the force field. The air on the far side of the force field was full of blue-white smoke, or fog, moving fast, blown by the wind, and there was more blue-white stuff underfoot. "It's like being inside a lightbulb," Kit said.

If it is, then I'll avoid it in the future, Ponch said, looking around him with distaste. *It smells bad here.*

The wind dropped off briefly, and Kit was able to look out of the lightbulb and see that the two of them had stepped into a snowfield. *Except that snow isn't blue,* Kit thought. Ponch, though insulated from the cold around them by the force field, nonetheless shifted uncertainly from foot to foot in the robin's-egg blue stuff. Kit felt the odd soft squeak of it under his sneakers, and understood Ponch's confusion. *It feels more like talcum powder than snow. Or, no, more like cornstarch*—for that strange squeaky sensation persisted no matter how the stuff packed under Kit's feet.

The wind rose again, reducing the visibility to nothing as it picked the snow up and started blowing it around in the air. The snow was as fine as powder on the wind, finer than any powdery snow that Kit had ever seen, even in blizzard conditions. The stuff piled and drifted in spherical sections around Kit's force field, gathering like swirls of smoke, abruptly dissipating again like smoke blown away. Suddenly Kit realized what he was seeing, and realized, too, why the snow's texture was so strange. *This isn't water snow. It's too cold here for that. This is methane . . .*

The wind howling around them gusted for a few breaths more, blowing the blinding snow shrieking past Kit and Ponch, and then dropped off once more, just briefly giving Kit the wider view again as the snow drifted back out of the air to the ground. *We might as well call it air,* Kit thought, though he knew that if he tried to breathe it at this temperature, it would freeze his lungs to solid blocks of blood and water ice. He popped his manual open to a premarked page for reading environmental conditions and let it take a moment to do its sensing while he turned in a circle, looking at the landscape.

There wasn't much of it. Nearby, black crags of stone stood up here and there, shining with blue ice that seemed almost to glow on its own in this fierce sourceless light. Kit glanced up at the sky, wondering whether there was a star up there somewhere, on the far side of what might be a "greenhouse" layer like Venus's upper atmosphere. But there was always the possibility that this wasn't a planet at all—just some kind of Euclidean space, another dimension that just went on eternally in all directions. *Whichever it is,* he thought, *it has weather, and the weather's bad. Even Titan's weather is better than this.*

Kit glanced at the manual page again, read the words in the Speech that began to spell themselves out there.

Nitrogen atmosphere. No oxygen. Methane and some other hydrocarbons frozen out to make the snow... Kit shivered despite the force field: The temperature outside was about two hundred degrees below zero centigrade.

"I'm glad I brought a coat," he said softly.

I wish I could grow mine thicker, Ponch said, looking around him with distaste. *I didn't like that other place, the hot one, but it was better than* this.

"Believe me, we won't stay long," Kit said. "Just long enough to talk to Darryl." The contrast between the room-temperature range that the two of them needed to function and the temperature of the space around them was as extreme as the difference between room temperature and a blowtorch...and this meant that keeping his own environment and Ponch's tolerable would require Kit to spend a lot of energy in a hurry. He was going to have to keep a close eye on the energy levels of the force field; this was no kind of place to have it fail suddenly. Whether they were genuinely in some other universe or just inside Darryl's mind, the cold would kill them both in seconds if their protection failed. "Let's get going. Where in all this *is* he?" Kit said to Ponch.

That way, Ponch said, turning. *The contrast in temperatures stands out. But so do other things. There's company here.*

"The same company as last time?"

The same. A heart of cold.

"Great," Kit said under his breath. "Well, let's head

that way. I'll put the stealth spell up around us again, though in these conditions, it may not work a hundred percent."

If you could make the wind drop...

It was worth a try. Kit paged quickly through his manual to the environmental management section and looked for the spells that involved short-term weather control. He found one that looked likely, started to recite it— And then stopped, shocked. Something that had accompanied every spell he'd ever done, that growing, listening silence—as the universe started to pay attention to the Speech used in its creation—was suddenly missing.

Blocked, Kit thought. *But how?!* Not even the Lone Power Itself should have been able to keep a wizardry from executing. Once executed, of course, it might fail, but—

Kit tried the spell again, and again got no result. Yet his force field was working fine. If it hadn't been, he and Ponch would both have been frozen solid by now.

"Weird," Kit said, closing the manual for the moment. "Looks like this environment's been instructed not to let itself be altered."

Could the Lone One have done that?

Kit shook his head. "I don't know."

Never mind, Ponch said. *I don't need to see, to lead us. And as for the Lone One...* Ponch's nose worked. *It's distracted,* Ponch said. *And Darryl's moving. Come on.*

Ponch pulled on the leash, and Kit followed him across the squeaking blue snow, while every now and then a new and ferocious gust of wind blue-whited everything out. "Snow tonight," a voice said from somewhere immeasurably distant.

"You heard it that time, right?" Kit said.

I heard something, Ponch said. And then he paused in midstep. *I hear something besides that, too.*

Kit waited.

Wings—

Kit listened, but couldn't make anything out except that the wind was rising, the hiss scaling up to a soft roar. The last time he'd heard a wind like this was when the hurricane had come through three years ago. The hurricane, though, had at least sounded impersonal in its rage. The sound of this wind had a more intimate quality, invasive, as if it was purposely pointed at Kit. And the voices were part of it.

"—won't be able to—"

"—and in local news tonight—"

"—wish I could understand why, but there's no point in even asking, I guess—"

"—come on, love, we need to get this on you. No, don't do that. Remember what we talked about—"

The voices somehow both spoke at normal volume and screamed in Kit's ears, intrusive, grating, maddening. He couldn't shut them out. He opened his manual and hurriedly went through it to the section that would allow him to soundproof the force field, for the voices were scaling up into the deafening range now, an ever increasing roar. The noise wasn't just made up of voices, either. Music was part of it, too, but music gone horribly wrong, screeching at him, and also sounds that might have come from Kit's own house, a door closing, someone opening a drawer, sounds that were magnified past bearing, intolerable—

Kit recited the wizardry, having to do it nearly at the top of his lungs to hear himself think. To his great relief, it took; he could tell that the sound all around him outside the force field was still rising, but now at least it was muted to a tolerable level. "Wow," he said to Ponch, who was shaking his own head, also troubled by the noise.

I lost him, Ponch said. *He moved again. He moves very fast sometimes. He—*

Ponch's head whipped around. Kit looked the way his dog was looking, through the blowing blue snow, just in time to catch sight of the thin young shape running past them, dressed in nothing but jeans and a T-shirt, running through the terrible cold and wind, running headlong, a little sloped forward from the waist as Kit had seen him running for the van at school.

"Darryl!" Kit shouted. "Hey, Darryl, wait up!"

Darryl turned his head for just a flash, looking toward Kit. For a fraction of a second, their eyes met.

Darryl ran on. Kit reeled back as if someone had hit him across the face, and staggered with shock and pain. He had felt, for that second, what Darryl had felt: the unbearable pain of another person's regard.

Kit had sometimes found it hard to look into someone else's eyes, but that was nothing like this. This pain denied even the existence of the one who looked back. For Darryl, even meeting the gaze of his own eyes in the mirror was impossible, nonsensical, painful. Yet Kit also thought of the blind looks of the statues at the edge of the world of dunes, and suddenly realized that maybe it was only to him that their blindness seemed creepy. To Darryl, in his autism, maybe they were as close as he could comfortably get to the experience of being looked at by another being. *It's something he wants, even though it hurts.*

At least he wants *it, though. If he didn't—*

Kit shook his head. "Where'd he go?"

That way.

"Come on!"

Kit and Ponch ran after him. But it seemed as if, in this world, Darryl could run a lot faster than they could. "The wind's filling in his tracks," Kit gasped.

I don't need them. Listen, though!

Kit could hear very little now that he'd turned the sound down inside the force field.

"What?"

The wings! They're here—

The first of them roared overhead, trailing noise like a passing jetliner. Kit looked up and saw, dimly, through the blowing snow, what Ponch had been talking about. He was tempted to duck. The thing wasn't big, maybe only six feet long or so, but it looked deadly. It was as if someone had taken the three-finned symmetry of a standard paper plane and brought it to life, but with wings that were clawed on the forward edges. The creature was a furry blue white, just paler than the snow, and eyeless, though it had a long, nasty, many-fanged mouth that ran down the length of its body between two of the wings. And it brought the terrible noise with it as it shot overhead and past, dragging behind it still more of the torrent of voices and sounds that threatened to drown whatever lay in their wake. It tilted one wing, and started to circle Kit.

Basilisk! Kit thought, having seen the creatures' images in the manual more than once, and having thought every time that he'd rather not see them in the flesh. They weren't the heraldic beasts that went by the name, but a worse thing that the Lone Power had constructed from spare parts in Its spare time—a minion-creature that served as mindless messenger and doer of small dirty deeds. *And it sees me. The stealth spell isn't working, either—*

There were three kinds of basilisk: hot, cold, and starry. It was plain enough to Kit which kind he was dealing with here, and he knew the remedy for them if they got too close. *Heat—*

Kit flipped his manual open to its notes and storage area. Some time back during the summer, his pop had been having a lot of trouble keeping the barbecue lit, and Kit—unnerved by the overconfident way his pop sprayed the lighting fluid around in his attempts to re-light it—had started working with some of the wizardries that temporarily "set" air solid and selectively reflective, so that it could be used to produce laser beams. When the barbecue season had come to an end, Kit had stored those wizardries in his manual for the next year. Now he hurriedly pulled one of them out, shook the long chain of characters out until it solidified into a rod, and twiddled its end to reset the air variable. Fortunately it didn't take long: All he had to do was deduct the oxygen and add some hydrocarbons. *Right. Here we go—*

Kit stuffed his manual into his parka pocket, shouldered the bright-glowing rod of the laser, and waited for the basilisk to swoop at him ... and then was disappointed when it didn't bother, but just went screaming on past. Several others followed, all heading in the direction Darryl had gone. Kit stood there for a moment and let out a long breath that was as much frustration as relief. It was annoying to have something to shoot with, and something worth shooting at, and then not have an excuse to shoot at it.

He's stopped running, Ponch said suddenly.

"What?" Kit said. "They've caught him!"

I'm not sure, Ponch said.

"Come on!"

They ran the way Darryl had gone. As they ran, something occurred to Kit. *The stealth spell hasn't been working since we got here—otherwise, Darryl wouldn't have seen me, either.* Kit wondered if these places where he kept finding Darryl weren't just rigorously constructed landscapes of the mind, obeying natural law, but genuine alternate universes, custom-made, the kind of places Nita had been working with to help her mother—the kind of thing Ponch had started creating on his own. *Places where even the way wizardry works can be changed—*

As Kit ran, he found his endurance wasn't what it normally would have been. He was tiring. He couldn't get rid of the sense that, whether real or inside Darryl's mind, this universe was much farther away than the last one. There was something inherently wearying about this space itself, as if its structure sapped the energy of anyone unfortunate enough to stray into it. Or maybe it was just the noise—the wind, the roaring of the voices outside, getting louder again—

Kit stopped for a moment to readjust the force-field wizardry, then went on again at a dogtrot behind Ponch. "You doing okay?" Kit said.

So far, no problems.

"You feel all right?"

So far...

Ahead of them, dimly, through the blue-smoke swirling of the methane snow, Kit thought he could see the basilisks diving and swooping at something, fluttering at it. Kit couldn't make out what it was.

Then, as he got a little closer, he could.

Darryl was standing there with his arms up over his eyes, twisting, turning from side to side...and then he stopped. Between one breath and another, he had become encased in what looked like a solid block of ice. The basilisks were scrabbling at it with the claws on their wings, screaming, and the thunder up in the sightless, coldly burning sky beat in the air like a heart, deafening.

Suddenly the basilisks flapped away, up into that blue-white haze, as a shadow approached them out of the blowing snow. Kit gulped and put the laser away in his otherspace pocket as the form became distinct, gathering Its darknesses together out of the snowy air.

The Lone Power came striding up to that block of ice, looking as Kit had seen It a long time ago—like a young-looking human, red-haired, handsome, but with cruel, cold eyes and a smile you did not want to see. It was wearing the same dark suit Kit had seen It wear on his own Ordeal, but this time with a long, black winter coat over it, and a scarf wrapped around Its throat. The Lone One's eyes were still angry and chill, but right now they also held an oddly weary and annoyed expression that intensified the closer It got to Darryl. A few feet away from the block of ice, It stopped and stood, and put out Its hand, which was suddenly filled with the hilt of a long, black-bladed sword.

The Lone Power stood there in silence for a moment, gazing at Darryl's silent form with narrowed eyes.

"So it comes to this," the Lone One said. "For a while, at least, you tried to fight. I'll give you credit for that. But now you've given up. What were you thinking of? That I'd be merciful now, that I'd let you off easy because of your 'problem'? You should know better. When people give up around me, the poor fools pay the price." It took a step forward, slow, menacing, savoring the moment. "Not that *not* giving up helps them, either, of course. Even for those who pass their Ordeals, there's no escape; I get them later. All they ever manage to do is delay the inevitable."

A chill, which had nothing to do with the local weather, went down Kit's back as the Lone Power took another step forward, and another, hefting the sword, lifting it in slow preparation to strike. "In your case, though," the Lone One said, amused, "there won't be any further delay. You should never have accepted the power if you weren't willing to use it. And you weren't...so now you lose it."

I can't stand it, Kit said silently to Ponch.

But I thought Tom said—

I don't care. I'm not going to just stand here!

Kit had already made sure the shield around him was secure. Now he was paging hurriedly through the manual to a section he looked at fairly often but had very rarely used, the offensive weaponry. It was the Lone One Itself he was going to be dealing with here, so Kit chose a quark-level dissociation tool—the wizardly equivalent of a low-yield tactical nuke—hooked his "canned" description of himself into it, told the wizardry to take as much of his power as it needed for one good shot, and then swallowed hard once, because this was scary stuff. *You ready to get us out of here in a hurry if you have to?* he said to Ponch.

Say the word.

I may not have time—

I'll be ready.

Kit took a deep breath—then dumped the stealth spell. He took a step forward, and another, and then walked right up to It, where It stood.

"Fairest and Fallen," Kit said, trying hard to keep his voice even, "greeting and defiance."

It didn't even look up.

Kit stood there breathing hard. "I said, greeting and defiance—"

No answer. The Lone One was intent on Darryl. It lifted that black blade high. Darkness ran down it, sweeping after in a trail as It brought the sword swinging around. Kit swallowed one more time and spoke the first of three words that would activate the dissociator, as the sword struck the middle of that block of methane ice—

—and shattered.

Kit stared.

The Lone Power straightened up from the stroke—and looked, suddenly dumbfounded, at the broken stump of a sword in Its hand. The block of ice wasn't marred, not even scratched.

If It was astonished, so was Kit. *Could it be that the Lone Power can't see you when you're in someone else's Ordeal?* he wondered. *But Tom would've said something.*

Or is this space just the way it is because of Darryl being here? If Mama's right, if some autistic people have trouble with the concept that other people might be or think differently from them, then maybe nothing It does to Darryl here can hurt him... because the things It does aren't things he'd do—

Kit looked at the Lone Power, wondering in a scared way what was going through Its mind. It regarded the broken sword for a moment, then flung it furiously away. Where the hilt-shard came down in the blue snow, there was a brief and noisy explosion. But the Lone One ignored that. It put Its hands up against the front of the block of ice and spoke softly to the small shape entombed there.

"Are you really stupid or crazy enough to think I'm just going to walk away?" the Lone Power said, and the menace in Its voice made Kit's hair stand up all over

him. "I have centuries, *aeons* at my disposal. I can
hound you from life to life if I chose, until for the sake
of a moment's peace you *beg* me to destroy your soul!
Is this what your precious Powers gave you your wizardry for? To stand here inactive as a statue, refusing
the inevitable? Well, it won't help you. Coward! You
can't come out the other side of this until you confront
me. And you *won't* confront me! You'll just stay in here
like the pitiful reject that you are, while outside in reality your darling mother and father grieve over you every
day. You're not being very considerate of them, are you?
After everything they've gone through? Now you have
a chance to stand up, to conquer me, to come out the
other side of your power, and you won't take it."

Kit was having trouble believing what he was hearing. The Lone Power was *frustrated.* He saw the unbe-
lievable—saw the Power that invented death start
hammering with Its fists on the upright coffin of ice.
"Come out!" the Lone One cried, and thunder cracked
in response, high up in the wind-torn air. The snow
blew around again, hiding nearly everything but that
relentless, furious, stymied darkness. "Come out and
let's finish it! *Come out!*"

The thunder of Its voice started to drown out even
the thunder up in the turbulent atmosphere. How long
this went on Kit wasn't sure, but finally It fell silent,
looking once more at the small, unmoving shape in
the ice.

"It doesn't matter," the Lone One said. "I can wait.
I have all the time in all the worlds. Sooner or later,
you'll drop this ploy and try another that's less effective.

Sooner or later, in life or after, you'll be forced to face me…and when you finally do, you'll wish your soul had never been created. For that day, I'll wait as long as it takes."

It turned and walked away into the blue-white snow. Kit lost sight of It within seconds, and a few seconds after that, by a lightening of the spirit that was impossible to mistake, Kit knew that It had left this space. Next to him, Ponch was shivering with a combination of nervousness and amusement.

"Wow," Kit said.

Yes. Let's get him out of there! Ponch said.

"Absolutely."

Kit dismantled the dissociator, and he and Ponch hurried over to the block of ice. But the closer Kit got to it, the stranger things started to seem. That weariness that Kit had been feeling, to a certain extent, since he got here, now got stronger with every step closer to Darryl.

He rubbed his eyes, staggered over to the block, put a hand on it. It was frozen methane, but the force field protected him from its touch. "Darryl," Kit said. "*Dai stihó,* guy. I can't believe you held It off like that. Nice going."

But Darryl didn't so much as twitch an eyelid. And as Kit bent over the block, trying to figure out how to get rid of it, or at least how to rouse Darryl, he found himself having more and more trouble believing in any of this. It started to seem as if none of it was real: not the cold, not the wind, not the single small, still, cold shape standing there rigid in the ice, expressionless, unmoving, unseeing. And as for the concept of the Lone Power banging on the block of ice, not only frustrated but powerless—that couldn't have happened, either.

"Darryl," Kit said. "Come on, buddy, this is no place for our kind of people."

But the feeling began to grow in Kit that this wasn't really Darryl, that he wasn't here—which was something Ponch had said the last time. Now, though, Kit could feel for himself what Ponch had meant. Darryl's presence here was illusory. None of this was real. *What a relief, because this is all just too weird—*

Kit straightened up, passed his hand over his eyes. He was incredibly tired, and there was nothing he could do here. Outside the force field, the noise was scaling up again. Somehow it didn't seem to matter, though.

Kit.

"What?"

We have to go.

"Go where?"

Kit! We have to go home. The wizardry's failing. Come on!

"What?"

Ponch turned, leaped at him, knocked him over. For a moment the two of them fell through darkness. Kit flailed for balance, found none, cried out—

And came down, *wham,* into something cold and wet. At first Kit panicked, because with a terrible suddenness his mind became clear again about two things: that the force field had failed, and that he was lying in the snow, which meant that in about another five seconds he would be dead. But then Kit realized that this snow was so much warmer and wetter than the snow where he'd just been that it might as well have been steaming; and the silence surrounding them was so complete, compared to where they had been, that Kit's ears rang with it.

Ponch was lying on top of him, licking his face in apology and fear. *Are you all right? Boss! I had to get us out of there. Are you all right? Kit!*

"Oh, wow," Kit whispered. "Okay, yeah, I'm okay." He pushed himself up on his elbows with some difficulty, dislodging Ponch in the process. Kit was lying in his driveway, in approximately three inches of snow, and as he looked over at the corner streetlight, he saw that more snow was falling, in big flakes, through still and silent air.

He turned around to look at his house and saw that all the lights were off except for the one in his parents' bedroom. "Oh, *no*," he said. "What time is it?"

Kit looked at his watch. It was two-thirty in the morning.

"Oh, god, the time flow in there wasn't what I was expecting. I'm going to get it now," he muttered as he staggered to his feet. "I'm completely wrecked. And they're going to kill me."

Not if I can help it, Ponch said.

"Buddy," Kit said, "I don't think even the Powers That Be could prevent the massacre at this point. Let's go in and get it over with."

Together they made their way up the driveway.

Elucidations

NITA LOOKED UP from her reading and glanced out the window into the darkness to see that snow was just beginning to fall. She sat still in the pool of light at her desk, for the first time in hours really paying attention to the silence that had been settling down outside— that particular muffling effect, possibly something to do with the low clouds, that always seemed to accompany a heavy snowfall from the very first.

Nita sighed at the sight of the big flakes coming gently down. The first really decent snowfall of the winter, and her mother wasn't here to see it. First snowfalls had always been an event for her mom. She would bundle herself up and go out and play in the snow like a crazy thing until she was worse soaked than either Nita or Dairine ever let themselves get. Over the past few years, Nita had heard her mom complain more than once to her dad that the greenhouse effect was screwing up the winter weather. "We just don't get snow like we used to, Harry," she would say. "We have to do something, or future generations won't know what it's like to get slush in their socks."

Nita held still a moment longer, listening to the quiet of the house around her. Her dad and Dairine were both in bed, and outside the snow kept on falling. After a few moments, Nita sighed again and pushed her manual away. For hours now she had been up to her eyes in more research on the contextual variations of the Speech—in noun paradeclensions, and judicial imperatives, and the history and use of the Enactive Recension. It was all fascinating, and she had no idea how she was going to stomp all this information into her head soon enough to be of any use. At any rate, it was late, and she wasn't going to get any more of it into her head tonight.

Nita got up...and her bedroom went away, fading around her into a darkness through which, bizarrely, snow continued to fall.

Standing there in jeans and one of her dad's big sweatshirts, Nita looked all around her in shock, and then realized what had happened. Her hand went to her throat, where the "necklace" of the lucid-dreaming wizardry rested. *I forgot about this. I turned it on, and then I fell asleep while I was reading,* she thought. *I'm dreaming already. Isn't that wild?*

Nita glanced around at the endless dark stretching away from her on all sides. Off in the distance she saw light coming from somewhere to fall on the dark surface on which she stood. The source of the light was itself invisible, but in its beam she could see more snow gently falling.

Okay, she thought, and for lack of anything better to do, she started walking toward the light. As she went, Nita became aware of a low mutter of sound out in the further reaches of the darkness. It took some minutes of walking through the dark before she recognized it as human voices speaking: a slow, muted sound of conversation, coming from somewhere else, but not seeming to matter, particularly. It was as if Nita was hearing these voices through someone else, filtered, and the filter made it all seem not so much unimportant, but simply unreal, unrelated to anything that mattered, as if a TV show about some subject that bored you was blathering away in the background, while you were too busy with other things to turn it off.

She shivered a little, recognizing the kinship of this filter with the one she'd been seeing life through lately. *Can something like this get stuck in place?* Nita wondered. It wasn't an idea she much liked. And suddenly it made that don't-care, don't-feel-like-it attitude seem not so much like a self-indulgence as a danger. *What kind of wizard doesn't care?* she thought. *What kind of wizard—*

The sound of the voices began to dwindle, just as Nita thought she was about to understand what they were saying. She breathed out in frustration, and kept on walking. The light was a little closer now, and she could see the white spotlight it made on the black floor; the snow kept gently falling through the light, though as far as Nita could see, it vanished as soon as it came in contact with the ground. "Hello?" she said. "Anybody here?"

No answer came back. She kept on walking. That spot of light had been about a quarter mile away when she noticed it. Now it was maybe a short block away, and as she peered at it, Nita thought she saw something sitting in it, a starkly illuminated shape—mostly white and black and red, with discordant splashes of other colors—sitting there in a pool of its own shadow.

It was the clown.

How about that, Nita thought. She didn't hurry. That was a good way to wake up prematurely. She just kept on walking, and when she was about ten yards away, what seemed like a polite distance to her, Nita stopped.

"Hello?" she said again.

The clown sat in the middle of the spotlight and didn't look up.

"I talked to you the other night, right?" Nita said. "Or you tried to talk to me, anyway."

The clown just sat there. Its face was immobile. The big red nose, the bizarre purple wig sticking out from under the absurd little derby hat, the painted tear, all were exactly the same as they had been before. The clown sat there cross-legged in brightly patched, baggy pants, rocking very slightly in the stillness, while the snow falling all around began to taper off.

"I'm on errantry," Nita said, "and I greet you."

Nothing. The clown sat there, didn't even turn its head toward her.

What's the matter with you? Nita thought. *I'm going out of my way to help you get through to me, here.* She thought for a moment, and then tried the on-duty wizards' identification phrase in another of its commoner forms. "I am on the Powers' business," Nita said, "walking the worlds as do They; well met on the common journey!"

The clown just sat there with its head turned away, rocking. Nita started to get annoyed. *Okay,* she thought. *Let's try this.* Nita thought for a moment about what she was about to say in the Speech, wanting to make sure she got it right the first time, as she wasn't sure what would happen if she mispronounced it.

"In Life's name and the One's," Nita said, "I adjure you to speak to me!"

It was astonishing how just uttering the phrase made a kind of shocked silence after it. The manual had said there was no resisting such an injunction. Nonetheless, there followed one of the longest silences Nita could remember hearing. It took a long time before the clown looked up. Its eyes didn't come to rest exactly on Nita, but looked a little way over her shoulder, and the voice that replied, not from the clown itself but from the darkness all around, was absolutely flat.

"I am One," it said.

Chills ran up and down Nita's back at the sound of a phrase unnervingly close to the one reputed to have caused the Big Bang, and much else. "Uh, I doubt that very much," Nita said. "At least not the way I understand the term."

"Then *you* are One."

Nita's expression was rueful. "Not by a long shot," she said. "I'm just one more mortal...and a wizard."

The clown still didn't look right at her. But Nita felt a change coming over the darkness around the clown, or in the way she saw it. Instead of being frightening, now the shadows outside the light were filled with potential and promise, and the light now seemed painful and arid, an expression of everything stuck and hopeless—a scorching-bright loneliness that didn't even have a word for itself. The clown looked at her helplessly, and though it seemed frozen in place, except for the rocking, the painted tear was real. All the darkness shivered with its pain.

"What's a mortal?" it said.

Nita actually winced. That was a question the answer to which she'd had entirely too much of lately. Yet Nita also could sense that out here, pinned down in the unforgiving light, was someone or something as vulnerable as a butterfly with glass wings. An angry or thoughtless answer could shatter it.

She thought about her response for a moment. "We're the impermanent ones," she finally said. "The world may last, but we don't."

The eyes in the painted face widened.

The painted mouth went wide, and a great cry of anguish burst out of the clown. Nita took a breath, terrified that she'd screwed up, despite her caution.

Then she caught her breath again, because without warning there was suddenly another clown there, identical to the first one. It was standing, not sitting, and with an interested expression it watched the first clown scream. "I heard about the impermanence thing," said the second clown. "The Silence told me. What went wrong?"

Nita was finding all of this unusually weird, even for a dream. *The Silence? What's that supposed to mean?* She sat down outside the circle of the spotlight, not far from where the second clown stood in the "twilight zone," halfway between the light and the shadow. "There are a lot of answers to that one," Nita said. "One of them's simple. Somebody invented Death."

As she mentioned It, Nita heard that low menacing growl coming from somewhere out there in the shadows. Invoking the Lone Power, however obliquely, and even in dream, always had its dangers. But the growl seemed to have no real teeth in it. *It sounds almost tired,* Nita thought. *Weird.* But of much more interest to her, though the second clown wouldn't look directly at her, either, was the sudden live look in its eyes—a flash of recognition, a scowl of rejection.

"I know," the second clown said. Its voice, his voice, was fighting with that robotic quality, the life in it struggling to get out.

Just for a moment it succeeded. Nita got a quick flicker-rush of images and sounds: dawns and sunsets, objects shaped roughly like the clown all rushing hither and yon on unfathomable errands, shouting at one another about incomprehensible things. All kinds of pain were tangled up with the rush and roar of perception, but strangest of all, it was pain that the one who experienced it actually welcomed. For the clown, that pain was a lifeline, something it clung to—as a way to temporarily mask out sensations it couldn't bear, and as something that could sometimes pierce through the muffling blanket of nonfeeling that kept draping itself over the clown's body and mind. Nita could feel that the clown hoped there might be more to life than hurting...but it was also willing to suffer the hurt if that meant staying alive to get its own job done.

The storm of pictures and feelings faded, leaving Nita staring down into a roiling, scary darkness. But the darkness was oddly ambivalent, as filled with possibility as with terror.

And I'm the one who finds that strange, not him, Nita thought. Whoever this was, however simplistic or not his view of the universe might be, he was braver about it than she was.

"*I* didn't know everything was like this for you," Nita said.

The clown winced, as if something had pained it. "I? But I *did* know. There is no other *I.*"

Nita blinked. It was remarks like this that kept making her wonder if she was dealing with a human or an alien—that, and the way the clown seemed able to cope with some concepts one moment, and then would lose them again the next. Yet again she had to remind herself that there was still no guarantee she was dealing with a human. All the imageries so far—the clown, the robot, the knight—were ones this entity could have pulled out of her own head as possible ways to communicate. And she still needed to be careful not to hurt whatever it was.

Well, I wonder if the version of the Speech I've been

using is too local, too humanoid? I could try one of the broader recensions. Or the broadest one.

She pulled out her manual to make extra sure of the phrasing. The Enactive Recension was the form in which it was said the One did Its business. Nita was a little nervous about using it, because she could, apparently, make serious changes in her local environment if she was careless while speaking in Enactive. According to an old joke, the asteroid belt had been a planet once, until one of the Powers That Be misconjugated a verb—

Well, I can't blow anything up if I keep the phrasing simple enough, Nita thought. *This phrasing should be real inoffensive.*

"There are more than one of us," she said.

There was the briefest pause—and this time *both* clowns put their heads up and screamed. While Nita watched, her mouth open, the first one actually shredded away on the air, in torment and shock.

The second one stood there screaming away, and Nita watched, wide-eyed, wondering if it was going to shred, too. But it didn't. The scream didn't stop, either. After a few moments, as her own shock wore off, the noise began to remind Nita of her earliest encounters with Dairine...or rather, with Dairine after she'd first become aware that Nita might possibly be in competition with her for their parents' attention. Dairine's lung power at the age of two had initially caused Nita some innocent wonder, but this was a phase that had lasted about five minutes, and now, as the scream just kept on going, Nita let out a long breath and invoked the remedy she'd learned way back then. "All right," she shouted in the Speech. "Shut UP!"

The second clown fell silent in complete amazement.

"There *is* more than one of us," Nita said, into the abruptly echoing silence. "*Are.* Whatever. I'm sorry if this poses some kind of problem for you. But screaming's not going to make all the rest of us go away."

There was another of those long, long pauses.

"Tried that before, huh?" Nita said, not without some amusement.

"And ignoring you," the clown said, looking past her, and looking annoyed. "That didn't work, either."

Nita found herself remembering how desperately she had wanted to ignore the preparations for her mother's funeral, to the point where she had actually partly succeeded and the funeral itself had begun to seem unreal, like a bad dream. It was after that that the remoteness began to sink into her. *That feeling of nothing mattering, of not wanting to deal with anything,* she thought, *the filter I've been stuck with . . . that's what this guy and I have in common. That's what's been drawing us together . . . even when he's tried to break the link himself. But somehow it seems important for it not to get broken now.* "Why ignore everybody?" she said.

"Because you're a distraction."

"As for the first part of that," Nita said, "sorry, but you're confused. I'm here, believe me. And as for the second—a distraction from what?"

The clown looked around at the darkness. "This."

"Meaning what?"

Out of the darkness, ever so softly, came that growl again.

Nita glanced out into the dark, slightly unnerved. *But this is still my dream,* she thought. *If It tries something cute, I can just slip out. I hope.* "Now there are some contradictions in what you've been saying," she said. "I thought you said you were all by yourself."

"I am." This time the phrase, in the Speech, was identical with the Self-declaration of Life. Nita, even more unnerved now, half expected to hear thunder, but none came. The One was either otherwise occupied, or not particularly concerned about having Its lines stolen. "But That, out there... *That's* different."

Nita wasn't sure that the clown was able to perceive the contradictions. *Maybe it can't. Or maybe* different *and* other *don't mean the same thing for it.* Certainly they were different words in the Speech.

"All right," Nita said. "I won't argue that." She noted that the clown wasn't wincing quite so badly now when she said "I." "But, look, you don't have to stay here."

And suddenly there were two clowns again. One of them was back in the middle of the spotlight. Nita made a silent bet with herself as to which one would shred next. The spotlit clown said, "But this is all there is." The one standing in shadow said, "If I go there... *That's* waiting."

One more tiger growl sounded from out in the darkness: Nita's dream-image of the Lone Power, patient, hungry, willing to wait. *But still a little tired,* Nita thought. *Interesting...*

"Yeah, well, so is What's older," Nita said. "And doesn't die, no matter what one of Its older kids intended for the rest of creation."

This time the screaming didn't surprise Nita when it started. This time it was the clown in the shadows that shredded. The one in the spotlight looked at Nita in genuine shock. "Where'd you come from?" it said.

"Don't ask *me*," Nita said. "Theoretically, I'm asleep. Look, now that you're over not being the only thing in existence—for the moment—do you wear that costume all the time?"

The clown looked at her in astonishment. "You can tell it's a costume?"

"Under the costumes," Nita said, "even clowns have lives. Outside the circus, anyway."

The clown was silent again, for even longer than before. Nita waited, untroubled. This far along in her practice, she had learned that a lot of wizardry wasn't speech, but silence. "It seemed right," the clown said. "The body I wear usually doesn't work real well, and that makes people laugh. They may as well laugh for a good reason as for a bad one."

And suddenly it wasn't a clown standing there, but a boy of maybe eleven. He was handsome, in a little-kid way, skinny and sharp-faced, with a short, restrained Afro cut high in the back. But his eyes were younger than his body. "Nothing works," he said, sounding abruptly matter-of-fact—or maybe it was just the loss of the clown suit that reinforced this effect. "Everybody laughs. Especially the ones who don't do it out loud; they do it the loudest."

Nita's surprise at the change of clown-into-kid was muted a little by what he was saying, because she knew something about this, though not in regard to laughter. Some of the kids at school and family friends who'd tried over the past month to treat her as usual, as if nothing had happened, had hurt her far worse than those who'd let their discomfort show. "Well," she said, "they're idiots."

"They're all That," the little kid said, pointing with his chin into the darkness. He didn't move much; he stood with his hands hanging down by his sides, like he wasn't sure what to do with them, and his face was fairly immobile. "The Thing out in the darkness, That's been chasing me forever."

Nita wasn't sure what to make of this.

"I'm not sure you're not That, too," the kid said.

Nita raised her eyebrows. "Either I'm the One, or I'm That," she said, frankly amused at the possibility that she could be either, "but I don't think you get to have it both ways."

The kid looked at her with an expression that wasn't entirely convinced. "It's tried a lot of costumes in Its time," he said. "It looks out of everybody's eyes. I tried looking back for so long...but I couldn't do it any-more. I had to get away by myself." He looked away from Nita again. "At least when I'm all by myself, It can't get at me. Everybody wants me to come out, I know...but every time I do, It's waiting, and I just can't. It hurts too much."

Nita said nothing. Finally, after what seemed ages of silence, he turned toward her. He didn't quite look at her as he said, "It's looking out of your eyes, too. It's always been close to you. Lately It's been closer than ever."

Nita swallowed hard. This would not be the moment to break down. "You're not the only one It chases around, you know," she said. "It's after everybody else, too, one way or another. Eventually It gets us all. But if we pay attention to what we're doing, we can make a whole lot of trouble for It along the way." And Nita couldn't help grinning a little, however strange that felt. If she had one satisfaction in her life these days, it was the knowledge that the Lone Power found her a personal pain in the butt, annoying enough to try to do one of Its crooked deals with.

The kid looked up at Nita with startling suddenness, and she caught the force of his glance full-on as he grinned back. "I know," he said.

Nita actually had to stagger back a step to keep her balance, mentally and physically. Meeting his gaze was like being hit over the head with a brick, but a *good* brick—an abrupt, concentrated, overwhelming onslaught of cheerful power with a slight edge of mischief in it. Nita had hardly ever felt so intense a wash of emotion or attitude from any being, human or otherwise.

"I know," he said again. "I'm doing just that. I do it all the time, now." If anything, his grin got more jubilant, though he looked away again. "And it's a *whole* lot of fun."

Nita was on the point of saying, *Don't start enjoying it too much*—and then stopped herself as she saw his smile start to fade. The sight pierced her to the heart. "But I always have to make sure I stop having the fun before It notices," he said. "Every time I find out again that I'm not alone, I let the knowledge go."

That explains it. That's why he keeps forgetting things, and has to ask questions over and over. "But why?" Nita said.

"Because it's what always happened when things got bad for me," the boy said, "when It first turned up in my life, the way It turns up at the bottom of everything bad. I was fine, I always knew who I was...until the world started screaming at me, making it impossible to think, to be with people...to *be.* I would forget myself, again and again. I couldn't help myself. I would forget everything that hurt...and everything that didn't. But then that started to change. I started to remember again, for a while. And It was still in here with me."

His eyes glinted with brief amusement. "Then I saw how to repay the little 'favor' It did me. It can't stop coming back to deal with me...and I never let It close the deal." He grinned. "The only problem is that I keep getting better, keep sliding back toward the way things used to be when I was normal. And every time, to keep It interested, I have to let go of a world that has other people in it..."

"*Don't* let it go!" Nita said. "Not being alone is the best part of being a wizard!" She swallowed. "Or just being a person."

"Am I a wizard?" he said, a little sadly.

Nita shook her head in admiration. "If you can speak in the Enactive Recension, you're sure on the right track!"

The growl out in the dark sounded more annoyed

now, and it prolonged itself, not fading away. "It's been following me around," he said. "Around and around... It's really funny. Especially when I forget."

I can't get off, Nita remembered the clown crying in the dark. Now she began to wonder whether the despairing voice was all the boy's... or some frustrated aspect of the Lone One's.

And her eyes widened. *It's been chasing him... and he runs and runs. All the time I've been assuming that it's the Lone Power in control here. And maybe it's not...!*

He started to fade out. "Wait! Don't leave yet!" Nita cried.

"I have to. It'll realize something different is happening if I stay here too long."

"Then at least don't let yourself go again!"

"I have to," he said. "If I don't, It'll realize what's happening, and all this will have been for nothing."

He smiled that delighted smile as he turned away. Then he was gone. Nita found herself standing alone in the darkness, and nearby a spotlight out of nowhere shone on the dark floor: just a pool of light. What briefly had made the light special was now gone.

Oh my god, Nita thought.

It really is him—the kid Kit's been hunting. It's Darryl! And now I think I understand "the Silence"! she thought. Wizards got their information from the universe in a lot of different ways. On Earth alone, the manual in either its printed or online versions was only one method. Whale-wizards heard the Sea speak to them; the feline wizards had told Nita about something called the Whispering. *This has to be like that...*

But she was still left with entirely too many mysteries to solve. Nita stood there wondering what in the worlds to do next, then shook her head.

Waking up would probably be a good idea.

It took Nita a few seconds to remember the way to break the dream without waiting for a normal awakening. When she opened her eyes, she was looking sideways at the wall beside her desk, having put her arms down on the desk and her head down on her arms as she initially slid into sleep.

Nita rubbed her eyes, blinked, stretched. *I'm completely wiped out,* she thought. *I've got to get some real sleep, now, or I'll be useless tomorrow. But Kit's got to hear about this.*

She glanced down at her manual. "What time is it?" she said.

The page cleared and showed her the time in every zone on Earth, as a Julian date, and on all the planets in Sol system.

"Show-off," she said softly, glancing at the local time for New York. The readout said, "0223."

It was late, but this was important. *Kit?* Nita said silently.

Nothing. But it wasn't the "asleep" kind of nothing: Kit was missing.

"Message him," she said to the manual.

The page blanked itself, then showed Nita the words, "Subject is out of ambit."

That "error" message she now recognized. Kit and Ponch were off world-walking somewhere, out of this universe proper. Nita sighed. *I'll have to catch him in the morning*, she thought. *But bed first…*

She slept hard and deep, and for a change woke up not in the dark, but just after dawn. *I still wish spring would hurry up*, Nita thought as she swung her feet out of bed and rubbed her eyes. *This winter seems to be lasting forever.* But at the same time, it was hard to dislike a morning like this, when there was what looked like six inches of new snow outside, and it was Saturday as well. The snow was wet, clinging delicately to the bare branches of the trees out in the backyard, and everything was very still, the sky a pure, clean blue behind the white branches. *Who knows? Maybe I'll sneak out there, make a snowball or two, and stick them in Dairine's bed. Give her about three seconds of thinking I've had second thoughts about her, her bed, and Pluto.*

Nita threw last night's sweatshirt and jeans on and went downstairs to the kitchen, manual in hand. Her father was there, making his own coffee for a change. He looked at Nita with some surprise when she came in. "You're up early for a Saturday," he said.

"Not that early. I got some sleep for a change."

"You don't look like it."

Nita yawned and stretched. "I don't feel like it, either," she said.

"Just a long week at school, maybe?"

"I don't know." She went over to put the kettle on for herself. She ached all over, as if she'd had a particularly bad gym class, and she just felt generally weary. *As if I was a long, long way away last night.*

But if that really was Darryl, then I was only two towns away, in his mind.

Or possibly in an alternate universe he created, one a whole lot further away than that—

"How are you coming with what you were working on yesterday morning?" Nita's dad said. "Any progress?"

"Yeah," Nita said, "but I don't understand it." She opened a cupboard and tried to decide what kind of tea she wanted. She finally decided on mint, and got the tea box down, fishing around in it for the right tea bag.

"Your alien, or the progress?"

"Both. And it looks like it wasn't even an alien, if I'm right. It's a little kid who lives over in Baldwin."

Her father looked surprised at that as he went to get his coat from the rack by the door. "Another wizard?"

"Supposedly not yet," Nita said. "Assuming this is the person who I think it is. I have to check with Kit." But that brought up another odd problem for Nita to consider. From her own experience, Nita knew that being on Ordeal imparted a certain tentative feel to your wizardry, even when your power levels were at their highest. Even Dairine's use of wizardry, when she was on Ordeal, had exhibited that tentative quality. But it was completely missing in Darryl. *That's something else to ask Tom and Carl about.*

Her dad put on his coat. "Well, that sounds encouraging, anyhow," he said. He came over, gave her a hug and a kiss. "Leave me a note if you have to go anywhere. Is Dairine going to be getting involved in this?"

"Jeez, I hope not," Nita said. "It's confusing enough already."

"Okay," her dad said. "She has some school project she's supposed to be working on this weekend. If you want to just have a look at one point or another and make sure she's staying on track..."

This was, in fact, the *last* thing Nita wanted, but she nodded. "I will."

"Thanks, baby girl. See you later."

Nita wasn't sure, as her father went out, whether to bristle or smile. *When's the last time he called me "baby girl"?* she thought. It was one of those nicknames that Nita had complained about forcefully for years when she was younger, until her dad finally stopped using it. *And now I'm not even sure I mind anymore,* she thought. *I wonder if somehow he's trying to remind himself of how things were when Mom was still here.*

After a moment she laughed at herself for thinking such "shrinkly" thoughts. *Millman is affecting me,* Nita thought.

She made a face then, as the kettle came to a boil. *Oh god... Millman and the card tricks. But how long can it take to learn a card trick? I'll do it later. I have other things to think about right now.*

Nita glanced at the digital clock on the stove. It read 7:48. A little early, but then Kit did tend to get up early on the weekends. *Kit?* she said.

For a moment there was no response.

Hnnnhhh?

I'm not sure, but I think I may have found your guy.

A pause. When he answered, he still didn't sound incredibly awake. *When?*

Last night. The time's hard to judge, but I think it would've been around two-thirty.

There was a much longer pause that made Nita think Kit might have gone back to sleep. Finally he said, *It couldn't have been. I was with Darryl around then.*

Nita blinked at that. *You sure?* she said.

Yeah, I'm sure. He sounded cranky. *Neets, look, I'm completely wrecked, and I had trouble with my folks last night. I want to go back to sleep. Call me back, okay?*

Uh, sure, but—

The connection between them didn't so much break as dissolve in a returning wave of sleep. Nita stared at the tea bag in her hand, bemused. "Well," she said.

She made her tea and sat down at the dining room table with the mug, the manual, and a banana. Nita didn't go straight into the manual, partly because she wasn't yet clear on where she should start looking. She was still trying to sort out some things about her experience last night.

There had just been something about Darryl. Nita kept coming back to the impact she'd felt when he'd finally looked right at her. It wasn't power, not strength, in the usual sense. She was well down the cup of tea before she found the word she was looking for.

Innocence . . .

Talk about the innocence of childhood tended to pass right over Nita these days. Her own childhood was behind her—rather to her relief, because of all the beating up. And her memory of Dairine's childhood was too fresh; anyone putting that concept and the word *innocence* together in the same sentence would simply have made Nita laugh. Her sister's behavior aside, Nita knew perfectly well that most kids were no innocents.

But then most of the talk you heard on the subject came from adults, most of whom were entirely too hung up on the concept of childhood as this pure, untroubled thing that Nita wasn't sure had ever existed. Plainly, like the counselor that Dairine had been complaining about, too few of them really *remembered* what it was like to be seven, or nine, or twelve.

Nita could understand that perfectly. Large parts of childhood hurt, and adults did with that remembered pain exactly what kids did when they could: Let whatever good memories they had bury it. Oh, the moments of delight, of pure joy, were there, all right, but what adults seemingly couldn't bear was the idea that their *whole* childhoods hadn't been that way, that the trouble and sorrow of their adult lives, the result of the Lone Power's meddling in the worlds, wasn't something they'd always had to deal with, right from the start. So despite whatever kids tried to tell them, adults just kept on reinventing childhood as something that was supposed to be happy all the time, a paradise lost in the past.

Yet in very small children, there was something that Nita had to admit she'd seen...even, occasionally, in Dairine. Last night, in her dream, Nita had looked at

Darryl and had seen the same thing in his eyes, un-
alloyed—a sense of living in the morning of the world, a
time or place either uncorrupted or redeemed; unafraid,
and with no reason to be afraid; a person grounded im-
movably in the sense that the world worked, was just
fine, would always be fine. . . .

Poor kid, Nita thought. *Wait till reality hits him.* Yet,
remembering the look in those fearless eyes, she found
herself having an unaccustomed second thought. Reality might hit him, might, indeed, have hit him hard already—but *it* might be what shattered.

Boy, would I like to be there to see that.

Nita began to peel the banana. *But all that aside, Kit
said he was with Darryl when I was,* Nita thought. *So
if he's right, then who was I with?*

She took a bite of the banana and considered. *And
that's not the only thing about this that's strange. It's Kit
who's been looking for him. If this really is Darryl, then
why have I been seeing him, too?*

But now she thought she had an answer to that. *The
filter,* Nita thought. *We've both been holding the world
at arm's length . . . trying to get it to leave us alone.* She
shook her head. *And making ourselves more alone
while we do it. But the wizardry knew what it was
doing better than we did. One wizard alone found another one . . .*

Nita sat there for a moment, staring at the banana
without really seeing it. *Okay. But that brings up another question. If this is Darryl, then how come my vis-
its to his world are so different from Kit's?*

She had another bite of the banana, reflecting. *Unless*

it's just that I didn't know *that the person trying to contact me was autistic. I didn't have any preconceived ideas about what the world would look like to him. So maybe I got something that was more like Darryl's own ideas about himself... just translated into my own images: the uncomplicated, scared-kid stuff. Whereas Kit's been getting stuff that looks more like it belongs to someone really troubled... maybe because he's known from the beginning that Darryl's autistic.*

To Nita this sounded so commonsense that it seemed very likely to be true. *So now if I could just figure out how Darryl can be with both me and Kit at the same time.*

Maybe he was time-slipping somehow? Nita thought. But that would have taken a wizardry, and a considerable amount of power to fuel it. And the only thing Nita was now certain about, as far as her dream went, was that Darryl hadn't actually been *doing* any wizardry at the time.

No. Something else was going on...

Nita finished the banana, got up to dump the skin in the kitchen garbage can, and came back to her tea and the manual again. *What other ways are there for someone to be in two places at one time?*

She had to laugh at herself a little as she reached for the manual. *It would be a great trick if you had a busy schedule,* Nita thought. *Or you could be in school taking a test while you were also lying on the beach with a good book, working on your tan.*

She started paging through the manual again, idly at first, then with more concentration. After about fifteen minutes of this, as the sun got brighter on the snow outside and the dining room filled with its light, Nita realized that she still wasn't sure exactly how to find what she needed. She went to the back of the manual, to the page that handled search functions.

"I need all the references that have to do with being in two places at one time," she said.

The page cleared itself, and new words appeared. "Apparition or co-location?"

There it was, yet *another* word Nita hadn't ever heard of before today. "Apparition first," she said.

"See highlighted section," the page said, and her manual was abruptly about an inch thicker.

"Oh, no," Nita said. "I think I need another banana."

It took three more. Nita was grateful that Dairine seemed to be sleeping late, as she was the big banana fan in the house and would not have been pleased that Nita had made such inroads into the supply. The three bananas gave Nita time to discover, mostly by skimming the material as fast as she could, that there were an unnerving number of ways to appear in two places at once, if you felt like spending the energy. But that was the factor that kept everyone from doing it all the time. The universe had a basic bias against the same thing being in more than one place at once—this singularity of location being one of the ways that matter defined itself to begin with—and if you wanted to bend that bias in your favor, you would be heavily penalized, in terms of having to use a huge amount of effort to build a very complex spell.

It doesn't matter, Nita thought as she turned over the last twenty pages of the section, doing little more than glancing at them. *I'm sure he wasn't doing a wizardry last night, so none of this stuff applies.* She turned back to the search page again. "Give me the co-location stuff now," she said, not seeing any great point in it, but unwilling to stop until she'd read everything that could have a bearing on the problem.

The manual reduced itself to something more like its normal size, and laid itself open at a much shorter section. Nita glanced at the title page and table of contents for the section, momentarily confused. It was a classifications section on the Orders of Being.

Huh? she thought. Nita had been through this section every now and then. The time she'd been most interested in it was just after passing her Ordeal, when she was trying to sort out some of the finer details of how wizardry was organized. That version of the information had been thinner than this one, a sort of beginner's guide; this one was considerably more detailed.

Nita turned the pages, glancing at the master classification listing of created beings in the universe. The listing didn't go by species, but by type. Good old-fashioned mortals naturally had all the other types outnumbered, but there were still a surprising number of modified mortals and other conditionals. Then came wizards, of which there were hundreds of different types, even within single species. Among her own species, with which Nita would have thought she was moderately familiar by now, there were more classes of wizard than she'd realized.

The standard classes—probationary, post-Ordeal, full wizard, expert wizard, Advisory/Senior, Regional, Planetary, Sector—those she'd known about for long enough. But there were also splinter classifications, some categories that didn't quite fit among either mortal wizards or the Powers That Be. The Transcendent Pig, of course, Nita knew. She smiled slightly as she turned past his page. *The picture doesn't do him justice. Maybe it's old.* But there were many other classifications in this section, too, some of them most obscure. *Principalities, thrones, dominations— Thrones? Who wants to be a chair? But maybe I'm missing something here. Who knows? Maybe it's fun to be furniture.*

Nita turned the page over. *Pillars? What is this? First furniture, now architecture . . .*

Abdals/"Pillars"—This category of created being is independent of wizard status but still included because of the sharing of various functions and qualities across species and eschatological barriers. The sobriquet "Pillars" refers to the immense supportive strength inherent in these creatures wherever they appear. The physical and spiritual structure of the Universe and its contents is strengthened against the assaults of evil by the Pillars' presence, and weakened by their loss. While they occasionally may also be wizards, abdals display no unusual aptitude for the Art: Their value lies elsewhere. Their status comes from direct endowment by the One; their power is derived strictly from the incorrupt nature of their personality. Some have unusual abilities of perception reaching into other universes, while still seeing the entire physical world as mirage. Some have sufficient control over their physical natures to change their bodies at will, without recourse to normal wizardry, or to travel great distances, or to appear in two places at the same time. . . .

Certainty went straight through Nita like a lightning bolt, and not only because of the two-places-at-once line. It was everything else in combination with that. She thought of the knight, of the strength and bravery she'd sensed in that version of Darryl, and of the power inherent in the robot. All those experiences were fragments of this bigger picture, pieces of the jigsaw. Nita glanced on down the page.

> The Pillars are rarely recognized as such by their contemporaries. Should they become conscious of their own status as abdals, the realization itself renders them ineffective in their role, which is to channel the One's power without obstruction into the strengthening of the world. Their portion of that power is then lost to the Worlds, and with its loss, the abdal dies.

Nita slapped the manual shut and sat there, actually sweating, for a few moments. The language of the manual could be obscure sometimes, but this time Nita was sure she knew perfectly well what it was talking about when it said the Pillars' power was "derived strictly from the incorrupt nature of their personality." *It means what Darryl's got,* she thought. *Innocence. That plain, straightforward innocence that just goes right through whatever comes at it, like a knife, or bounces any attack off it, like a shield. And that really, really pisses off the Lone Power, so that It just keeps coming at him again and again, which is just the way Darryl wants it—*

Nita pushed back from the table a little, leaning back in the chair and considering. Normally when the Lone Power turned Its attention to destroying a wizard during his or her Ordeal, It would lay out no more energy than It absolutely had to. The tendency not to waste energy unnecessarily was one It still shared with the other Powers. It didn't waste Its time spending a lot of power on one wizard unless It knew that person was going to be something really special. *Dairine, for example,* Nita thought. *It gave her a lot of grief because she was so young when her Ordeal hit. The kind of power she was going to have, even just for a while, was worth trying to knock out.* But Darryl didn't give Nita the same impression of huge and abrupt power that Dairine had, and the manual confirmed his power levels as being, while not unusually low, not unusually high, either.

So these repeated attacks suggest that the Lone Power knows Darryl's one of the Pillars, Nita thought. *And killing an abdal has to be worth more to the Lone Power than just killing a wizard on Ordeal. Getting two for the price of one must look like an awful lot of fun to It.*

But the game's changed. Darryl's not the only stuck one now!

Nita sat looking out into the front yard, watching the maple tree there shed little sparkles of snow into the air as a faint breeze moved its branches. *If the Lone One finds out about this, It's going to go ballistic,* Nita thought. *It's been having so much fun toying with Darryl that It doesn't realize he's turned the tables on It.*

The Enemy will fight and fight again. I will hold It here, he said. *He's prolonging his Ordeal on purpose, running the Lone Power ragged—*

But that can't last forever. If there's one thing the Lone Power hates worse than anything else, it's someone laughing at It. *The minute It discovers that Darryl's tricking It, It'll just kill him outright in the nastiest way It can.*

Nita bit her lip. *And that would be for It to make Darryl find out that he's one of the Pillars. He loses the power. He dies. And the Lone Power gets back at the One, too, through Darryl's death.*

Her eyes narrowed as she remembered that mischievous smile, the courage in those dark eyes—and thought of how long Darryl had been alone there in one or another of his worlds, fighting, forgetting, fighting again, an endless battle with no hope of relief, no way to win...but with that valor always there, like shining armor.

Well, It's not going to get Its way this *time,* Nita thought.

She got up and started picking up the banana skins lying around the dining room table. *There's been enough dying around here,* she thought. *No more of it! As soon as Kit gets up, we're going to sit down and make a plan.*

She headed upstairs to get dressed.

Complications

KIT STOPPED IN the middle of the jungle path and looked around him. "We're lost," he said.

I don't know if I'd say we, Ponch said, sounding ever so slightly reproachful.

Kit wiped the rain off his face and turned to look back the way they'd come. It was nearly impossible to see where that was, for the path they'd been following was scarcely any wider than he was. The jungle all around them was a tangle of dark reds and dark greens, huge trees and undergrowth, vines and creepers and strange-looking plants. High above, the upper canopy of broad leaves held away the burning whiteness of the sky. Down here, precious little of that light reached; all the plants were in mud and blood colors, depressing... and the shadows in between them were worse. There were creatures in this jungle that had messy eating habits, and Kit had stopped looking into the shadowy places at the bases of the immense trees unless he absolutely had to.

"Where is he?" Kit said.

Ponch stood there with his nose working. *I'm not sure,* he said.

"*You're* not sure?"

We didn't do this the usual way, Ponch said. *For one thing, neither of us is awake. For another, you went in first, and I followed you because I didn't want you going in here alone. And you didn't bring the leash.*

Kit sighed and put out his hand. "Leash," he said.

Nothing happened.

You tried that before, Ponch said, *and it didn't work then, either.*

Kit sighed and wiped the rain out of his eyes again. At least the rain was warm, which was a good thing because it never really stopped; even when the hot sky above it wasn't actively raining, the jungle floor got more or less constantly dripped on.

So which way? Ponch said.

"We might as well keep on down this path," Kit said. "We're bound to run into Darryl eventually."

A high-pitched scream came out of the gloomy creeper-hung darkness ahead of them. *Assuming* that *doesn't run into him first,* Ponch said. *Or that it doesn't run into us first.*

"Come on," Kit said. He slogged down the muddy path, and Ponch padded along behind him, glancing nervously into the shadows of the trees and the undergrowth on either side of the path.

The path made a curve around one unusually large tree. Kit paused, looking at it, and went slowly around the curve. "Darryl?" he shouted. "Where are you?"

There was no answer but another of the blood-curdling screeches from up in the canopy. Kit knew, in a general sort of way, that there was no guarantee that what he was hearing up there was a carnivore...but there was no guaranteeing that it *wasn't,* either. He reached sideways to his otherspace pocket, thinking about the barbecue-lighting laser...and couldn't find the pocket, let alone the laser.

You tried that before, too, Ponch said.

"I forgot," Kit said. He wiped his face again. It wasn't rain he was wiping away this time, but sweat. The heat here was terrible—stifling, muffling, like wearing a portable electric blanket—but far worse was the humidity. If there was anything in the normal world that Kit really hated, it was hot, humid weather. In this place, though, it seemed like all the spare humidity from any number of jungle planets had been gathered up and dumped here. The sweat was running into his eyes, making them burn. Kit paused long enough to wipe his face again, then continued around the tree, looking at it suspiciously. "I keep expecting Darth Vader to come out of one of these and chase me with a light saber."

I don't think that's a good thing for you to be imagining, Ponch said, sounding unnerved. *Let's stick to Darryl for now. And once we've found him, let's get out of here!*

They went on under the trees. Not far ahead, trees shorter than the gigantic two-hundred-footers were gathered together in a cluster, and the path wound through them. It seemed to Kit that this looked like a perfect place for some kind of ambush...yet somehow he felt unable to take the prospect seriously. He slowed down a little, but kept walking.

Something smells bad here, Ponch said.

"*Everything* smells bad here," said Kit. The whole jungle had a smell like wet laundry that had been left in the washing machine too long, a stagnant scent. Some of the creepers were even festooned with something that might have been mistaken for wet laundry, though the growth was actually some kind of nasty, flabby fungus. Kit looked now with some loathing at the vines hanging from the red-trunked trees ahead of him; they had that fungus all over them, curtaining away the view of whatever might be further down the path.

"You smell anything?" Kit said.

Mold, Ponch said, his nose wrinkling. *And other things. I don't want to talk about it.*

Kit walked forward a little more slowly, looking at those trees, then looked over his shoulder again, back down the path. "I wish Nita were here," he said.

I don't! Ponch said. *I wouldn't want anyone I liked to be here. And I don't want us to be here, either! We're not going to find him this way, boss. Let's go home!*

"Just a little while more," Kit said. He was beginning to agree with Ponch, though. He was so tired. *I should have walked out of here the minute I found my-*

self in here, he thought, *except I don't remember how I* got *in here.*

No, wait. I do remember. The dream. I dreamed I saw Darryl running into the jungle. I went after him...

There was a rustling among the trees that lined the path ahead of them. Kit reached sideways for his other-space pocket. Then, as he was feeling around for it, he remembered that it didn't seem to be there in the dream. *I keep forgetting things,* he thought. *I guess it's just that I'm so tired. After yesterday, and the days before. But I can't help it. We can't leave him stuck in this. We have to find him!*

There was definitely something moving around in those trees, though Kit couldn't see what it was, and he didn't want to go any closer without some kind of weapon. He had a memory that there should have been wizardries that he could use for self-defense, but he was just too tired to think of any of them right now. Kit looked around him, saw a fallen log to one side of the path. There was a branch sticking out of it that looked big enough to use as a club. He got down on one knee and struggled with the branch for a few moments until it snapped off the log. It was covered with dark brown goo, yet more mold of one kind or another. Kit made a face as he rubbed it off the branch as best he could, rubbed his hands more or less clean on his pants, and then got up. "Come on," he said to Ponch.

High up in the jungle canopy, one of the invisible monsters started screaming again. Kit wanted to hold his ears against the noise of it, though that would have meant dropping the branch. Shortly the screamer was joined by a second, and they screamed at each other more and more loudly as Kit got closer to the trees.

One big creeper was hanging down over the path. It was well draped with the dirty-laundry fungus, and looked almost like a curtain. They were going to have to push through this. There was no avoiding it. Kit reached out one hand to the creeper, while above him in the trees the intolerable screeching got louder and louder. *If there is something in there,* Kit thought, *I'm not going to be able to hear it if it's coming for me.*

Yet he felt he had to go in. "You ready?" he said to Ponch.

I'm right behind you. Be careful!

Kit pushed the creeper aside. The gloom beyond the curtain of fungus was even worse than that out in the shadow of the trees; it was danker, more stifling and breathless. Kit edged into it, let the curtain fall—

Darkness. Ponch was close behind him, crowded up against his legs. Any hope that Kit had had that being in this closed-in place might somewhat muffle the awful screeching from outside was in vain; if anything, it seemed worse. He moved softly among the trees, brushing past the down-hanging loops and rags of fungus, trying not to touch them more than he had to. Where the fungus brushed him, he got an uncomfortable itchy feeling even through his shirt.

Kit started to move faster, though the weariness that had started to bother him when he came into this place was getting worse all the time. He was sure he could see shadows moving just beyond the trees that hemmed in the path. It might just have been more of the fungus, shifting in the wind, except that there was no wind. Something *was* moving there. Then, even over the screaming from above, Kit thought he heard a breathing sound—

He couldn't bear it anymore. He broke into a run, and Ponch plunged along behind him. The awful fungus slapped him in the face and upper body as he ran; Kit swatted it aside as best he could, but somehow it always seemed to get him anyway. Once he nearly throttled himself by running into a creeper that was hanging exactly at throat height. Kit reacted just in time to grab it, and used it to swing himself a little sideways—but then he banged into one of the closer trees and fell, and from above he could hear the screaming, louder than ever, sounding like laughter now.

Kit staggered to his feet and wobbled down the path again. His body didn't seem to be working right, and he couldn't understand why, unless it was just the weariness that was getting to him. His legs almost seemed to belong to someone else. His brain was full of noise that he couldn't stop. He knew Ponch was behind him, but he had to keep reminding himself of that. He couldn't get rid of the idea that he was all alone here, had been alone forever...

...except for something that hated him. It was hiding in the shadows. It was up in the furious brightness above the trees. It was dripping from every leaf, underfoot in every square inch of mud, looking at him with cruel, small, burning eyes from up among the branches of the trees. Kit ran, but his body wouldn't obey him, wouldn't let him run fast enough; he staggered along like some broken mechanical thing, and the screaming voices up above all laughed at him, and eyes, eyes he didn't dare meet, eyes whose contact was infinite pain, were staring at him from all around in the dark. He would come out into the open again in a moment, but there would be no respite for him then, either, no escape. The worst of the eyes would be there, waiting for him, in the shape of what was going to kill him at last.

Kit tried to stop, but he couldn't. Ponch blundered into him from behind. Kit's own momentum combined with the push from Ponch sent him forward, through the last curtain of creeper and fungus, down onto the path, and he was helpless in front of the merciless thing that waited.

Hands came down, grabbed him by the arms. *"No!"* Kit cried—

—and then realized that nothing had happened to him, and that he was facedown in the mud, and that the screaming above him was just screaming again—and that the hands were Darryl's.

Darryl was stronger than Kit would have expected. He hauled Kit nearly upright, but Kit didn't have the strength to stay that way; he collapsed down onto his butt again in a most undignified manner, and stayed there for a few moments, just panting and trying to get his breath back.

"Have to get up now," Darryl said. "It's coming."

Kit tried, and had trouble. Once again Darryl reached down to him and took Kit by the forearms. This time he swung him right up to his feet. Kit staggered a little, but managed to stay there, marveling again at how strong the youngster was. "Thanks," Kit said. "Darryl, I've been trying to catch up with you for a long time. I'm on errantry, and do I ever greet you! Now can we go somewhere quiet and have a talk, because—"

"No," Darryl said.

"You don't understand," Kit said, getting his breath again, but only slowly. "You really ought to get out of here while you've got the chance. It's not here yet, but I think It's coming—"

"That's just why I can't leave," Darryl said. "There are still things I have to do here, and in all the other heres. It doesn't matter whether—" He stopped, as if searching for words. "It doesn't matter what else might be here. It doesn't matter if there's a way out. I can't take it. I have to find the thing that still needs to be done before I can go."

Kit had been tired enough to start with, but now the exhaustion was coming down on him hard. *He means it doesn't matter who else is here,* Kit thought, *but he doesn't really believe in anyone else. Not me, for sure. Maybe the Lone Power ... but in some way that I don't understand, which is a problem, because when the Lone One gets here—*

"I said I'd stay until what I came to do was done," Darryl said. "The Silence said, 'So here's what it's all about. Here are the words. What're you going to do about them?' They were clear that first time, but after that it was hard to hear them all at once. Every time I tried to make sense of them, the noise would get in the way. Once or twice the shouting got so loud that I thought I'd die of it. Maybe only once or twice after that, it got quiet enough for me to think. But finally I knew those words were what needed saying, though I had trouble visualizing what they meant. It took a long time to picture them, longer to say them...days and days. I kept forgetting. But finally I got them all together and said them. 'In Life's name...'"

Kit sat there listening to the words. Part of him knew them better than he knew almost anything else. But another part of him thought, wearily, *Why does that sound familiar?* And the roaring and screeching in his head were once again making it hard to pay attention, hard to care about anything.

"...I will fight to preserve what grows and lives well in its own way..."

It was amazing the way the incessant howling of the world could weary you, until you would do anything to distract yourself from the noise of it—bang your head on a wall, hammer your fists on a table, scream to drown it out. That noise got into your head and wouldn't let you alone, wouldn't let you *be*. In the face of that torment, you quickly got to the point where the pain was itself reassuring, something you could rely on, something less stressful than trying to think anything or do anything through the cacophony of life. And when you come right down to it, it doesn't really matter. Nothing matters that much. Nothing's worth that much struggle....

"...To these ends, in the practice of my Art, I will put aside fear for courage, and death for life..."

Not that any of those matter. The world seemed dim and far away, this world, *any* world.

"But I don't think anyone else should be here now," Darryl said, and he came over to Kit. Kit turned his head away.

"There was— Someone was...here before," Darryl said. "In other 'heres.' It was..." He paused, as if hunting for the right term. "It was appreciated. But this isn't the right way to be here. It's dangerous like this. It's a way to get linked to me...by a link that can't be broken, to keep getting sucked back into the trap I've set—" Darryl turned him around, pushed him. "Go," Darryl said. "Go. It needs to—"

And Kit saw Darryl catch sight of Ponch.

Darryl froze.

Kit turned to look toward him, dulled, not understanding what he was seeing. Darryl and Ponch looked at each other. Ponch stood there with his head up, his tail wagging. It was a speculative look on Ponch's part. He was no more sure what Darryl was reacting to than Kit was.

"You," Darryl said. "*You* have to go."

Up in the trees, the screaming was scaling up again. "Go on," Darryl said—not to Kit, now, but to Ponch. "Don't wait. I recognize you—what you're becoming. But you can't stay. It'll be here soon. This time you're here the wrong way, you've been sucked in with him, and It'll see the two of you for sure. Go on!"

We will, Ponch said.

Above them, the gloom started abruptly to get darker. *But we won't leave you here,* Ponch said. *We'll be back.*

Ponch turned around and grabbed Kit by the wrist, gently, with his teeth. He pulled Kit back into the dimness of the stand of trees that surrounded the path.

The darkness increased behind them, and the screaming. Finally the blackness became total, and Kit staggered through it, blinded, deafened, being led by the hand, aware of nothing except that he was being led, and hoping it was to somewhere better.

Eventually Kit found that he was looking at the wall by his bed. He'd been looking at it for a long time; there was no telling how long. Ponch was licking his ear, and there was no way to tell for sure how long that had been going on, either, except that the side of his head felt pretty wet.

I don't think we should go there like that again, Ponch said.

It took Kit a long time to collect his thoughts enough to answer. *I think maybe you're right about that,* he said. But at the same time, he found it hard to get excited about the concept. It just didn't seem to matter that much.

Nothing seemed to matter that much.

Kit lay there for a long time, staring at the wall.

As Nita came through the dining room again, the phone rang.

She hurried over to answer it before it woke Dairine. "Hello?"

"Nita, it's Carl."

"Hi, Carl. What's up?"

"Uh, have you seen Kit today?"

He sounded reluctant to be asking. "Haven't seen him," Nita said. "Heard from him, though. I think he had a late night last night."

"Tom was expecting him for a debrief," Carl said. "That hasn't happened yet, though, and Tom was called away, so I need to handle it. You have any idea where Kit is at the moment?"

"I think he's still asleep." She paused a moment, checked to see if that was true. "Yeah," she said. "He's still out of it."

"Okay," Carl said, but he sounded uncomfortable to Nita. "It can wait a few hours, I suppose...but when he wakes up, make sure he gets in touch with me, all right?"

"Sure. I want to talk to him, too, because I found Darryl last night, and I think he's an abdal."

"You think he's a *what*?"

"An abdal. You know...one of the Pillars."

There was a brief silence at that. "Would you mind coming over here and telling me how you came to that conclusion?" Carl said.

There was something peculiar about his tone of voice. "I'm not in trouble, am I?" Nita said.

"What? No. But do me a favor? Bring your manual with you."

"Okay. See you in a while."

Nita pulled on her boots and parka and then made her way over to Tom and Carl's house the quick way, popping out into six inches of untouched snow, and was very glad she'd remembered the boots. Carl was standing inside the door, looking out at the backyard, as Nita came up to the sliding doors. He pushed one aside for her. "It's pretty out there, isn't it?"

"Yeah. But cold." She came in and stomped her boots on the tile floor of the kitchen to get rid of the snow as Carl closed the door. "Where'd Tom go? Anything important?"

"He's meeting with the Sector Advisories," Carl said. "Administrative business . . . something to do with reorganizing some planets' worldgating systems. Nothing wildly exciting, but he'll be gone for a couple of days."

Nita went to the table, taking off her coat and hanging it over one of the chairs. "You've got some wires hanging down there," she said as she sat down, noting the tangle extending from underneath the cupboards.

"Yeah. I've made a mess, and now I have to clean it up. Does your mom or dad know a good electrician?" Carl said wearily. And then stopped, and looked at Nita in shock, and passed a hand over his eyes.

"Oh, Nita," he said. "I'm sorry. I'm so sorry. Habit . . ."

"I know," she said. "I know." She swallowed. "It's okay. I'll ask Dad. He just had a guy doing some stuff to our garage. He thinks he's pretty good."

"Thanks."

Nita reached into the empty air beside her and pulled her manual out of the claudication that followed her around. "Here," she said. "Is something wrong with it?"

Carl sat down. "I don't think so," he said, "but

there's something I want to check. Tell me what you've been up to."

Carl opened Nita's manual, turned to one particular page, and spoke to it softly under his breath. Nita watched this curiously. The page filled up with characters in the Speech, cleared itself, and filled again, while Nita told Carl about the dreams she'd started having, how she'd decided to look into them more closely, and what she'd found. Well before she was finished, Carl had pushed her manual to one side and was giving Nita his undivided attention. When she finished, he let out a long breath.

"Well," he said.

"What were you looking for?" Nita said, feeling slightly nervous.

"It's all right. It's nothing bad." Carl folded his arms and sat back in the chair. "It's just that the information you've been given normally isn't made public."

"Been *given*?" Nita said.

Carl nodded. "But someone at a higher level has seen to it that you got it. So I see from the authorization logs."

Nita thought about that for a moment. "So he *is* an abdal?" she said.

Carl got a brooding look. "Tell me how he seemed to you, in twenty-five words or less."

"Innocent," Nita said. "He's absolutely innocent. But he's *fierce* about it. It just rolls off him." She shook her head. The impact of his personality, as communicated by just that one brief direct glance of Darryl's eyes, was difficult to describe without sounding silly. If it was light, it would have been blinding. "And it's not just the innocence. Even when he was screaming, I still liked him a lot. He's really *good.* And he just doesn't notice, doesn't seem to get it..."

"That would seem to clinch it, wouldn't it?" Carl said. "The definition out of the manual, practically word for word."

"That's what I thought. And it scared me somehow."

Carl smiled a little. "Possibly a healthy response," he said. "And one that convinces me you're right. You met him out of the flesh, without the protective coloration that a body provides for a spirit like that. At such times you would get the full impact...and I imagine it's an eye-opener."

Nita nodded. "I never thought goodness could be so *tough,*" she said. "So strong. But then again...I guess goodness isn't something I'd think about a whole lot, anyway. Nobody uses the word much unless it's in a commercial, and then they're just trying to convince you that something has a lot of milk in it."

Carl nodded, looking wry. "Virtue," he said. "The real thing. It's not some kind of cuddly teddy bear you can keep on the shelf until you need a hug. It's dangerous, which is why it makes people so nervous. Virtue has its own agenda, and believe me, it's not always yours. The word itself means strength, power. And when it gets loose, you'd better watch out."

"Something bad might happen..."

"Impossible. But possibly something painful."

Carl fell silent for a moment. "The manual makes the abdals sound like saints," Nita said.

"Oh, they *are* saints," Carl said. "That aspect of their power doesn't have anything to do with wizardry as such, though it can coexist with it, the same way you could be, say, a mathematician and a really nice person at the same time."

Nita made a face. "You haven't met my statistics teacher."

"I hear you. I still hate anything more complex than long division. But the trouble with sainthood these days is the robe-and-halo imagery that gets stuck onto it." Carl got that brooding look again. "People forget that robes were street clothes once...and still are, in a lot of places. And halos are to that fierce air of innocence what speech balloons in comics are to the sound of the voice itself. Shorthand. But most people just see an old symbol and don't bother looking behind it for the meaning. Sainthood starts to look old-fashioned, unattainable...even repellent. Actually, you can see it all around, once you learn to spot it."

"You make it sound like there are saints all over the place."

"Of course there are. You don't think it's just wizards that keep the universe running, do you? But saints tend not to be obvious. For one thing, they don't want to draw the Lone One's attention to them. Also, they tend to be too busy. Mostly sainthood involves hard work."

Carl leaned forward to pick up Nita's manual again, paging through it. "Anyway, I think you can understand why information about the abdals would be pretty carefully controlled, most of the time. The whole point of the way they function is that they're not supposed to know what they are. And the more mortals who *do* know, the more might let it slip. Darryl is important. Far more important, in the larger scheme of things, than you or I, or than just about anybody else I know, or am likely to know. Abdals don't exactly grow on trees." Carl looked suddenly thoughtful. "Well, actually, some places they do. What I mean is, they're not commonplace. The One invests a lot of power in them. There wouldn't be many of them on a given planet at any one time . . . and we want to keep the ones we've got. Or the *one* we've got, because as far as Earth goes at the moment, Darryl may well be it. And his presence here, even when he doesn't seem to be doing anything, is important for the world, because through him, the One channels into the world some of the power *we* use. If you'll pardon the plumbing analogy, think of us as faucets and Darryl as the reservoir, or the well. Cut that off, and—" Carl shook his head.

Nita was silent for some moments, digesting this. "So what do I do now?" she said at last. "I don't want Kit to think I'm horning in on his assignment or something because I'm worried about him. But I think maybe I am. He was okay when he started this, pretty much . . . as far as I was able to tell anything clearly about his state of mind when I was so stuck in my own. But now . . . he doesn't feel like he usually does. And I can't tell for sure whether that's good or bad."

"I wouldn't be sure, either," Carl said. "Well, the first thing you can do is, when he gets up, tell him I want a word with him, pronto. I don't like to lean on my wizards as a rule, but Kit's been a little less careful than usual, and with what you've discovered about the situation, he'd better sharpen up. The stakes have been raised."

She came back from Tom and Carl's the quick way, popping out into the backyard. The snow there was untouched, rather to her surprise. Dairine was as much a snow fiend as their mom had been. It was unusual to find that she hadn't been out here at least long enough to make a couple of angels. Under more normal circumstances, there would have been a whole snowman by now. *But the circumstances aren't normal...*

Nita went in, shucked her parka off and left it by the back door, and went up the stairs to see what Dairine was up to. She found her in her bedroom, staring at her desk. Spot was sitting in her lap, also staring with its little stalky eyes at the construction sitting there.

Nita looked at the desk. It was covered with tinfoil. On the foil and on a subsidiary bed of newspaper rested what appeared to be a model volcano sculpted out of wet papier-mâché. The volcano was extremely broad and flat, of the shield type, and Nita recognized it immediately.

"How does it look?" Dairine said.

"Not bad," Nita said. "What's it for?"

"We're doing a geology unit in our science class."

Nita raised her eyebrows. "Bending the rules a little, Dair?" she said. "That's Olympus Mons. It hardly counts as geology."

"Okay, areology, then." Dairine sat there wiping her hands on a towel.

"It looks a little bare right now," Nita said.

Her sister turned a look of withering scorn on her. Spot cocked one eye in Nita's direction as if to suggest that she'd asked for this. "Of course it looks a little bare," Dairine said. "I have to paint it first. My *real* project for today is constructing an airbrush out of nothing but wizardry."

"Sounds like a moderate challenge," Nita said.

"And when the volcano's done, I'm going to make it blow up in class," Dairine said.

Nita's eyes widened slightly at the first image that occurred to her.

"With lycopodium powder," Dairine said, more scornfully than before, if that was possible. "Sheesh, Neets."

"Just checking," Nita said.

"Yes," Dairine said, "I know you were." She rolled her eyes. "Tell Dad I'm being good."

"If you're good enough, I won't have to tell him anything," Nita said. She turned away.

"Wouldn't it be fun to do it with real lava, though?" Dairine said from behind her as Nita headed to her room.

"There are times," Nita said, "when I think a nice big lava flow would improve that school a lot. You know any card tricks?"

The silence in answer to that question was unusually eloquent.

Nita sighed and sat down in her room. *You awake yet?* she said silently to Kit.

She waited for a few seconds.

Huh? Kit said.

Well, that's half my question answered, Nita said. *You sound pretty tired. You okay?*

I guess so.

Nita raised her eyebrows. This wasn't exactly a normal response for Kit. Either he was okay or he wasn't, but the middle ground wasn't usually an option for him, in Nita's experience, especially when he sounded as dulled as he did. *I'm coming over in a while,* she said. *There's some stuff I have to show you.*

Okay.

And that was it.

Either he's exhausted, Nita thought, *or there's something wrong…*

She knew what her present hunch suggested, though. She was starting to get worried about him. *He's been hitting this problem with Darryl so hard,* Nita thought, *that he's just been wearing himself down. That's one possibility.*

Why don't I think that's what's really going on?

Nita headed downstairs to make herself a sandwich. "By the way," Dairine said in a piercing voice as Nita went past her door, "someone seems to have eaten all the bananas."

Nita sighed. "I'll stop by Brazil on my way home. Or Panama."

"Costa Rica."

"Please," Nita said as she went down the stairs. She had never been any good at remembering which exports came from which countries. It struck her as information that, for someone in junior high, was about as useful as dissecting the history of the gold stan-dard. *When I get a job at an import-export firm,* Nita thought, turning the corner into the kitchen, then *I'll worry about who exports bauxite and who exports tin. Not before.*

She opened a can of tuna fish, drained it, mashed it in a bowl with mayonnaise and Tabasco sauce, made herself a sandwich with it, and ingested the sandwich without paying it much attention. Darryl was on her mind. *He's more important than all of us, Carl said.* The thought was sobering. She and Kit had done some mod-erately important and useful things in their time work-ing together, but what Carl seemed to be describing was a different level of function, one in which just being there, just being alive and breathing, could be more important to the world than any amount of running around doing things. It made a strange kind of sense when Nita put it together with what Tom had been saying about the Powers finding the difference between active and passive work "illusory." *If just by being here, Darryl is channeling the One's power into the world, then if something were to happen to him suddenly...*

It was a scarier thought than any Nita had had in quite some time. *Whatever else I do,* she thought, *I've got to find a way to help him.*

Because he doesn't know it, but he's helped me...

Nita went to get her coat, and then went out to walk over to Kit's.

"Hola, Carmela. ¿Qué pasa?" Nita said as she came in Kit's back door.

"*Watashi wa ureshii!*" Carmela said, more or less dancing past Nita into the living room, with the TV remote in her hand.

Nita blinked as she slipped off her coat and dropped it on the floor beside the dining room sofa. The Japanese thing was something Carmela had been working on for a while, and now that she was getting good at it, you never quite knew which language you were going to get from her. "Let me guess. You're saying you're going to turn into a giant robot?"

"No," Carmela said, "that would be, *Watashi, imakara sugo-ku o-kina robotto ni naruno!*"

"I'm impressed," Nita said.

"If I really did turn into a giant robot, I bet you would be," Carmela said, heading back into the living room.

Nita followed her. "Oh," she said. "Is this the new TV?"

"*Ohayō gozaimas'!*" shouted the TV and the DVD player together.

"Oh," Nita said. "Hi, cousins. Nice to meet you."

"*Dōzo yoroshiku!*"

"Uh, yeah." To Carmela she said, "Don't you find that a little unusual?"

"I'm used to it now. Kit says he thinks we're having some kind of wizardry leakage in the house," Carmela said, very matter-of-fact. "Mama can hear Ponch. And Pop and I can hear the TV when it shouts at the DVD. Mostly it's friendly shouting now, since Kit fixed the remote." Carmela plunked herself back down on the sofa, stretching out her legs.

"*Fixed* it," Nita said, still having some trouble with this concept.

"It was a lot worse before. He said he was going to ask Tom what was going on. Meanwhile, in case you're wondering, Kit's in his room. Mama and Pop are out shopping, and they did not take Kit with them because they are *annoyed* with him." She lowered her voice. "But also because he slept real late, and he looks like hell. Mama thinks he's coming down with something."

"Thanks for letting me know," Nita said. "Uh, have you been having any trouble with—?" She glanced in the general direction of the TV and DVD while turning enough to conceal the look.

"Trouble? Not at all. Weird stuff turns up sometimes, but all the regular TV's there, the cable and all. I don't care how many aliens I see, as long as I've got my MTV and the shopping channels."

Nita grinned. This was Dairine's attitude as well, though it was the music channels that interested her more than the shopping. "Half the time, with some of those videos, you can't tell what planet they're from anyway," Nita said.

Carmela snickered. "Later," Nita said, and went back to Kit's room.

He was lying on the bed, his manual open and facedown on his chest, looking up at the ceiling. Ponch was lying next to him on the bed, with his head on Kit's chest. Ponch's eyes shifted to Nita as she came into view, but he didn't move or say anything.

Nita paused in the door and knocked on the door frame. "Hey," she said.

Kit glanced over at her. It was the least-interested glance that Nita could remember seeing from him in some time. *Why doesn't he just come out and say that he wishes I wasn't here?* Nita thought, shocked. But it occurred to her then that she'd been distant enough with him lately. Maybe he was giving her a taste of her own medicine. *That wouldn't normally be his style, either. But if he's really feeling sick, maybe he's just saying what's on his mind, stuff he'd keep to himself otherwise.*

Nita felt briefly guilty, then put the feeling aside. "You look kind of out of it," she said.

"Yeah," Kit said. "I feel that way, too. I didn't sleep real well after I got in last night."

"Late?" Nita said, going over to sit in the chair by his desk.

"Yeah."

She waited a moment to let him tell her what he'd been doing, but he just turned his head away and looked up at the ceiling again. He wasn't going to tell her. "You have any luck with Darryl?" she said.

"Not really."

Nita started feeling around for something sarcastic and angry to say to Kit, and then she stopped herself. *He didn't push me when I didn't want to talk,* she thought. *I'm not going to push him now.*

But there's still something that needs saying. "Kit," she said, "about Darryl...I'm getting the feeling that you going after him the way you are isn't doing you any good."

"Uh-huh."

Nita pursed her lips. That was the same "uh-huh"

that she used on Dairine, as code for the message, "I am not listening to you. Bug off."

He doesn't mean to be rude. He just doesn't want to tell me what's on his mind, or hear what's on mine.

Did I sound like this? He should have hit me on the head with something until I paid attention.

Nita let out a breath. "Okay," she said, "forget about it for now. But I have a message for you. You need to go see Carl."

That finally made Kit look at her again. "Huh? How come?"

"Tom's out of town," Nita said. "Some Advisory or Senior thing. Carl's handling his interventions for the next day or so. You owed Tom a debrief on what's up with Darryl, and Carl wants to know where it is. Just between you and me, I think he's steamed. So if I were you, I'd get over there and take your medicine."

"I've taken enough medicine for one weekend," Kit muttered.

"After you got in late?"

"Yeah. My pop didn't say much, but my mama did."

"Tore a few strips off you, huh?"

"It wasn't my fault, Neets," Kit said. "The timing got blown, that's all." He sighed. "But it doesn't really matter."

Nita looked at Kit with concern. That was a theme she'd been singing too much herself lately, and Nita wasn't going to be indifferent to it when someone else started in on it.

"They didn't ground you or anything?"

"No. Anyway, they would have done that *how,* exactly?" Kit said.

Nita had to smile, despite her worrying. It was extremely difficult to ground a wizard without the wizard's consent. Still, you had to live with your parents... and rubbing their noses in the fact that they couldn't control you no matter how much they wanted to wasn't a great way to make that life an easy one.

Kit sighed. "Neets, I'm sorry, I'm just..." He trailed off. It wasn't that he was too tired to pursue the thought. It was just that he didn't care.

"Okay," Nita said, and got up. *At least he talked to me a little. It's possible he really is coming down with something... Well, we'll see.* "Look... call me when you feel better. There's stuff we have to discuss about Darryl."

"Sure."

"But go see Carl first."

Kit turned his attention to the ceiling again.

Nita gave him one last look as she turned away. As she did, Ponch glanced up at her. His eyes had been all for Kit until now, but the look Ponch gave her had even more concern in it than Nita was feeling.

Nita met the gaze, glanced fractionally at the door, and went out.

That could have turned into an argument, Nita thought, *if he'd had enough energy to bother. But he didn't.* She passed through the living room, where Carmela was curled up on the sofa, watching the TV, where models in frilly things pounded up and down a catwalk. Nita paused briefly, eyed the things the models were almost wearing.

"Not for me," Carmela said, not taking her eyes off the screen. "Drafty. How is he?"

"He looks tired," Nita said. "Anyway, tell your mama and pop I said hi."

"Sure, no problem."

Nita got her coat and headed out the back door. She didn't shut it right away, because after about half a minute, Ponch came trotting out of the dining room and headed outside, past Nita.

She closed the door, brushed some stray snow off the back steps, and sat down. Ponch sat down next to her.

"Ponch," Nita said in the Speech. "What's with the boss?"

He's sad, Ponch said. *But there's more to it than that.*

Ponch looked down the driveway toward the street. *I'm sad, too,* he said. *And I'm afraid. Something's happening to him, and I don't know how to stop it.*

Somewhere down the street, a dog began to howl in a high little voice, like something out of a cartoon.

"It's about Darryl, isn't it?"

We were there again this morning.

"Again? I thought you went last night."

We did. I took him there. But the second time we went, he started to go by himself. I had to follow him. Ponch licked his nose nervously. *It wasn't easy. He wasn't going the way I go.*

"Was he dreaming?"

Yes.

"Lucid dreaming, though? The guided kind?"

No. He was worried. His dream took him there without him wanting to be there, at first. Then he couldn't get out. They were getting alike . . .

Nita pondered this. Her own nonlucid dreaming had brought her to Darryl, or Darryl to her, and those dreams hadn't been good, either. But this experience, at least as Ponch described it, sounded slightly different. *I bet their minds are starting to get locked together because of all the time Kit's spending in there,* Nita thought. *This is not good . . .*

And reality doesn't feel terribly real to Darryl, Ponch said. *I think it's starting to feel the same way to Kit.*

"That would make a nasty kind of sense," Nita said. "Ponch, I don't think you should take him back in there for a while. At least not until he's feeling better. And when you go, I want to go with him."

I want you to do that, too.

Nita lifted her head, listening, realizing that the howling of dogs down the street had increased. Three or four more dogs had joined the first one. "What's the matter with the dogs?" Nita said. "Is someone using one of those silent whistles or something?"

No. I think it's because I'm afraid, Ponch said. *I think they hear me being that way, and they're upset for me.*

"But that's not all, is it," Nita said, looking thoughtfully at Ponch. "Something else is happening to you besides just being afraid for the boss. Isn't it?"

There was a long pause. *I don't know,* Ponch said. *I don't know what it means. I don't have the words. But I'm frightened for me, too.* He licked his nose again.

The howling down the street got a lot louder, and Nita suddenly found herself thinking that it wouldn't be smart right now to press the question any further. She put an arm around Ponch and roughed his fur up a little. "We're both nervous about a lot of things, big guy," she said. "I'll be glad when the boss is better. But listen. Right now, as soon as he gets up, Kit needs to go see Carl. He's not in the mood to listen to me right now. I know how that is. But he needs to go, anyway. Will you nag him? Get him to go over there?"

I will.

"That's my boy." She rubbed Ponch behind the ears and pulled the door open for him. He went back into the house.

Nita shut the door and headed home. She was almost halfway there before, as she went over the conversation with Ponch in her mind, she realized that at least once Ponch had answered a thought in her mind—not something she'd actually said out loud.

Nita shook her head, sighed, and walked in the direction of the neighborhood deli, to see if they had any bananas.

Entrapments

KIT AND CARL were sitting together in Tom and Carl's dining room, later that afternoon.

"Kit," Carl said, "it's all very interesting what you've told me. It throws a lot of light on Darryl's problem. I'm going to look into this myself, as far as possible. In the meantime"—he frowned—"I want to know why it took you so long to get in here and tell Tom or me about this. We've been working together on power-sensitive issues long enough that you ought to know better than to let a situation of this kind go for so long without a debrief."

"I've had the manual on record-and-report," Kit said.

Carl shook his head. "Not good enough," he said. "The manual, powerful as it is, is context-poor when reporting on experiences like this. Especially considering that what you've been doing with Ponch is unique as far as I can tell. For maximum effectiveness in assessing Darryl's status, I need to know how things looked and felt to you *after* the fact, as well as during it. So you'd better start getting serious about this, Kit. It's not like you to let things slide."

"Okay," Kit said.

Carl looked at him with an expression that suggested he was expecting to hear something else. At last he said, "Which brings me to the next thing on the list. The Powers certainly don't expect you to work on a project so hard that you neglect your own well-being. Neither do I. You look terrible; you've been spending too much time chasing around outside of your home space, and it's affecting you. I appreciate your efforts, believe me...but I want you to take a couple of days off."

"But—"

"*No* buts," Carl said.

Now it was Kit's turn to frown. Possibly Carl read the expression as rebelliousness. "Kit," he said, "as a Senior, it's not beyond my abilities to put a freeze on your wizardly exertions for the next day or three. I would prefer not to have to do that: It's undignified for both of us, and it also sends a signal to the Powers that there might be a problem with the way you're using the Art. I would much prefer to hear you tell me that you won't do any further exploration of Darryl's inner worlds until Tom and I have had some time to work out what seems to be the best way to proceed. This may sound cruel to you, but he's been holding his own for the past three months, at least; I would guess he'll hang on for a day or two more. You, on the other hand, need to leave his problem with me for the next couple of days."

Kit let out a long breath. "So," Carl said, "do I have your word?"

"Mmf," Kit said.

Carl gave him an exasperated look. "Even among nonwizards," Carl said, "it's considered impolite to grunt."

"I promise," Kit said.

"Good," Carl said. "Thanks." He relaxed a little. "Kit, go home, get some rest. It's not that you did a bad job...it's just that you got a little too wrapped up in this one. Take two days or so and get your objectivity back. Then you and Tom and I will sit down and work out what to do next." And he saw Kit out the sliding doors into the backyard.

Kit used his transport wizardry to get home, then walked slowly down the driveway to the side door, with Ponch trotting along behind him. He was feeling rather bruised. But to a certain extent, bizarrely, part of him felt grateful. Carl's very understated annoyance had shaken Kit a little way out of the feeling that had been creeping up on him that nothing particularly mattered. However, that was the only good thing about it. Kit felt very much as if he were in disgrace.

You look sad, Ponch said.

"I don't know," Kit said. "I think I'm just tired." Even as he said it, though, Kit wondered how true this was. Ever since he woke up from his jungle dream, he had been moving through a world that seemed oddly dulled around the edges. The daylight seemed to be reaching him through some kind of filter; sound seemed distant, and he didn't even seem able to feel his clothes properly—they seemed to bother his skin where they rested on it. The feeling was like what he got sometimes when he was coming down with a cold. *Maybe Mama was right...*

He went in the back door, took off his coat and hung it up, while Ponch trotted over to his dog food bowl and started to chow down on dry food. Kit's mama, in the kitchen in her nurse's pinks, looked up at him from the business of making a sandwich. "How are you feeling, sweetie?"

"Maybe a little better," Kit said, thinking that possibly this was true. "Getting out in the air was nice. Where's Pop?"

"He's lying down reading a book, waiting for the basketball game."

"Okay."

His mama gave Kit a glance as he went and flopped down on the dining room sofa. At first Kit thought she was going to bring up once more the subject of the discussion she and Kit's pop had had with him earlier. "I meant to thank you, by the way," his mama said as she opened a drawer to get a plastic bag to put her sandwich in. "It's been so much quieter."

His mama's voice had a strange grating quality to it, which Kit couldn't remember having heard before. *Is she coming down with a cold, too?* Kit thought. *It wouldn't be great if we all got sick at once.* "Sorry?"

"The little dog down the street."

Kit was bemused. "Tinkerbell, you mean? I haven't talked to him."

"You haven't?"

"Sorry, Mama, I've been busy."

"Well, he got quiet again. Relatively quiet, anyway. There was some howling earlier, but it didn't last long."

"That's good," Kit said. He stretched, but far from making him feel more comfortable, it made him feel less so; he felt very out of sorts, as if his skin didn't fit him, as if his bones weren't fastened together correctly. "Mama, I think I might go lie down again for a while."

That got her attention. She finished wrapping her sandwich and came over to feel his forehead. "Do you feel hot, sweetie?" she said.

Kit shook his head. If anything, he felt chilly, though not to the point of shivers—he felt a strange kind of still numbness that left him unwilling to talk about what was bothering him. Indeed, talking about *anything* seemed more trouble than it was worth. When his mother took her hand away, Kit got up and went to his room. There, as he lay down on his bed, he reached out for his manual and started paging through it to find a diagnostic to run on himself. *I won't be any good to anybody if I just lie around feeling like this.* But, shortly, Kit was lying on his back again, gazing at the ceiling, the manual lying open, pages down, on the bed beside him. He didn't even hear Ponch come in and circle around once to lie on the braided rug by the bed, looking up at him with troubled eyes. And after a while Kit turned over on his side again and just stared at the wall....

The next afternoon, Nita was sitting at her desk, cutting a deck of cards. She had reached the point where what she really wanted to cut them with was a meat cleaver, but that would simply have meant that she'd have to get another deck of cards from somewhere.

Nita cut the cards again. *There's an art to this,* she thought. *The only problem is, it isn't* my *Art. And no matter how I do this, when I think of why I'm learning it in the first place, it feels like cheating.*

She was working on her false shuffle. From what she'd been able to find out on the Web, many of the simplest card tricks depended on shuffling the cards in such a way as to make the card you wanted come up in the right place. This, in turn, involved protecting some of the cards with one of your hands while you shuffled. So far, Nita had gotten to the point where she could protect about a third of the deck, keeping the cards stacked there from being shuffled out of order. *In about three hundred years,* she thought, *I'll be ready to let some other human being see me do a trick. Why did I ever mention magic to Mr. Millman?*

The only good thing about having to sit here doing this was that it gave Nita something to occupy her hands while she worried about Kit. She'd called him late yesterday afternoon to make sure he'd gone to see Carl, and had been very concerned about the tone of his voice. It had acquired a strange monotonous quality, one that made her think of ...

A robot? she thought, unnerved. She stopped shuffling for a moment and thought about that. It occurred to Nita that the more contact they'd all had with Darryl, the better his ability to express himself had become... and the more adverse effect it seemed to be having on Kit.

If he goes in there again, she thought, *he's going to lose it.*

And he's going to go in there again. I'm sure of it.

Nita cut the cards again, looking to see if the ace of hearts, the card she had been protecting, came up. What she got was the three of clubs. She made an annoyed face and pushed the cards away. It wasn't just a matter of Kit's stubbornness now—not that that couldn't be formidable when he was in the right mood. She was also dealing with something else she was less familiar with: Darryl's stubbornness. He had been holding off the Lone Power all by himself for a long time now, and Nita didn't think he was going to stop for their sakes. *And why should he?* she thought. *From his point of view, or what's been his point of view for a long while, he's all there is. He might as well be the only wizard alive. He may briefly realize there are more of us... but it doesn't last.*

Because he keeps making himself alone again every time. Nita thought about what that must cost him. Such loneliness would have crippled her a long time ago. *But he bears up under it,* she thought. *He just keeps fighting.*

That stubbornness had found a resonance in Kit. He and Darryl had become linked in more ways than one.

His promises to Carl aside, Nita had a feeling that Kit was going to find himself in Darryl's mind again shortly. *At which time,* Nita thought, *I'd better be ready.*

She picked up the deck again, took a couple of minutes to find the ace of hearts, repositioned it, and reshuffled, carefully protecting the back third of the deck. Then she put the deck down, cut it twice so that she had three piles, reached out to the leftmost pile, and turned the top card over. It was the four of diamonds.

I hate *this,* Nita thought. She stood up from her desk and went across the hall to Dairine's room.

Her sister was sitting at her own desk, which was still completely covered by the papier-mâché version of Olympus Mons. It was no longer gray-white; Dairine had done a fairly credible job with her wizardly airbrush. Now the mountain lay there nicely colored in shades of red and pink, its huge crater looking entirely ready to spill out lava. Spot was sitting up on one of the bookshelves, peering down at the volcano with his little stalky eyes.

"Dair?"

Dairine looked up at Nita with a weary expression.

"I think I'm going to need some help," Nita said.

"As long as it doesn't involve me painting anything," Dairine said, "you're on."

Nita came in and sat down on Dairine's bed. It creaked.

Dairine looked at her.

"Don't start," Nita said. "You know what's on my mind."

"Darryl," Dairine said. "Or the ace of hearts."

"Please," Nita said. "Dair, I need to ask you a favor." Her sister gave her a slightly suspicious look.

"He's going to go in there again," Nita said.

"Kit?" Dairine put her eyebrows up. "I thought he promised Carl he wouldn't."

"Dairine, I don't think he's entirely in control of what's going on with him. Darryl is very, uh, single-minded. And that single-mindedness strikes me as really likely to affect Kit. I think we need to be ready for that."

"'We'?" Dairine said.

"Dairine, he's sure not listening to *me* right now—"

"I guess you know what he felt like with you over the past month, then," Dairine said.

Nita grimaced at that, taking the point. "So we've got to arrange some kind of connection, ideally with an integrated power feed, from you to me—for when he goes in again. Think of it as a lifeline. I need to make sure that there's somebody on the outside who can yank us both out of there if we get stuck too deep."

Dairine, sitting there with her hands in her lap, looked up at Nita. It was an unusual position for Dairine; usually, even when she was talking her hands were doing something. But now she sat quite still, looking at Nita steadily, but a little bleakly. "Are you sure you want my help?" Dairine said.

Nita looked at her strangely. "Are you crazy?" she said. "Of course I do."

"I just wasn't sure," Dairine said, and looked at the floor. There was nothing overtly guilty or upset about her face, but all the same, Nita saw there was trouble underneath the expression. "I warned you, Neets. Right now I'm paying the price for a big showy start, just as Tom said I would not so long ago. I can do basic wizardries well enough, but as for anything really high-powered—" She shook her head. "I don't know if you want to be depending on me right now."

"I will depend on you any time," Nita said.

The look Dairine gave Nita had a certain amount of good-natured scorn about it. She opened her mouth. "Do I have to say it in the Speech?" Nita said.

"Nita," Dairine said then, very softly, "*Mom* couldn't depend on me."

Nita shook her head. "If you mean you couldn't just make a wish and save her life," Nita said, "then you're right. If you really thought that it was going to be that way, then, yeah, you made a mistake. But that hardly means that she couldn't depend on you. Or that I won't."

"*You* may be the one making the mistake, depending on my power right now," Dairine said.

Nita rolled her eyes. "I don't know if I'm exactly a model of stability right now myself," she said, "but I can't afford to just stand around wondering. Will you help, or am I going to have to do this without a net? Because more depends on this than just me or Kit. Darryl is apparently..."

Nita trailed off. She was uncertain exactly how much she wanted to tell Dairine about why Darryl was special.

"Something unusual," Dairine said. "A lot of power...

or something else. He would have to be unusual, to have attracted so much attention from Tom and Carl."

Dairine sat quietly for a few seconds, then nodded. "I'll work something out for you," she said.

Nita nodded. "Thanks," she said. She turned away.

"It kills you, doesn't it?" Dairine said. "Asking me for help."

Nita gave her sister a very slight smile. "Better it should kill me than Kit," she said.

Then she went back into her room to start yet another futile search for the ace of hearts.

We have to go.

Kit sat up suddenly on the bed, looking around him. His glance wandered past the clock on his wall; it was around four-thirty in the afternoon. *Where did the day go?* part of him wondered, but that part seemed very remote. Much more important was the need to go looking for Darryl. Darryl was in trouble, he was stuck, and Kit had to get him out of there. In a world where nothing much seemed to matter, that suddenly mattered a great deal.

He could almost see that other world, here in the room with him, as if he were in two places at once. The world had changed again, or rather, *he* had changed it, Darryl had changed it, to put the One who was pursuing him off the scent. It always realized what had happened eventually—that Darryl had It trapped—and then Darryl had to change everything again, making a new world, a new self, in which the Pursuer would once again be confused. Each new world was better than the last, with new rules to impede the Lone One's power and to keep him occupied longer. He wished, sometimes, that Darryl didn't have to do it again and again. It gave him no time to find out what else wizardry might be for. If it *was* for anything else...

We have to go, Kit thought, and got out of bed—

—and tripped over Ponch, who was lying on the rug, watching him. *Boss!* Ponch yelped. *Where are you going?*

"We have to go," Kit said. The bedroom was already beginning to fade a little, like something that didn't matter. What mattered was elsewhere. The Pursuer was coming again; all his attention now had to be given to the creation of the new illusion, at the expense of the old one.

You promised you wouldn't! Ponch whimpered, jumping up and down. *You told Carl you'd stay here!*

But it seemed now as if a different person entirely had made that promise. In fact, someone different *had* made it: another person, in another place...different from this, the only reality that really mattered, now re-forming itself around him. The last time, he'd gotten a little careless, and the dark Other had found Its way in, and out again, too easily. This time, the place to which he found his way had to be a little more challenging. The idea had come to him that morning in the bathroom, as once again he faced what he couldn't face in the mirror on the wall, in which he had to see, every day, human eyes with the dark Other looking out of them. *This is Its weapon against you,* the thought had come to him. *Turn the weapon against It...*

That other reality, glassy, gleaming, was becoming more and more real around Kit as he stood there. It was only a matter of moments before he would be able to step wholly into it, such was the other's power and his need for help. Distressed, Ponch said, *The leash! Boss, let me get the leash! Wait for me—*

The voice in his head seemed to Kit to come from almost too far away to matter.

Stay there, boss! Kit—stay! Stay!

The urgency of that voice was just enough to keep Kit where he was, to prevent him from taking the single step forward that would bring him into the gleaming maze now being constructed for the Other's confusion. That was all that could be hoped for—to befuddle It, wear It down until eventually It would stop coming and just leave him alone. There was no telling whether the hope would ever be realized. But it was the only hope in the world, and hence it was worth clinging to.

The sound of paws scrabbling up the steps was as distant as everything else. Kit watched the shining unreality forming around him, watched his bedroom fade away, a backdrop without meaning. Into that backdrop burst something that shone, a line of blue light around a dark creature's collar. The creature looked up at him, the only gaze he could stand, the only eyes that didn't hurt him. *Boss, take the leash! Take it, put it around your wrist.*

Kit couldn't see the point, but the creature's eyes were so beseeching that he did as he was told. As he looped the other end of the line of light around his wrist, the world in which he was standing finally became totally irrelevant. Kit took the step forward into the real world, or into the one that had become real, and the black creature beside him stepped through, too—

"Kit," his mama's voice said from down the hall, "I'm going out now. You call me if anything comes up here. Can I bring you anything back on my meal break?"

No reply.

"Kit? Sweetie, are you asleep?"

No reply.

Kit's mama came down the hall. "You know, I brought that cold medicine home, the one with the zinc in it," she said. "I wonder if maybe you should just take some, so you can head this thing off—"

She stood in the doorway of his bedroom, looking in at the empty bed.

"Oh, no," she whispered.

At Nita's house, the phone rang. Her dad, sitting at the dining room table and working his way through the Sunday paper with a beer and a sandwich, got up and answered it.

"Hello? Oh, hi, Marina...No, he's not, as far as I know. Wait a minute..."

Nita's dad looked around the corner into the living room, where Nita was sitting on the rug, playing an extremely frustrated game of solitaire as relaxation from nearly an hour of utterly unsuccessful attempts at getting a simple "guess the card" trick to work. "Nita?" her dad said. "Is Kit here?"

Nita was surprised. "No."

"His mom's looking for him."

Nita's heart went cold inside her. "I thought he was going to be home all day today."

"He's not there, his mom says."

Nita sat still for a moment. *Kit?*

There was no answer.

She broke out in a sweat. There was no way to be absolutely sure where he was, but she thought she could guess. And it upset her to be right so quickly. "I don't hear him nearby," she said. "Wait a minute, Daddy."

She went to get her manual, paged through it to the messaging section, and said to it, "Kit, where are you? Urgent!"

"Send message?" the manual page said.

"Send it!"

"Recipient is out of ambit. Please try again later."

Nita swallowed. She got up and went into the dining room. As she did so, she suddenly started to hear something she hadn't been able to hear in the living room; the sound of dogs howling a few streets away, more and more of them.

She took the phone from her dad. "Mrs. Rodriguez? It's Nita. I just called him, but I don't get any answer. And the manual says he's not in this universe. He's gone again."

There was a long, frightened pause on the other end of the phone. "He said he wasn't going to do that until Tom and Carl gave him the word," Kit's mama said. "But he really hasn't been...himself, these past couple of days."

That was exactly Nita's worry at the moment: that Kit wasn't himself, but somebody else. She had started wondering last night, as she wrestled with the cards, what possible effect autism might have on an abdal's ability to be two places at one time. If that ability could start "slopping over" onto another party, one already susceptible to the abdal's worldview, from having been inside it a few times—

She held still. *I have got to keep my cool here,* she thought. *It's the only way I'm going to find him.* "I'm going to go look for him," Nita said. "It may take me a while to find him. I can't do it the way he does it with Ponch; I've got to be asleep."

She heard Kit's mama take a long breath, the sound of someone else controlling herself as tightly as Nita was having to right now. "I have to go to work," she said. "I'll be back around midnight. But if you hear anything before then, will you call me? I think Kit gave you my work number."

"Yeah," Nita said. "Mrs. Rodriguez, please...don't worry." *It's going to be all right,* Nita wanted most desperately to say, but she couldn't say it: It might not be true.

"Okay," Mrs. Rodriguez said. "Thank your dad for me, sweetie. Good-bye."

Nita hung up the phone. Outside, faint but clear, the howling continued. Her father was looking at her in distress.

"Where *is* he?" he said.

Nita shook her head. "I don't have a name for it, Daddy. It's not another planet or anything like that. I wish it were, because it'd be easier to get to. It's somewhere inside of Darryl, which means it's closer to us in some ways, but in some ways much further off than anything that would just be way out in conventional space. And it's a lot more dangerous, in its way. If Kit's stuck in there, and I can't get him out..."

She began to shake. Here it was, full-blown, what she'd been most afraid of—a crisis that she was terrified she wasn't going to be able to handle. *And you're all alone on this one,* she thought. *Dairine may be able to offer some support, but* you're *going to be the one who has to figure out what to do with it. And if you* can't *figure it out...*

Her father saw the look on her face and came over to her, put his arms around her. "Nita," he said. "Listen to me."

She looked up at him, rather shocked at his tone of voice. It was unusually stern for him.

"You're tough," her dad said. "You're tougher than you think. That's what you need to hang on to now. That's what I've been hanging on to the best I can, and as far as I can tell, it turns out to be true every time if you just don't let the idea go. What you have to do now is take one thing at a time—don't let the stress overload you. Will Tom or Carl know what to do? Call them."

"Yeah," Nita said, and went back to the phone, dialed it hurriedly. A moment later, Carl's voice said, "Hello?"

"Carl," Nita said, "we've got trouble. He couldn't hold it. He's gone again."

Wizards tend not to swear, since the results are likely to be unfortunate if they slip into the Speech while doing it. Nita, however, distinctly heard several swearwords in Carl's silence. "When did he leave?"

"It might have been just a few minutes ago."

"Okay. Wait a second."

Carl put the phone down. She could hear him going to the table, where his version of the manual usually lay hidden. She heard him flip one volume open and start going through it. Listening carefully, she could hear a hiss, the little breath-between-teeth noise that Carl made when there was trouble.

A moment later he picked up the phone again. "He's out of ambit, all right," Carl said. "And the energy signatures are too vague to track him with, in terms of getting an ID on a specific universe ... even assuming I could do that. The universes Ponch has been finding are nontypical, as is his mode of transit; the normal wizardry-tracking routines won't work. But this much we do have in our favor. Ponch went with Kit."

"I bet Ponch made Kit take him," Nita said, feeling sure of this without knowing why. "Carl, I'll go try to find them."

"I wouldn't do that right this minute," Carl said. "They might still be in transit. I can't tell. Give the situation an hour or two to settle."

Nita could see his point, but she didn't like it. "Carl, he's been really spaced-out since he came back from his last time in Darryl's universe. Anything could happen to him in a few minutes, let alone an hour!"

"Nita," Carl said, "take a breath or two and get a

grip on yourself. I know how you feel, but even if you'd already done the presleep preparation you need to do for a lucid dreaming session—which I don't think you have—you'd still need to get to sleep after that. And you know you can't induce it with a sleep spell when you're going lucid. You're going to have to relax a little, enough to sleep, or you won't be able to do anything."

She let out a long breath. "I hate it when you're right," Nita said. "Okay. I'll call you later and let you know what I find."

"Do that. I'll be up late."

She hung up, looked at her father. Dairine had come downstairs and was leaning in the dining room doorway, looking alert, with Spot peering into the kitchen from behind her legs. To Dairine, Nita said, "He's gone. Let's start building that power-feed spell; I'm going to need it in a couple of hours."

She and Dairine headed up the stairs.

It took Nita nearly four hours to get ready to go after Kit, and even then she couldn't sleep. Part of the problem was that she was very much a daytime person and found it tough to get to sleep before eight in the evening. The rest of the problem was her nerves.

When Nita first lay down, Dairine was still sitting in the chair by Nita's desk, looking over the lifeline spell she'd constructed. At any other time, Nita would have been annoyed enough by the elegance and speed with which Dairine had constructed it to try to find at least some fault with it. But there wasn't time for that, and right now she was simply grateful that Dairine was so talented in this kind of work. The bed was surrounded by a long, tightly knitted cord of words in the Speech, rather like Kit's leash for Ponch, but both more intricate and thicker. The wizardry had to handle much higher power levels than the leash did, and had no life-support functions as such—those Nita would be carrying with her on her charm bracelet, in a suite of interconnected shielding and atmosphere-maintenance spells.

Nita was also more heavily armed than usual, not knowing how many friends the Lone Power might have skulking around the borders of Darryl's mind, intent on keeping enemies out and friends in. From Nita's bracelet dangled a number of charms, each of which represented a spell almost ready to go, needing only one thought or pronounced syllable to set it going. It was wearying to carry this much nearly released power around, but Nita was beyond caring how much energy she had to expend. Her fear for Kit was growing by the minute.

After she'd finished looking over the lifeline wizardry and lay down on the bed, Nita took a last moment or three to check out the weaponry—the lightning bolt of the quark-level dissociator, the little closed spiral of a pinch-off utility that could seal a designated attacker or group of attackers into a "pocket" space, the little "magic wand" charm that contained a one-off terawatt particle-beam generator. Even in her present nervous state, Nita looked at that one with slight relish and wished she might have a chance to use it—the manual had been explicit about how dangerous it was, and how effective. The manual itself was slipped into her own otherspace pocket, inside the lifeline wizardry with her. Last of all she checked her throat, where the thin fine chain of the lucid-dreaming wizardry was fastened, and made sure it was charged and active. It buzzed slightly against her fingers, acknowledging that it was ready to go.

Nita settled herself back against the pillows. "How long's the lifeline good for?" she said to Dairine.

"You get six hours," Dairine said. "Then it's got to be dismantled and rebuilt, and I have to recharge it. It's..." She glanced at Spot, who was sitting on the desk with his screen up, running manual functions, among them a Julian date clock. "It's just past three-oh-three-point-three. You get until point-fifty-five, then you snap back here, no matter what you're doing. So keep an eye on your manual."

Nita nodded. She wiggled against the pillows a little and closed her eyes.

After about five minutes, she opened them again, and sighed. "Dari..."

"Is there something wrong with the spell?"

Nita made a face. "This is really dumb, but I can't fall asleep with you sitting there watching me. You're going to have to stay in your room, for a while anyway."

Dairine shrugged. "No problem," she said, and reached down to pick up one of the lines of light that was trailing away from the lifeline spell. Dairine walked out the door with the power-feed line in her hand. The line of light, the single character for *connection* in the Speech, stretched and stretched after her as she went.

Then Dairine stuck her head back in the room. "Good luck, Neets," she said.

"Thanks," Nita said. *I may need it...*

At first Nita concentrated on doing the breathing exercises that often helped her get to sleep when she was having trouble doing so, but tonight all they seemed to do was make her uncomfortably aware of her breathing. Finally she gave up on that and just stared at the ceiling, fixing her attention on one spot, the little flawed place where Dairine had once bounced a Superball too high and flaked off the ceiling paint. After a while, as Nita had expected, her eyes started tiring.

Eventually she found herself standing in the dark. That darkness was nearly complete: There were no spotlights now, no signs of anything being in this universe but her, and only the faintest, not-quite-black "background" radiance from the sky above. *Did I miss them?* Nita wondered. *Have they gone somewhere else?*

She looked around. It did no good standing still in one of these dreams, she'd found. You had to walk around to get anywhere worth being. So Nita reached into her otherspace pocket and came out with a favorite tool, a moonlight-steeped rowan wand lent her by Liused, the tree in her backyard. This one was getting close to its "use by" date—such wands routinely lasted for only three full moons and an intercalary day, unless burned out by overuse before then—and wasn't much good for anything but light at this point. But light was just what Nita needed. As she touched it and pulled it out, the wand came afire with a blaze of secondhand moonlight, enough to show Nita that she was standing on the same plain black surface that she'd seen here before, when meeting the clown, the robot, and the knight. But there was nothing else to be seen at all, in any direction.

"Okay," she said softly. "Let's see."

One of the ready-made spells on her bracelet had a charm that looked like a miniature radar screen. Knowing before she left who she was going to be looking for, Nita had wound Kit's name in the Speech into it. Now she reached down to that charm and, touching it, saw in her mind the single word needed to activate the spell.

She said the word. Immediately Nita was standing in the middle of a pool of faint light, very much like the big radar that air traffic controllers use. It was a life-sign detector, one that would tag any specific personality it had been keyed to. Nita looked down at it. Even though the steady glow of it was soft, it was hard to make out any specific indication from it. Nita whispered the light of the rowan wand down to nothing and stared at the detector for many long moments, until her eyes watered.

Finally, though, she spotted what she was looking for: a faint, faint patch of light, off in the two o'clock direction. The curling tracery of Kit's initials in the Speech were beside it.

He's a long way off, Nita thought. *But he's here.*

The trouble was that he seemed to be all by himself; there didn't seem to be any indication of Darryl on the radar screen. *He might still be by himself,* Nita thought. *Or if he has found Darryl, then Darryl's perception of his own isolation may have affected Kit so that he thinks he's still alone.*

It didn't matter. At least now Nita had a direction to walk in.

She spoke the light of the rowan wand back up and spent what seemed like the better part of the next fifteen minutes walking toward Kit. *But my time sense may be off, too,* Nita thought, pausing briefly at about the fifteen-minute point to check her manual.

She was shocked to find that it was nearly .40. *It's been nearly three hours outside!* she thought. *This is the problem Kit ran up against the other night. Time flow in here is getting strange.*

Nita walked faster. After what seemed like another five minutes or so, she started to see something right against the very edge of the dark horizon, like a very faintly seen thread or line of some different color. The closer she got to it, the more distinct it became; it was starting to pick up the light of the rowan wand.

Within a few minutes she found that the line was growing thicker and taller with every step, and brighter, too. Shortly she was close enough to start to make out what it was.

It was a wall. Perfect, white, featureless, stretching away from her—seemingly to infinity—in great curves on either side, the wall towered over Nita as she approached it. A few feet away from it, Nita stopped, bent her neck back to look at it.

It was not a physical thing, she knew, but a representation of some power or force that had been put here to stop any intruder. And there was no telling who had put it here—Darryl, or the Lone Power.

Nita stepped forward and cautiously touched the wall with a fingertip, like someone gingerly testing an electric fence. She could tell immediately that this construction didn't have anything to do with the Lone Power: There was none of the inimical burn she would have expected. Nothing else happened—no force attacked her—but Nita could tell by the feel of the wall that it was meant to be infinitely obstructive. She could try to levitate over it, but it would simply stretch up and up and up to match the height at which she attacked it; she could try to dig down under it, but it would extend that way, too. The only way to deal with this wall was to go through—if she had time.

Okay, Nita thought. *Let's see what works.*

She said the twelve words of a small-scale antigravity wizardry, wrapped them around the rowan wand, and hung it on the air to give her some light to work by; then turned the charm bracelet on her wrist. One of the charms, looking like a little lasso, was the representation of the lifeline spell. Touching it, Nita could feel the power feeding down it, and could faintly feel Dairine, in circuit with it back at home.

You okay? her sister said.

So far. I need some power now.

Take what you need. The wizardry's fully charged.

Nita held the charm between her fingers and said the two words that released the clamp on the power flow at her end. Her right hand started filling with a hot white glow, the representation of what Dairine's wizardry was sending her. Nita let it flow, squeezing the power down to compact it a couple of times and make room for more. Finally, after about a minute, she cut off the flow and stepped toward the wall, using pressure of hands and mind and a few sentences in the Speech to shape that power into a small, concentrated explosive charge of wizardry. She pushed it up against the bottom of the wall, like so much plastic explosive, instructing it to vent all its force away from her, and then retreated to a safe distance.

Nita spoke the air in front of her dark, and then said the explosive's actuator word in the Speech.

The result was a dazzling flash and impact like lightning striking six feet away. Dark though the air had been, Nita still had to shake her head and blink a few times, trying to get rid of the afterimages. When she managed it, she looked up . . .

. . . and saw that the wall was standing right where it had been, without so much as a dent in it.

Nita stared. *What?!*

The amount of power she'd planted in that explosive had been huge. She felt somehow cheated and really angry at the same time. "Okay," she said, "no more Miss Nice Girl. Let's try something a little more emphatic."

She reached down to the bracelet again and found

the charm for the particle-beam accelerator. As she touched it, the accelerator wizardry sprang into being in her hands, ready to fire—a long, narrow conical shape with a blunt stock. Nita snugged the stock of it up against her shoulder, and carefully took aim again at the base of the wall. She had invested a great deal of energy in this wizardry; now she would see what it was worth—

The world flickered, went abruptly bright. *What?* Nita thought.

Don't shoot! someone shouted into her mind. It was Dairine.

Nita looked around her in complete confusion. She was lying in bed, aiming the linac weapon at her ceiling.

Oh my god, Nita thought. She hurriedly lowered the accelerator and let the wizardry relapse. She lay there for a few moments while her pulse got back to normal, and then sat up and looked over at the small figure slumped in the chair by her desk.

"Dairine, *what am I doing here*?!" Nita whispered.

"Giving me grief, apparently," Dairine said, looking ragged. "I *told* you to watch your time. You spent a real long time getting wherever you were going." She let out a long breath. "And you didn't find any trace of Kit at all?"

Nita sagged against the pillows again, and shook her head. "I know he was there, but I couldn't get near him. We're going to need more power in that thing this time, Dari. Charge it up. I'm going out again."

Dairine shook her head. "Nita," she said. "It's

nearly three in the morning. And I'm wrecked. It's a strain holding that thing open." She looked miserable at having to admit such a thing. "I have to get at least *some* sleep, because I have to go to school tomorrow morning. Of *course,* I'd rather blow school off, but I promised Dad. You know I did. You know what'll happen if I don't go, or if I fall asleep in class."

Nita was so angry that she had to put her hands over her face to keep from screaming, or otherwise letting Dairine see how she felt. After a few seconds she felt sufficiently in control to uncover her face again.

"Okay," she said. "You're right. I have an early morning, too. We'll try it again tomorrow." And she let out a long breath. "But thanks, Dair. You did good."

"We'll do better tomorrow," Dairine said. "We'll find him then, and get him home. G'night."

She wandered off toward her room, closing Nita's door behind her.

Nita lay there for a while more. *Kit?* she said silently, out of desperate hope, nothing more.

Of course, no answer came.

She tried to sleep again, normally, but that was impossible for her now. All Nita could do was think about what Kit's parents must be going through, and wait for six-thirty to come....

Reconstructions

THE MIRRORS WENT on forever.

Kit and Ponch stood in a brittle glory of reflected light. Overhead was a bright gray sky, featureless. All around them, mirrors stood, as many mirrors as trees in a forest, set at a thousand different angles: tall ones, small ones, mirrors that reflected clearly, mirrors that bent the reflection awry; shadowy mirrors, dazzling ones, mirrors reflecting mirrors reflecting mirrors, until the mind that looked at them began to flinch and sicken, hunting something that wasn't just another reflection of itself.

Kit and Ponch wandered among them, searching for something, but Kit had forgotten what it was they were looking for, along with everything else. Ponch wasn't sure what his master wanted—wasn't even all that sure, anymore, why they were there. Together the two of them wandered through the glittering wasteland, seeing their shapes slide and hide in the mirrors, images chasing images but never meeting, never touching, fleeing one another as soon as any got close enough to make contact.

"—don't want to—"

"—when do you think he might—"

"—that hurts, why do you have to—"

Splinters of conversation and fragments of personality hid in the reflections and fled from mirror to mirror. Kit and Ponch moved slowly among them, looking in some, avoiding others. Some had too many eyes to look into comfortably. Not all the eyes seemed human. It was as if alien logics looked out of some of them, either irrational or briefly revealing rationalities that were more painful than the human kind, and these were the glances that made Kit and Ponch shy away most hurriedly, looking for somewhere to hide. But there was nowhere. Light and merciless reflection filled everything; and everywhere the two of them walked, a soft rush of sound ran under all other sensation, like water running under the mirrored floor, a river of words and noises trapped there under the unforgiving ice. All they could do was walk and walk, the thoughts in their minds being washed away as fast as they formed by the relentless flow of sound. They could hear the voices of other wanderers, elsewhere in the maze, but there was no way to find them, no way even to tell where they were.

"—have to get out, if they don't they'll—"

"—find him, and when I do find him I'll—"

They walked for a long time, seeking those other

voices but never finding them. Finally, exhausted, Kit sat down against the "trunk" of a mirror-tree, leaned back, and closed his eyes. His mind was full of the painful rush of voices and noise; it was a relief just to sit here, his eyes closed so that he didn't have to see the eyes in the mirrors, his body rocking a little and letting the motion distract him from the myriad other distractions around him that were fraying the fabric of his mind. Ponch sat down next to him, on guard and frightened, but not so frightened that he would leave his friend.

Finally someone came. Kit didn't open his eyes; every time he did, he saw other eyes staring at him, and he couldn't bear the invasiveness of their gaze. But he heard the footsteps even through the rush of noise.

Whoever it was stood there, not looking at them straight on—that much Kit could feel on his skin, even without looking.

"I asked you not to come," it said.

But he had to, said Ponch. *And so I had to.*

"I've filled this whole place with one version of what happened to me," said whoever was speaking. "The Other followed me right in here, the way It always does...and now what happened to me has happened to It." There was a kind of sorrowful amusement about the speaker's voice. "I did a really good job this time. I don't know *how* long It'll be stuck in here. But no one can get out from inside: It's sealed."

We have to stay here forever, then, Ponch said.

"I don't know about you," the voice said. "Your

eyes aren't anything like his, or the Other's. You're something different. But me, and him, and the Other... yes, we'll have to stay forever."

If he has to stay forever, Ponch said, *then I'm not leaving.*

And he lay down beside Kit, huddling close to him, and started to wait for forever.

Nita got her dad up at the usual time. She was already dressed for school at that point, having been unable to get to sleep. "Anything?" he said.

Nita shook her head. "I'll call you," she said, and she couldn't bring herself to say much of anything else. Her dad hugged her and went to work.

She made her own breakfast and ate it, thinking over what had happened the night before. *If Darryl put up that wall,* she thought, *who's he shutting out?*

Or shutting in? There was always that possibility—that the Lone Power was in there with him again, right then, trying to destroy him one more time. *And Kit and Ponch are stuck in there with them...*

Nita shuddered. But another problem had occurred to her, one that kept nagging at her now, though it wasn't specifically about any kind of danger. *How's Darryl getting the kind of power he needs to do this kind of wizardry?* Nita wondered. *Especially since he's not even a full wizard yet? Is it something to do with being an abdal—with the fact that there can be two of him? If there really are.* It was a good question, whether co-location really did mean there were two of you, or just one of you in two places at the same time.

Even the manual hadn't been as clear as Nita would have liked on the subject; the terminology got very dense. *Or maybe I did...*

She drank about half of a mug of tea, put it down. *Anyway, that universe seemed farther away than the last one, somehow. He's withdrawing. He's doing it on purpose.*

Why?

Nita mulled that over, but no clear answer suggested itself. *Well,* she thought at last, *even when I do get in again this afternoon, it's possible that brute force won't work against that wall. I may have to try to get myself directly in sync with Darryl, the way I did before, when he was a clown.*

The danger, of course, is that if I get too well synced with Darryl's mind, then what's happened to Kit will happen to me, too. And neither of us will ever get out...

That thought left Nita morbidly considering what would happen afterward in such a case. Both of them would simply have disappeared without a trace. What remained of their families would wind up going through endless anguish as the police investigated the disappearances...and they would never be able to share with anyone that they all knew exactly what had happened to their kids—

Nita pushed *that* idea away hard. *That's* not *an option,* she thought.

Fine. So what is?

That endless wall was very much on her mind. *If I'm going to do anything about it, anything that'll let me get through it in time to find Kit, I've got to find a way to get there without walking forever and ever!* The problem was that, from the feel of it, Darryl's interior space wasn't allowing quick transits—just long slogs through forbidding or sterile terrain. *It might even be intentional,* Nita thought. *Maybe he's set it up that way so that every time the Lone Power comes after him, It gets drained by the effort...has to stay in there longer, and take longer to find him—*

There Nita stopped abruptly, staring at her mug of tea, which was rapidly going cold. In either a real physical universe or an interior space, there were ways to briefly change the laws that ran that space. And the best of these was to get your hands on the universe's "kernel," the little tight-wound wizardly construct that encapsulated that universe's physical laws. Lately Nita had had entirely too much experience manipulating those. Her work with the kernel of her mother's personal universe had bought her mom a few extra months of life.

A stab of pain answered that thought almost immediately: *It wasn't enough to buy her anything else.* But Nita pushed the pain aside for the moment. If she could get into Darryl's interior world and find its kernel, she could at least temporarily make changes to the way its physical characteristics worked...enough to get her where she needed to be in a hurry: the wall. Maybe even beyond it. Other changes would probably require Darryl's permission before she could make them. But this would do for a start.

Nita glanced up as Dairine came downstairs, showered and dressed for school, but still looking fairly terrible. "Did you sleep at all?" Nita said, going to the fridge to get Dairine a glass of milk and a banana.

"Yeah," Dairine said miserably. "I couldn't help it."

She stared at the milk. "Drink it," Nita said. "I'll be back home at three-thirty. We have to try again."

"Yeah," Dairine said.

"Will you have enough power?"

"Yeah," Dairine said. "But— Neets, it should have worked last night! We were all set."

"We didn't realize how far there was to go to the wall," Nita said. "I missed a trick last time: I'll make better time today. And I'll go more heavily armed. Now finish that stuff up and then go on. You're going to be late."

Dairine nodded, finished her breakfast, and left. Nita was left in the quiet again, alone, a state that she preferred for the one task she had to do before she left: call Kit's mother.

The phone there rang only once before someone answered. "Hello?"

"Mr. Rodriguez," Nita said. "Hi."

"Nita. Have you got any news?"

She had been hoping against impossible hope that Kit's pop would tell her that Ponch had brought Kit home. Hearing the carefully controlled desperation in his voice, Nita felt even lower than she'd felt when she'd picked up the phone. "Not yet," she said. "I tried to find him last night. I know sort of where he is, but I couldn't get through to him. I'm going to try again this afternoon."

Kit's pop paused for a long moment. "Are you able to tell anything about whether he's all right?" he said.

"Not yet," Nita said. "I'm sorry. I'll call you right away this afternoon, as soon as I know something. Bye."

She hung up, heartsore, put on her boots and her coat, and headed off for school.

Nita went to her Monday morning meeting with Mr. Millman full of dread. *He's not blind: He's going to see that something awful's wrong with me,* Nita thought, *and I'm not going to be able to tell him what it is. And then I'm going to have to do stupid card tricks. Can anything be worse than this?*

She found him in the little bare office, on time as usual, stuffing a magazine back into his briefcase. In front of him were the remnants of the bagel with cream cheese that he'd brought along for his breakfast before their appointment. "Nita," he said, "good morning."

She didn't answer immediately. He glanced up from closing his briefcase.

"I hate to say this," he said, "but you look awful. I won't insult your intelligence by asking if you're all right."

Nita raised her eyebrows in mild surprise at this opening gambit. "Thanks."

"Dairine acting up again?"

"No, actually, she's fine," Nita said.

Mr. Millman just looked at her quizzically. Abruptly Nita wondered if near-total honesty might possibly be of some use.

"I really don't feel like talking to you this morning," Nita said. "I wish I could make up some dumb story and tell you that, instead."

Mr. Millman shrugged and sat back in his chair with his arms behind his head. "Everyone else does. Why shouldn't you?"

Entirely against her will, Nita had to smile at that. "Just as long as you don't expect me to come up with something original."

Mr. Millman allowed himself just a breath of laughter. "That's the last thing I'd expect. Ten or fifteen billion of us, now, must have lived on this planet, and the more you look into the stories we tell one another, the more like each other they look. Everybody repeats the same basic themes."

Nita said nothing.

Mr. Millman raised his eyebrows. "But maybe that's how we know humanity is still in its childhood. You know how it is when you're little, you want to hear the same story over and over again?"

"My sister used to do that."

"So did mine. Partly it's because they know how the story ends. There's always tension when you're not sure about the ending, and little kids don't want too much of that tension... but they do want *some*. So this is a solution to the problem. When you know the ending, you get the tension of the middle and the relief at the end... theoretically. Did you have a book like that, that you kept wanting to hear at bedtime?"

Nita nodded. "It had a horse called Exploding Pop-Tart in it," she said. "My dad said he wanted to explode every Pop-Tart he saw after a while, because he was so tired of that book."

Millman nodded. "Mine was the one about the bat that wouldn't go to bed," he said. "My mother told me she hated bats for the next twenty years. Fortunately she didn't see a lot of bats in her line of work."

"What was her line of work?"

"She was a concert violinist."

Nita had to laugh.

"One laugh, one smile," Millman said. "Not bad for the way you looked when you came in. Look, don't bother to tell me any story if you don't want to. You'd probably just repeat one of the favorite themes. Life, love, death..."

"Death," Nita said softly.

The image of the Lone Power was suddenly before her eyes. She glanced at Millman then, wondering if she'd had time to cover over her expression.

"The same story," Millman said. "And the only one we all know the end of, once we're older than about three. But, boy, the way people behave, you wouldn't think so! Adults refuse to talk about it... even with people your age, who really want to hear about it, and about the other important things—the beginning of life, the relationships in the middle. We try to distract ourselves by wasting our time on all the other less important stories, the incidentals—who 'failed,' who 'succeeded.' It's a pity." He shook his head. "We hardly ever do right by kids. All you want from us is to tell you how life works. And one way or another, the issue of life and death makes us so uncomfortable that we find a hundred ways to keep from telling you about it, until it's too late."

Nita swallowed. "My mom was good about telling me the rules," she said. "She— My mom said..."

Nita stopped, waiting for her eyes to fill up. But it didn't happen. And for a weird, bitter moment, that it *wasn't* happening felt strange to her.

She looked up. Mr. Millman was simply looking at her.

"My mom said it was important to die well," Nita said at last, "so she wouldn't be embarrassed later."

Mr. Millman just nodded.

For a few moments they sat there in the quiet. "She had it right, I think," he said. He paused, then, looking at Nita. "*Now* it makes sense to ask. Are you all right?"

Nita thought about it. "Yeah," she said. "For the time being."

"Okay," he said. "Let's cut it short for today. One thing, though."

"What?"

"What about the card tricks?"

In the face of the more important things that were presently on her mind, the question seemed so annoying that Nita nearly hollered at him, "*Don't you think I have better things to do than card tricks?*" But she caught herself.

"Okay," she said. "I've got one here..."

She fished around in her book bag and got out the deck of cards. Nita slipped it out of its packet and began to shuffle, hoping that the motion would help her hide the fact that her hands were actually trembling with rage. *Okay,* she thought. *Calm down. You knew he was going to ask.*

But Kit—!

"Am I supposed to pick a card or something?" Mr. Millman said.

"In a minute," Nita said. She shuffled, then said, "Okay, name one."

"The five of clubs."

Nita knew where that one was because the deck had been stacked when she took it out of its little packet. She put the shuffled deck down on the desk, wondering whether she'd protected the back end of the deck well enough. Then she realized she should have asked him what card he wanted before she started shuffling. The trick wasn't going to work.

I don't care if it does or not! Nita thought. *I should make him play Fifty-Two Pickup with the whole deck.*

She controlled herself, though with difficulty. She finished the shuffle and cut the cards into three piles. Then she narrowed her eyes and did a single small wizardry that she had sworn to herself she wasn't going to use.

Mr. Millman turned over the third card. It was the five of clubs.

"That was fairly obvious," Mr. Millman said, "that anger. And fairly accessible. We were talking about the stages of grieving earlier, how they don't always run in sequence. Let me just suggest that when anger runs so close to the surface that it's easily provoked by unusual circumstances, you're quite possibly not done with it yet."

Damn straight *I'm not,* Nita thought.

"It's not a good thing, not a bad thing, just what's so," Millman said. "But you might want to think about what result this kind of emotion has produced in the past. Or might produce again in the future."

"Right," Nita said. Whatever good humor had come and gone during the course of the morning's session, it was gone for good now. She picked up the cards, got up, and stalked out, making her way to her first-period class.

Right through history class, and right through the English literature class that followed it, Nita stewed. She was furious with herself for having lost her temper over Millman and the card tricks. She was furious that she had let him see how furious she was. She was furious over the maddeningly calm and evenhanded way he had dissected her anger. She would almost have preferred that he yell at her. At least she would have had an excuse to walk out of there ready to, as her mother used to put it, "chew nails and spit rust." She was so mad—

Nita stopped, literally, in midthought.

"What result this kind of emotion has produced in the past..."

She thought of the fury and desperation that had driven her, in the time before her mother's death, to try the most impossible things to stop what was happening. *And they still didn't stop.*

But some amazing things happened, anyway...

She had gone from world to world and finally from universe to universe, learning to hunt down and manipulate the kernels that controlled those universes' versions of natural law. And now she had to admit that it had been her grief and anger at what was happening to her mother that had made her as effective as she'd become.

The thought unnerved her. Nita wasn't used to thinking of anger as a tool. It had always seemed like something you didn't want to get accustomed to using, in case it started to become a habit, or started twisting you and your wizardry in directions you didn't want to go. *But if you're careful,* she thought, *if you stay in control, if you manage it carefully enough—maybe it's okay to use it just every now and then. Maybe managing it, rather than letting it manage you, is the whole idea—*

Nita sat there staring fixedly at the blackboard. Her English teacher was illustrating the scansion of a sonnet there, but Nita wasn't really seeing it. *Okay,* she thought. *I forgive Millman his dumb card tricks. He's given me something useful here. Now I just have to use it…*

The bell rang, and her English class filtered out, muttering about the pile of sonnets they'd been given to analyze by the end of the week. Nita's next class was statistics; she shouldered her book bag and wandered out into the hall, unfocused. Her anger was still running high, but it was strangely mixed with a sense of readiness. Nita couldn't get rid of the feeling that time was suddenly of the essence, that she had to make the best of her present emotional state—in which she had been given a weapon that was primed and ready to go, a weapon too good to waste.

I don't want to lose this, Nita thought, making a

sudden decision. *This is important. I'm going to ditch the rest of my classes. I don't care if they call Dad. He'll know what's going on.*

Meanwhile, I need somewhere private to teleport from.

Nita hurried for the girls' room. Between periods it was always full of people who didn't feel like going through the hassle of getting a hall pass in their next period, and as Nita pushed into the smaller of the two girls' rooms on that floor, she saw a couple of girls she knew there: Janie from her chemistry class and Dawn from gym. She nodded and said hi to them, found herself a stall, and sat down on the rim of the toilet, keeping the stall door pushed closed with her foot.

Well, this *is one of the less dignified moments in my practice of the Art,* Nita thought, resigned. Nonetheless, she sat and waited. As the five-minute period between classes went by, the room outside the stall door got very briefly busy, then less busy...then the room emptied out altogether. A few seconds later, the beginning-of-period bell rang. *Okay,* Nita thought, standing up, *here's my opportunity.*

The door to the hallway pushed open a little. "Room check," said an adult voice.

Nita flushed hot with annoyance. It was one of the teachers who checked the toilets after the change-of-class bell to make sure no one was hiding in there and smoking or doing something even less healthy. *Who needs this?* Nita thought, getting furious all over again. Her hand went to her charm bracelet just as the teacher pushed open the stall door.

The teacher—it turned out to be one of the gym teachers, Ms. Delemond, a tall, blond, willowy lady—stared in at Nita, but saw nothing, because Nita had just climbed up on the toilet seat, to avoid the door, and had availed herself of the simplest way to be invisible. A second or so later, Ms. Delemond turned away, went to check the next stall, and the next. Finally she went outside again, and Nita could hear her footsteps going down the hall.

Nita got down off the toilet and let out one small breath of annoyed laughter. Then she reached into her claudication pocket, came out with the long chain of the ready-made transit spell she kept there, and dropped it on the floor around her. The chain of words knotted itself closed and blazed with light...

Nita came out in a sheltered part of her backyard, ankle-deep in snow, and the air-pressure change caused by the air she had brought with her from school made snow fall off the trees above her and onto her head. She spluttered as the snow got down her collar, finding it funny and getting angrier by the second. *Good. Use it. It's a tool—*

Nita's house keys were inside her locker at school, along with her coat and her boots. *Forget it,* she thought as she went around into the driveway and up to her back door. She pulled the screen door open and put her hand against the wood of the inside door. "I just need to walk through you, if you don't mind," she said in the Speech, while she reached down to the charm bracelet for another wizardry she'd been keeping there, this one with a charm like a little cloud. "Is that okay? Thanks, just bear with me."

She said the three words that turned the low-level dissociator loose. Nita waited a moment for the itching to set in—the sign that every atom in her body was willing to move aside for atoms of other substances. In this case, Nita wanted to walk through the atoms of the door. She went through it like so much smoke, itching fiercely all the way, and when she was standing inside the back door, she let the wizardry go, then just stood there and scratched for a few seconds until she felt like all her molecules had settled themselves back into place.

She headed upstairs to her room, got her manual, and lay down on the bed. *This had better work,* Nita thought, *because Dad's probably going to go intercontinental when he finds out I cut school. But I can't help it. What's the use of behaving myself and losing my best friend?*

She lay there and realized it was just too bright for her even to think about going to sleep. Nita opened her manual, went to the energy-management section, and turned pages until she found the wizardry she wanted.

She recited it, feeling the universe leaning in around her, paying attention, slowly muting down the light in her room as if someone was turning down a dimmer switch. *Anyway, this is all my fault,* she thought as the room got darker and darker. *If I hadn't been so wrapped up in my own troubles, I'd have been with Kit on this job from the start. Yeah, okay, I have a right to grieve. But do I have a right to dump my friends until*

I'm finished with it, until it's convenient to listen to them, to care about them again? If I'd listened to Kit—

"He wouldn't listen to me," Nita had said. And "Now you know how *he* felt before," Dairine had said to her, as blunt as always, and accurate. Kit had come right out and said that he wished he had backup on this job. She'd ignored him, and he'd gone ahead with what he was doing and gotten in too deep. *I should have been paying attention to what was going on around me, no matter how awful I felt. I've been indulging myself. I've almost been having* fun *hurting. That's so stupid.*

Nita stopped herself. There was no point in rerunning the "guilt movies." They always ended the same way. And a new guilt movie was no better than the old ones.

But she was still left with her anger at herself. Nita lay there just breathing, just feeling it, letting it build. Well, she'd been in too deep herself, not long ago, unable to see the trouble she was getting into ... and Kit had pulled her out. Now she was going to be able to return the favor. But it wasn't about scorekeeping at all; there were much more important issues. *I've already lost one of the most important people in my life. I'm not going to lose another!*

Nita was briefly distracted by the burning at her wrist and throat.

She glanced down in surprise. All the charms on her bracelet, the symbols for all the prefabricated spells she was carrying, were glowing considerably brighter than usual. And the necklace of the lucid-dreaming wizardry was running hot, too.

"Think about what result this kind of emotion has produced in the past," Millman had said. "Or might produce again in the future."

Nita smiled a small angry smile.

I could get to like this, she thought. *Maybe it's better if I don't. But today... today, I'm going to like it a* lot.

She closed her eyes and pushed all her available power into the lucid-dreaming spell.

Nita's intention and the force of her anger briefly turbocharged the spell, and it drowned her consciousness in dream. The effect wouldn't last, she knew, as she opened her eyes in a different darkness; the spell would relapse to its normal levels momentarily, but it wouldn't matter. She'd stay asleep. The important thing was that she was dreaming *now.*

She stood there again by herself in that great dark space inside Darryl. Far off to one side, somewhere, she knew that the infinitely obstructive white wall was waiting. But this time she wasn't going to waste her time: There was more important business.

For a long few moments Nita quieted herself, opening her mind to listen, as she'd been taught. Then, eyes closed, self-blinded, she turned, waiting for the sensation she knew would come.

It took less time to find it than she'd hoped it would. Nita had been banking on the idea that Darryl's grasp of worldbuilding was instinctive, not studied, and that if he even realized the heart of his universe for what it was, he wouldn't have thought to hide it. And he hadn't. When she finally sensed what she was looking for, Nita took the time to actually walk to it, not wanting to attract any possible unwanted attention by using a transit spell. She was glad that the spot she was hunting was only a couple of miles away, not a couple of light-years.

She knew it by feel when she reached it, which was just as well; physically and visually it was indistinguishable from any other part of that tremendous darkness. Nita grinned, though, as she came close, feeling up close the faint, lively, burning, buzzing sensation she'd been seeking. She rolled up her sleeve, thrust her arm elbow-deep into the darkness, felt around for a moment, and came out with a bright, tight, surprisingly large tangle of silvery light.

"Will you *look* at this," Nita said under her breath, turning the kernel over in her hands and looking closely at it to identify its major structural elements. The complexity of this kernel was by and large on a par with other personal kernels Nita had seen before. A couple of its sections were devoted to the mere physical business of running a human body. One of them seemed oddly augmented. *Maybe this is how an abdal does his co-location,* Nita thought. *He's got an extra set of "body software" in here. Interesting.*

But the power conduits were the real surprise. They were huge, far bigger than a physical universe's own conduits would have been, and they pulsed silently and blindingly with such force that Nita found it hard to look at them. *This is what an abdal uses. Or doesn't even have to use; just* has. *There's enough power in here, of enough kinds, to do . . . incredible things.*

Even to keep the Lone Power shut up inside for a while...

Nita shook her head. This much power could be used for a lot more important things than that, though. And she noted one more thing, now that she had the kernel in her hands. She teased some of the power strands out a little and looked closely at one tightly braided chain of characters that glowed calmly right at the heart of the kernel. It was the core representation of the Wizard's Oath, the heart of an Ordeal; and it was complete.

Nita grinned with sheer pleasure at having been right, remembering her earlier thought that Darryl didn't have that tentative quality about his use of his wizardly abilities. *So,* she thought, *he's already passed his Ordeal. Let's get moving!*

She turned the kernel over in her hands once more, finding the little strand of light that was the spell Darryl had, however unwittingly, enacted to create the wall. Nita pulled it a little way out of the kernel, like someone teasing loose one strand from a ball of knitting wool, and twisted it in such a way as to cause that spot to become this one.

Instantly the internal laws of that universe changed accordingly, so that Nita looked up and found herself staring at the wall.

She walked right at it as if it wasn't there. And when she touched it, it wasn't. It evaporated in front of her. The wall knew that the key to the physical structure of its universe was right in front of it, in the possession of a living being. Cooperatively, it got out of her way.

"Thank you," Nita said. She placed the kernel in her otherspace pocket and kept walking. In front of her the view opened up, distant and glittering, a view of what appeared to be a forest of glass trees, shining in that sourceless light she'd come to recognize.

Nita walked toward the forest, listening to the voices that she'd heard before in Darryl's worlds, and that were here, too, louder than they'd been before, an endless rush of them. If she let them, they blended into a white-noise sound like wind or water, indecipherable. But if she concentrated, they did make sense.

"—get tired of waiting sometimes, you know?" said one of them, a man's voice, Nita thought. "Sometimes I wonder whether any of it matters at all."

"Of course it matters," said another voice, a softer one, sadder, but more certain of itself. "We have to keep doing what we're doing. Someday..."

The voices got steadily more distinct as Nita got closer to the forest. Soon she saw that it wasn't a forest of trees, but of mirrors. "Someday! But no one can tell us when that day's going to be. No one has the slightest idea! And we're the ones who know him best. We're the ones who ought to be able to tell. For a while there it looked like it was working. A little. But since autumn, it's like we've hit a brick wall or something. No change. I can't help but think...can't help but think that maybe there's not going to *be* any more change. That this is as good as it's ever going to get. That he's going to be this way forever—"

The voice broke off, choked with pain.

"You know they told us this was likely to happen," said the other voice. "That there'd be plateaus...times when nothing would seem to happen for a long time."

"But *this* long?"

"Every case is different, they said. You know that, too." A long pause. "We have to have faith, honey. If we don't, if we lose it, no one else's faith is going to help."

The voices sounded two ways to Nita. On one hand, they were like any conversation she might have heard on the street. On the other, there was a terrible poignancy about them. Hearing their words was like being thrust through the heart with knives. *I'm hearing this not just as I would,* Nita thought, *but as Darryl would. And possibly seeing his inner world as he does, too.* Far from drawing her into Darryl's trap for the Lone Power, this seemed to be giving her a kind of immunity. *Good. If that just lets me see a way out...*

As she came closer to the fringes of the "forest," Nita saw that the trees weren't exactly just mirrored, either. They were half-mirrored. She could see partway through them, out their other sides, to the shapes that walked among them. And there were only four of those.

Two of them she knew instantly: Her heart seized at the sight of them. Ponch and Kit were wandering, sightless—or rather, it was Kit who looked and walked like someone blind, or like someone afraid to look at what he saw around him. Ponch walked ahead of Kit like a Seeing Eye dog, seeing for both of them. But something about the way the light fell on him made Nita wonder whether Ponch somehow saw *more,* in this chilly and sterile landscape, than any of them. *What is it with him?* she wondered. He hadn't been able to tell her the other day. Nita remembered Carmela telling her what Kit had said, that there was some kind of "wizardry leakage" going on in his household. Suddenly she felt sure that what was happening with Ponch was more than just a symptom of this.

She paused, watching the other two figures wander around separately in the light shining on and reflecting from the half-mirrored trees. One of them was small and dark, in jeans and a polo shirt. He looked less lost than Kit and Ponch... or the final figure.

That last figure was tall and looked human. He was slender, well-built, and extremely handsome. Nonetheless, Nita couldn't help but shudder at the sight of the Fairest and Fallen, the Lone Power, looking, in the dark suit he was wearing, like a businessman lost in a strange city and doomed to wander around because he was too proud to ask for directions.

The shudder passed, though. Nita's anger was still running high enough to wash it out and leave her mind clear. *All right,* she thought. *Nothing bad has happened yet. Let's think about what to do.*

Let's...

Nita's head jerked up, looking for the source of the word, and her hand went to her bracelet again. A second later she was holding the linac weapon, ready to discharge.

I am on errantry, she thought, glancing around, *and I greet you. Wherever you are...*

I am *errantry,* the Silence said.

Nita held very still. There was something familiar about that voice...though it wasn't a voice as such.

Then she remembered her earlier thought. "The Silence told me about that," the clown-Darryl had said to her. *You are the manual,* she thought. *Darryl's version of it.*

The Silence sang agreement.

Right, Nita said, lowering the weapon again. *Sorry, you startled me. How can I hear you now? I couldn't before.*

You are fully inside him now... because you have the heart.

Nita wondered about that phrasing, and then smiled. The heart of Darryl's universe: the kernel. *Yes, I do,* she said. *Now all I have to do is figure out what to do with it.*

He will know. He has full access now, as you've discovered.

Nita nodded and watched the four figures walking among the trees for a few minutes.... She was looking things over, assessing where the weak point in this scenario might be. That was how she saw something start to happen, something that initially scared her—an encounter that she normally would have done anything to prevent. The Lone Power in Its dark majesty came striding down between the mirrored pillars, to Nita's eye looking very much like someone who's trying to act like he knows where he's going when he doesn't. Toward It, ambling, unhurried, maybe even unseeing, came Kit and Ponch. Nita sucked in her breath and lifted the linac weapon into an aiming line, pointing it at the Lone One.

She watched with profound unease as Kit and the Lone Power got closer and closer to each other. They were no more than a few paces apart when the Lone One made a single sudden move.

It looked at Itself in a mirror as It passed, and smiled faintly. And Kit walked right on by It, unnoticing, unnoticed.

Nita had to just stand there for a few moments, calming herself down, nearly lost in admiration at the sheer power of the otherworld Darryl had created. *It's like that fairy tale about the guy who does some magic creature a good turn,* she thought, *and as a reward it gives him a bag that nothing can get out of. The guy lives a bad life, and when the devil comes for him, he tricks it into the bag, and it's stuck there until he lets it out.* But in this case, Darryl was in the bag, too—and apparently thought this a reasonable price to pay to keep part of the Lone Power out of circulation for days or weeks or even years at a time.

Carl had been completely right. *If that's not a saint,* Nita thought, *I don't know what is.*

I need to get them out of here, she said to the Silence.

You will have to break this paradigm, the Silence said. *Break the mirrors. That will release them. But it will also release the Lone Power back into Its full potency.*

For just a breath of time, Nita weighed the pros and cons of the problem. *Keeping It stuck in here, even just a fragment of It, couldn't be a bad thing.*

But keeping Kit here as well, and Ponch? And Darryl?

The price was much too high. *Especially,* Nita thought, putting aside her personal concerns for the moment, *in Darryl's case.*

Nita sighed. *Besides,* she thought, *like in the fairy tale, the Powers That Be will make them let the devil out of the bag eventually. It's still one of the Powers, and part of the world. Keep the Lone Power in here forever and It'll never be able to change...*

Nita stuck the linac weapon under her armpit and held it there against her side while she reached into her "pocket" again, found that tangle of light, and spent a few careful moments adjusting several of its properties. She altered the universe's time flow first, so it matched their home universe, then made a few additional changes that might come in handy later. When that was done, she put the kernel away and considered the maze of half-mirrored trees. It was vast, possibly even infinite, but Nita didn't let herself worry about that. All these mirrors, the Silence whispered to her, were clones of another one. At the center of the maze was the key to the secret, the way out.

We're short on time here, Nita said silently. *Tell me.*

In her mind's eye, she saw it.

Nita grinned.

She unlimbered the linac weapon again and started to make her way toward the spot she'd been shown. If she'd tried to search for it by sight, she might have passed it many times. But she closed her eyes again, so as not to be bewildered by the reflections, and found it the way the Silence showed her—by walking slowly, bumping into things sometimes, feeling her way. Once she bumped into a tall shape that burned her to be near. Out of reflex, she said, "Excuse me," to the Lone Power, and slipped on past It toward the heart of the maze.

It should be near here, shouldn't it? Nita thought.

You're close. Keep going...

She walked now through the darkness behind her eyes, slowly, taking her time. A few minutes later Nita came to the place she'd been looking for, and opened her eyes. They'd been closed so long now that she had to blink a little in the light as she looked at the one mirror—among however many uncounted millions in that place—that had no reflection in it at all, not even of any other mirror. This one was a plain bathroom mirror about three feet by two, hanging on a taller mirror-pillar and held in a steel frame—one that probably had a medicine cabinet behind it in the real world. Nita walked up to the rectangular mirror and waved at it, then jumped up and down in front of it. In the mirror, nothing showed at all.

That's the way it's supposed to be with vampires, Nita thought, intrigued. But, here, the mirrors themselves were vampiric, sucking up fragments of personality, snatches of conversation, the glances of eyes, leaving the originals devoid of words and glances afterward. Nita once more shook her head in admiration. Darryl had done a fantastic job constructing this trap. Even the Lone One, once inside this universe that so perfectly mirrored Darryl's autism, was vulnerable to it, slowly losing moments of Its vast existence, being worn down.

Okay, Nita thought. *Here we go.* The one thing she made certain of was that her other weapons were all ready to use as soon as she was finished with the linac. *I'll only get one shot with this,* she thought. *If it's a good one, all I have to worry about is what's handy to use next, when all hell breaks loose...*

Nita glanced around her to make sure no one was about to come wandering through one of the many openings of the maze that led into this central area. Then she lifted the linac weapon again, narrowed her eyes, took careful aim at the bathroom mirror, and fired.

The blast of energy that came out of the linac weapon didn't radiate in the visible spectrum, but the air in its path did, ionizing and spitting blue lightnings where the particle beam passed. The mirror leaped and split into thousands of fragments as the blast hit it, and the fragments in turn went white-hot and vaporized in the air—

—and as they did, every other mirror in that world shattered.

The noise was deafening, terrifying. Tons of razory glass exploded into millions of pieces and came raining down on the glassy floor. The fragments vanished as they hit it, as if falling into water. Moments later there was nothing remaining inside that whole space but five figures, standing on a dark floor and looking around in various degrees of surprise.

Nita stood there and chucked away the linac weapon, which vanished as soon as she let go of it, its wizardry now spent. She walked over to Kit and Ponch while reaching to her charm bracelet and activating one of the charms.

Ponch was shaking himself all over, as if he were wet. He turned and saw Nita, and began wagging his tail so furiously that it was mostly wagging him. He jumped up and put his forepaws all over her and started jumping up so that he could lick her face.

"Yeah, yeah, big guy, how you doing?" Nita said, sort of holding him by the ears and scratching them at the same time, in a mostly futile effort to keep his tongue out of her nose. "Kit? Give me a hand with this guy, will you?"

Kit was standing there, blinking at her, looking completely astonished. "What are you doing in here?" he said. Then he paused. "Come to think of it, what am *I* doing in here? I was home . . . I was lying down—"

The energy bolt came at them from behind.

And it splashed.

Nita looked over her shoulder at the Lone Power and couldn't restrain a grin. The alterations she'd made in the kernel had worked. And Kit was all right. Now she had backup—and she felt how *good* it was to have that again, after she'd been alone. *Now then!* she thought.

"Well, I guess if you're going to omit the formalities, so will I," Nita said, turning to face the Lone One. "I have to say, I would have expected a slightly higher level of function from you. But you've been running on half-speed ever since you got in here, poor baby. Take a few moments and try to pull your brains back together. We'll wait."

The Lone Power's expression set cold, as Nita had known it would; there are few things the Eldest hates more than being made fun of.

"Your insolence," It said, "is going to be short-lived."

"Compared to the age of the universe, yeah, I guess so," Nita said. "But I think we're going to walk out of here today, because *you* miscalculated. You never considered what might happen if Darryl ever realized that the door swings both ways. Or that the door can be locked. Ever since he took the Oath, ever since you decided to stop him from being a wizard, he's been keeping you stuck in here with him on purpose! He's been getting better and better at it all the time, and you never even suspected, because you thought you were in control. But this is his masterwork, no matter what I did to the fun-house mirrors, which were just a local feature. And you're *still* sealed in here until he lets you go."

The Lone Power looked at Darryl.

Nita looked over at him, too. "Darryl?" she said. "You okay?"

"Yeah," he said, though he sounded somewhat surprised. "I didn't know anyone else would be able to see what was happening."

"The Lone Power couldn't," Kit said. "You built this place in such a way that It wouldn't be able to tell what was happening. But you weren't expecting *us* inside your worldview. You left a loophole."

"And once we got in—though we came and went— our points of view stayed behind, at least a little," Nita said to the Lone Power. "While only you were in here, Darryl believed what you believed about this space, and about his Ordeal—"

Darryl had walked over toward Nita and Kit while Nita was speaking . . . and the smile growing on his face now was rapidly becoming a match for Nita's: angry, but still very amused. "I may be autistic," Darryl said to the Lone One, grim, "but I'm not stupid. You've invested a lot of energy in your little cat-and-mouse game. Well, I can play this game, too. Maybe I'll just amuse myself playing with *you* for the rest of my natural life. It's sure been fun so far!"

The Lone One's expression was indescribable. Nita felt like laughing out loud, but this would have been the wrong moment.

"You cannot," It said after a moment. "Now that I am alerted to this game of yours, it will never work again, even if I did allow you to escape with either life or soul intact." It raised Its hands, clenched Its fists—

And nothing happened.

Nita smiled gently, and from her pocket, she pulled out the kernel to Darryl's internal universe.

The Lone One looked at it in sudden furious surprise.

"You really are running slow today," Nita said. "*You* taught me how to deal with these things when you were inside my old 'friend' Pralaya. How to find them . . . how to manage them. Of course, you were doing it for your own reasons. Maybe it didn't occur to you that I was going to walk away after the dirty deal you offered me! Or that I was going to survive the consequences. Well, I did...and I remember everything you showed me, very well." She smiled. "Now I— excuse me, *we*—just have to decide what else to do with this besides making you temporarily powerless."

Nita stood there with the universe's kernel, the heart of the world, in her hand, juggling it like someone juggling a grenade with the pin pulled. "Make your stay here permanent, maybe?" she said, glancing over at Darryl. "By just wiping the whole place out?"

"You wouldn't dare," the Lone One said.

"I'd dare a whole lot at the moment, so don't push me!" Nita said. "Doesn't it strike you as likely that I'd have just a *whole* lot of fun killing you off? Oh, sure, it wouldn't be the *whole* you. Here you're just a fragment of your greater self; I know that. And I'd die, too. And so would Kit, and Darryl. But the power that the One has invested in Darryl won't be lost."

"That power is lost *now*! Boy"—the Lone Power turned Its baleful gaze on Darryl—"you are one of the—"

Then Its face suddenly went white, as if a whole universe had suddenly taken It by the throat and squeezed.

"You're not going to be able to discuss certain subjects," Nita said, "so don't bother. Now, I think we were discussing what happens when we blow up this universe with you inside it. The damage done to *you* by the total destruction of even just this fragment of you...well."

She smiled.

The Lone One trained that deadly look on Nita now. "If you did such a thing," the Lone Power said, "your father and sister would—"

"Spare me," Nita said. Her eyes narrowed. "Life hasn't been so wonderful for me lately that I need to cling to it for my own sake. And if I went out taking you down, my dad and Dairine would grieve, yeah, but they'd applaud, too...because they'd find out soon enough that what I did lessened your clout in this part of the solar system." Nita grinned. "You've underestimated me one time too many. Someone needs to teach you that *this* kind of behavior isn't going to get you anywhere. I think today we're the ones to do it."

She turned as the Lone One lunged at her and tossed the kernel to Kit. He fielded it expertly.

"Nice little universe you've got here," Kit said, tossing it up in front of him, and then Hacky Sack-ing it into the air a few more times, from his knee and elbow, and once from his head, while the Lone Power came toward him, a look of furious uncertainty on Its face. "It'd be a shame if something happened to it. Whoa!"

He flipped the kernel to Darryl. Darryl caught it, looked it over, and tossed it lightly in one hand. The kernel, which had been glowing only softly while Nita and Kit had been holding it, now blazed like a star in the possession of its rightful master and creator.

"I've learned a lot from listening to the Silence for the past few months," Darryl said. "About wizardry, and a lot of other things. But that hasn't changed the fact that I haven't lived long enough to be really attached to life. Maybe this is the other thing that makes wizards so powerful when they're young. It's not that we don't know about death. It's not that we don't believe in it. It's that we're still able to let life go, if the price is right."

He looked at the other two, looked in their eyes.

Nita nodded. She glanced at Kit.

Kit hesitated a moment...then set his jaw, and nodded, too.

The three of them looked at the Lone Power. It stood in the middle of them, trembling with rage...or with something else.

"You want to bargain," It said.

"*Our* terms," Darryl said. "Not yours."

"What's the price for my freedom?" It said at last.

"Once *they* leave, they stay unharmed," Darryl said. "No more than your usual attentions in the future. If you refuse, you stay in here with me until I die...and I chase you around and around forever."

It stood there, silent, brooding. "But you stay here, even if I go?" It said.

"This is my world," Darryl said. "Where else would I go? I'll stay here."

Nita and Kit looked at each other in shock.

"I can still make something of this place, with time," Darryl said. "Everything has its price. I'll stay."

The Lone Power's face was expressionless. "On the Oath, and in Life's name, you say it?"

"Darryl!" Nita cried.

"Don't!" Kit cried in the same moment.

"On my Oath," Darryl said, very deliberately, "and in the One's name, I say it."

The Lone Power stood there, staring at the floor. Then, slowly, It began to smile.

"Fooled," It said. "Fooled again."

It started to chuckle. "You've bound yourself to my will after all," It said. "What makes you think that just because you cast me out once, you can do it again? Manipulate your world's kernel as you please. I have something better to manipulate. Entropy is my tool. I'll wear away at the fringes of this place, at the edges of your life, until sooner or later you let your guard over the kernel's parameters drop. I'll be in here again within seconds. Then you'll still be trapped here forever... and I'll stay here with you, making every moment a torment, and reminding you every second of the rest of your life of the price of mocking the Eldest. Despair now, for you won't have time later."

"I'll get around to the despair thing when I'm good and ready," Darryl said. "Meantime, get your butt out of my world."

It gave them an ironic bow. "Once again," It said to Nita, "despite all the brave words, you've gotten someone else to save your little life at his expense. One of these days, someone will refuse you. I'll be waiting for you then. And for you," It said, glancing at Kit, "when she betrays you at last."

"*Out,*" Darryl said.

It looked from one to another of them. But It looked hardest and most cruelly at Darryl. "Don't get too comfortable here," It said. "I'll be along any day."

And It was gone.

They stood there, in the sudden silence, staring at each other.

Then, as if by prearranged signal, they all began to laugh.

"Oh, Neets!" Kit said, and he grabbed her and swung her around. "What a bluff! You were terrific!"

Nita was laughing, too, but there was an edge of pain on the laughter. "I'm not sure I was bluffing," she said. "I was just so angry right then that I believed it."

"You must have," Kit said. "There's no lying in the Speech. But Darryl…"

He turned to Darryl in concern. "That's the problem for you, guy. You promised to stay here."

"I did," Darryl said.

Nita let out a long, unhappy breath.

"But this isn't the only place I can be at the same time," Darryl said softly.

Nita's head jerked up.

"I thought I was hallucinating at first," Darryl said. "Now I know it's no hallucination. When the two of you started coming into my worlds, I was with you both at once." He shook his head. "I don't know if this is something most wizards can do—"

"It's *not*," Kit and Nita said simultaneously.

"But it's real useful," Kit said after a moment, intrigued. "Just think. If you were—"

"Kit, maybe we should save it for later," Nita said. This was a line of reasoning she didn't want him to go too far down just now. "Why don't we all get out of here first?"

Darryl looked at Nita in shock. "But I can't leave," Darryl said. "The Ordeal isn't over."

Nita looked at Kit, wondering if he'd realized the truth yet. From his blank look, it seemed he hadn't. Then she looked at Darryl, and laughed out loud for sheer delight.

"Sure it is!" Nita said. "You passed your Ordeal *weeks* ago! You passed it the minute you managed to say the Oath."

"Remember how you had to fight to get it out, word by word, phrase by phrase?" Kit said, slowly starting to grin. "How you kept losing it, forgetting it, having to start over again and again?"

"That was the Lone One interfering," Darryl said softly. He was wearing a listening look, as the Silence spoke to him.

Slowly, his face changed, and the joy in it was so dazzling that Nita found it hard to bear, and had to look away.

"That was the real battle," he said. "And I won it! I won…"

Nita had to smile, and for the first time in a long time, the smile didn't feel like it would crack her face.

Kit looked at Nita in some surprise. "I thought the Lone One only starts noticing a wizard when he first says the Oath."

"That's how it is for most of us," Nita said. "But it looks like not all Ordeals are alike." She was still treading cautiously around anything that would get too close to the subject of abdals, until she could get Kit somewhere private and give him the lowdown. *I'm pretty sure that since the Lone Power knew Darryl was an abdal, It wanted to keep him from taking the Oath any way It could, because who could tell how powerful he might become once he was a wizard? Maybe that's even why Darryl became autistic in the first place; maybe the Lone One did that to him. But I'd better not get into that just now...*

"And just the act of saying the Oath, accepting it, for someone autistic..." Nita looked at Darryl with renewed admiration. "You have to accept the concept of the Other, that there *are* others, to do it at all. It must have been like eating broken glass."

Darryl stood there looking as if a whole new world was opening up before him, as if his past pain was retreating into the shadows. "It *was* hard," he said. "The whole Oath is about doing things for other people..."

"But, Neets," Kit said. "Your manual, Tom's, mine, they all say that Darryl's still stuck in his Ordeal."

"Because *he* hadn't realized it was over," Nita said. "And because he just kept hitting the reset button in his brain, and losing his sense of self over and over again to keep the Lone One trapped in here, he never had *time* to let himself realize it. So his manual, the Silence, stayed stuck, too, and it couldn't update to the manual network outside."

Nita nodded. "The ones you couldn't look at, the ones you were afraid of because you saw It in their eyes, you had to promise the One and the Powers That Be that you would come out and do stuff for *them*. What could possibly have been harder?"

"This," Darryl said.

Nita and Kit glanced at each other.

"*That,*" Darryl said, changing his mind. "In here ... it's been safe. In here I never have to look, never have to be afraid I'll see what might be there. Rejection. The one who sees me and doesn't *want* to look back. Because he's bored with me, or I've hurt him, or ..."

"I will put aside fear for courage," Kit said.

"And death for life," Nita said, very softly. She swallowed. "When it's right to do so." She was silent for a moment, then said, "If it isn't right now, then when will it be?"

"We need you out in the real world with us, guy," Kit said. "We need all the wizards we can get ... now more than ever. Entropy's running ..."

"But I can't go out there!" Darryl cried. "It's in me! If I go out there, It'll be loose in the world in the worst possible way!"

Nita's heart squeezed inside her. "It's loose out there already," she said. "Your coming out, or not coming out, won't make the slightest difference to *that.* You can die with It at the bottom of your heart, out in the world with the rest of us, or you can die with It at the bottom of your heart, in here, alone."

He stood there, silent, his eyes averted.

"It's better not to do it alone," Nita said.

Darryl didn't look up.

"There's strength in numbers, Darryl," Kit said. "It's easy to forget that." He glanced at Nita a little shamefacedly. She gave him an amused look and raised her eyebrows. He turned back to Darryl. "There are a whole lot of us out in the world, giving It a hard time.

You were real good at doing that just when you were stuck inside and didn't have any clues about how the rest of us manage it. Come on out and give It a run for Its money! When you get right down to the bottom of it, that's nearly all we do. Which wizardries we use to do it...*that's* the cool part."

Darryl was silent for a long while. Eventually he looked up again, and as Darryl slowly started to let himself believe that this was the right thing to do, that innocent joy and delight in life simply poured off him, so that once more Nita had to brace herself against it.

She saw Kit wobble, too. Only Ponch stood there untroubled, wagging his tail.

"All right," Darryl said. "I'll come."

Ponch started to bark for joy.

Nita had to smile. "But one thing," Nita said, glancing at the kernel, "before you do anything final with that."

Darryl looked up at her, confused.

"If you have to leave part of you here," Nita said, "think about *which* part you might leave."

Darryl looked at her in confusion. "Which part?" he said. "I know I can be in both places with *all* of me, but splitting parts off—"

"Don't make reasons you can't do stuff, Darryl," Kit said. "Find reasons you *can*."

"You *made* this world," Nita said. "That's powerful stuff. And you can make the rules in here. You made them so strongly, without even being clear on what you were doing, that the Lone Power Itself got stuck in here with you and couldn't get out until you let It.

Now It's gone...and you're fully conscious, with the operating system for your own universe in your hands. You're not just inside the game anymore: You're outside it, too, now—you're in control of it when you've got the kernel. Even from in here, you can make this world anything you want!"

Darryl looked from Nita to Kit, and slowly, surmise dawned in his eyes.

"The autism..."

"Why not? You started ditching it the first chance you got," Nita said. "You ditched it on Kit, for example."

Darryl looked embarrassed. "I didn't mean to..."

"Darryl, I know you didn't mean it personally," Kit said. "It's okay. You were doing a sane thing, getting rid of it!" Then he glanced at Nita. "I still don't know *why* you didn't get it."

"It could have been that a lot more boys are autistic than girls," Nita said. "Or that Darryl and I already had something in common."

She wouldn't say it out loud. She didn't have to.

The pain, Darryl said silently. *The pain of being alone.*

Nita had to glance away.

"Yeah," Darryl said. "But giving it up..." He looked distressed. "I don't know if I can! It's part of me."

"So?" Kit said. "Is it a part you need?"

"*No!*" Darryl said.

And then he fell silent.

"I hear a *but* coming," Nita said.

"I don't know if I know how to live without it," Darryl said.

They were all silent for a few breaths.

"It's how I stood being alive," Darryl said. "It's how I *didn't* have to see the Lone Power at the bottom of everyone's soul, all the time. If I go back without it, I'm going to have to see that. Every day. Every time I look at my mom, or my dad..."

"Believe me," Nita said, very softly, "I'd look at my mom all day and every day no matter how much It looked out of her, if she were here to look at. Some things are a lot more important than others, Darryl."

"We all see It sometimes," Kit said. "We all run into It every day, in the people we know, in the things that happen around us. There's no escape. That's life. That's Life: what we serve. It's worth it."

Darryl was silent. "I don't know if I can stand how much it's going to hurt," he said. "I might lose it. I might fall back into being that way...and that would kill my folks."

"I'm guessing your folks are tougher than you think," Nita said, remembering the voices she'd heard on the way in. "Give them a chance. Give yourself a chance. If it does happen..." She grinned. "You're a wizard. Listen to the Silence. Pick yourself up and do what it tells you. You'll get out again...because you're tough, too. Tougher than you think."

Darryl looked at Nita with eyes that were beginning to believe. "Besides," Kit said, "imagine how funny it'll be when It finally gets back in here, and locks Itself in, and then discovers that what It's locked in with isn't you. It's your autism."

Darryl looked from Kit to Nita with that expression of absolute delight, edged again with mischief.

"Yeah," he whispered. "Let's do it."

"I don't think there's a lot of 'let's' about this," Kit said. "I think you get to do this part yourself. Otherwise, it's not going to take."

"Use the kernel," Nita said. "You set the configuration into it for the way you want this world to behave. The Silence will show you how. I had to take classes to find out, but this is your own world that you made. You're not going to need authorizations to work with it."

Darryl nodded, looking down at the kernel for a moment.

Then, "Oh," he said. "Oh!"

He was quiet for a long time. While he was concentrating, Kit bent his head over to Nita's and said, "Thanks."

"It was my turn to save you," Nita said, "that's all. Now I want a few weeks off."

Kit smiled a crooked smile at her.

Nita looked down at Ponch. "I thought you said you weren't going to take the boss out again without me," Nita said.

Ponch dropped his head a little. *He went,* he said. *So I had to go, too.* Then he brightened. *But you got here when I thought you would, so it's all right!*

Nita gave Kit a look. "Your dog has me on a *schedule*?" she said.

Kit shrugged. "He has a very well-developed time sense," Kit said. "Ask him about feeding time, for example."

Ponch began to jump up and down in excitement.

"Speaking of time," Darryl said suddenly, "I think this looks right..."

Nita glanced over at the kernel in his hands, judging the way the tangle of light looked and felt. "The parameters feel right," she said. "You ready?"

Darryl nodded, looking nervous and elated.

"Do it!" Nita said.

Slowly, all around them, the brightness dimmed down. "I left you a space to slip through," Darryl said, as the space darkened, like a stage at the end of a play. "Just behind you there. But this is what'll be left inside."

Darkness, and a spotlight.

In the spotlight, a clown rode a tiny bicycle around and around, never stopping, never looking up. Its eyes were empty. It was a machine, just a fragment of personality without the soul that had once animated it: hopeless, mindless, animate but insensate. Kit looked at it and thought of a windup mouse going around and around in little circles, waiting for the cat.

"Let's get out of here," Kit said. "Darryl? You know the way back?"

"In my sleep," he said, and grinned.

Kit held out a hand. "Welcome to the Art, brother," he said.

Darryl took the hand, then pulled Kit close and hugged him hard. He let go, turned to Nita. He hugged her, too.

"Later," she said. "Go home."

Darryl vanished with the ease of someone who's been doing it for years.

Kit and Nita looked at each other. "Your place or mine?" Nita said.

"My folks are going to yell at me," Kit said, "so let's do mine first."

Nita smiled a small wry smile. "You just want me to help you take the heat."

Mind reader, Kit said. *Come on.*

They vanished, too.

Some distance away, in a special-ed classroom in Baldwin, the afternoon routine was proceeding as usual when one of the teachers saw something unusual happen.

Darryl McAllister looked at him, looked at him straight on.

The teacher went over to the boy, and got down beside him where he had been sitting on the floor and rocking. "Hey there, Darryl," he said. "What's up?"

"I don't think," Darryl said, in a voice that cracked and creaked with not having been used for words for a long time, "I don't think I need to be here anymore."

The teacher's mouth dropped open.

"Can I go home now?" Darryl said, and smiled.

Liberations

THE EXPLANATIONS TO parents, Seniors, and others, as usual, took nearly as long as the events themselves had done, so it was several days before Nita and Kit found time to go off and relax. The chosen spot was a favorite one, by the edge of a crater close to a well-known site in Mare Tranquillitatis. They were leaning back against the very top of the upper crater wall, looking down over at the rising half-Earth, while Ponch lay on his back in the moondust, snoring, with his feet in the air.

A fourth figure suddenly stepped into the vacuum nearby, looking around him.

"Wow," Darryl said. He wandered over to where Nita and Kit sat, bouncing a little as first-timers tended to do, because of the lighter gravity.

"Are we allowed to be up here?" Darryl said, looking about half a mile away, toward where the feet and base of Apollo 11's lunar lander sat.

"As long as we don't mess it up," Kit said. "This is a heritage area."

Hearing that, Darryl burst out laughing, looking in mischievous admiration at the rough sculptures Kit had been doing on this site for some years. "*This* is what you do in a heritage area?"

"I'll clean it up before they build the hotel here," Kit said. "After that, I guess I'll have to amuse myself carving rocks on Mars into faces."

Darryl snickered.

"How are your folks doing?" Nita said.

"You kidding? They're in shock," Darryl said. He sat down on the rock beside Kit.

"I wouldn't have thought they'd let you out of their sight right now," Kit said.

"They haven't," Darryl said. "I'm home in bed."

"Oh," Nita said, and laughed. "Wow, that two-for-one deal really does come in handy, doesn't it?"

She'd already had a word with Kit about the genuine source of Darryl's ability to be in two places at once. They'd agreed that there was no need to be too cagey about mentioning Darryl's ability to co-locate, as long as they stayed away from discussing the reasons for it. If Darryl just thought it was a personal talent, that was fine.

"I looked at the transit spells," Darryl said. "But except for the air, they looked like a waste of energy. We're not supposed to waste. And besides, why go to all that trouble when I can just do this?"

For a moment he was standing behind a large boulder some feet away, while also sitting on the rock beside Kit. Kit shook his head in admiration.

"It's a slick trick," Kit said. "I'll do it my way for the time being, though. Seriously...are your parents coping?"

"They're coping great." Darryl's eyes shone. It was plain to Nita that this was an understatement. "My mom and dad are..." He broke off, shook his head.

"It's all new," Darryl said after a moment. "They hardly dare to believe it. And I can't really tell them why they *can* believe it, not yet. Eventually I will. But right now wizardry'd be one shock too many. They'd probably think I was coming down with some kind of nuts to replace the autism."

"Give them some time," Kit said. "Neither of us came right out to our parents, either. I think you're probably right, though. Too much strange at once isn't a good thing for them. There's going to be enough of that later, once you start getting into your serious work, whatever that turns out to be. For now, just enjoy how happy they are, and take it easy."

"Well, happy's good, but the 'take it easy' part's not going to last," Darryl said, and grinned. "I heard my mom thinking that if I was really going to be better now, she was going to start giving me *chores.*"

Nita and Kit groaned in unison.

"She was kind of nervous about it," Darryl said. "I think I get a few weeks of being lazy before they really start expecting me to be normal."

"Take advantage of it," Kit said. "Once they start, they never let up."

Darryl nodded, looked over at the Earth. "So now we get to take care of that," he said.

"That's the job," Nita said.

"I'd better get on with it then," Darryl said. "You guys come here often?"

"Often enough," Kit said.

"I might be needing some advice as I work into this job," Darryl said.

"For you, we're available any time," Nita said.

Kit grinned. "We're in the book."

Darryl nodded and waved. A second later he was gone.

"Nice kid," Kit said after a moment.

"No argument there," Nita said. "Come on, your mom said dinner was at six."

Kit was looking over at the Earth. "It really is the best job, isn't it?" he said.

Nita nodded. "None better. And the company's good, too."

"The best," Kit said. "Welcome back."

Nita smiled. "Come *on*," she said. "I want some of that chicken you're always raving about."

Kit stood up and dusted floury pumice dust off him. "Yeah, well, if you think you're going to get a bigger portion than I am, think again! C'mon, Ponch."

Ponch rolled over and bounced to his feet in a cloud of silvery dust. Kit and Nita vanished.

Ponch stood there, looking thoughtfully at the half-Earth for some moments...then wagged his tail.

Chicken! he said silently, leaped up, and vanished.

The next morning Nita walked to school quietly by herself, noticing a lot of things that had passed her by recently: the snow, the slush (of which there was a great deal), the icicles hanging down, glittering, from the eaves of people's houses; the color of the sky, the sound of people's voices as they said good-bye to each other on their way to work. *If it wasn't for what's been going on this past week or so,* she thought, *how much of this would I have noticed?* She had been locked up in her grief as surely as Darryl had been locked up in the otherworlds of his own making. It had taken a major blow to jar her loose, and Darryl had gone through something similar.

But he was free now. *And as for me...*

Nita mused as she turned the corner, thinking of Carl's mention of the concept that right across the fields of existence "all is done for each." As far as she could tell, that meant that every good thing that happened to everybody had some effect on all the rest of everybody, from here to the edges of the universe. It was like that saying about the chaos-theory butterfly in the rainforest, which, just by waving its little wings, contributes to the hurricane half a hemisphere away—if not actually causing the hurricane. But more specifically, the "all done for each" principle seemed to mean that the Powers That Be had designed the world so that everything that happened in it—every victory, every sacrifice, from the largest to the smallest—was pointed specifically at every separate living thing. At first Nita had found this almost impossible to imagine. Now she found herself wondering if what she'd just been through, besides being about Darryl's liberation, had been about helping her find her way out of her own pain as well.

Nita shrugged as she walked in through the gates that led into the parking lot. There was plenty of time to get into the highly theoretical stuff later. For now, she had work to catch up on...and some other business to finish.

She went down to the temporary office where she usually found Mr. Millman. There he was, sitting behind the desk and reading a magazine while eating the last couple of bites of a bagel with cream cheese.

He glanced up as Nita came in. "Morning," he said.

Nita sat down, put her book bag on the floor, reached into her jacket, and came out with the cards.

"Before you start in with those," Mr. Millman said, "one thing. We left on a slightly jangly note the other day..."

"Did we?" Nita said, refusing for the moment to smile at him, refusing to let him off the hook.

"I think we did, especially since you cut half your classes shortly thereafter."

Nita shrugged. Millman's eyebrows went up as he took note of the gesture. "I just wanted you to know something," he said. "Whatever the secret is about what's going on in your life right now—I want you to know that there's no need for you to tell me, ever, and I have no intention of pressing you."

Nita looked at him with surprise, because this wasn't what she'd been thinking. She also looked at him with amused suspicion. "What is this, some kind of reverse psychology?"

Mr. Millman looked at her in shock, and then laughed. "What? Like you're a three-year-old or something, and you'll do the opposite of what I suggest? Spare me. This is supposed to have been counseling, not brain surgery. I was merely saying that my intent was just to counsel you—not to dig around in your skull for juicy tidbits, like something out of a horror movie about bad Far Eastern food."

Nita snickered. "Okay," she said. "I thought you were going to say something about my anger."

"Anything that needs to be said," said Mr. Millman, "I'm sure you'll take care of it."

Nita slipped the cards out of their pack and started to shuffle them. It was surprising how easy the false shuffles were when you were really paying attention to them. "Name a card," she said.

"Five of diamonds," he said.

Nita nodded, put the deck down on the desk, and cut it twice, to the right, to make three piles. "Turn one card over," she said.

Millman reached out and turned over the top card of the leftmost deck. The top card was the five of diamonds.

"Not bad at all," Millman said. "Do I get to pick another one?"

Nita gave him a look. "I wouldn't push your luck if I were you," she said.

He grinned a little and sat back.

"You look a whole lot better," he said.

"I feel a whole lot better," Nita said. "And I think I don't need to be here anymore."

"What, school?" Millman said, raising his eyebrows.

"Not school here. *Here* here," Nita said.

"Oh, you're cured then?" he said.

Nita cracked up. "Why not?" she said. And then said, "Cured of what?"

"You would be the one to tell me that," Millman said.

Nita was quiet for a moment. "If you mean, am I over my mom dying? Don't be silly," she finally said. "She'll always be part of me. It's going to hurt for a long time that she's not still in my house. But nothing can take her out of my life. Am I over wanting to just sit and suffer and let life go by? I think so."

"Then I would say," Mr. Millman said, "that my work here is done. Insofar as any of it was *my* work."

He reached out and turned over the top card on the middle pack. It was the ace of spades. "Aha," he said.

"What?"

"Highly symbolic."

"Of what?"

"Well, that would be a long story. That little leaf-shaped thing, the 'spade'..." Mr. Millman picked up the card, looked closely at it. "The history of the word is tangled. But it goes back at least as far as the Greek *spatha*. That was a sword, once upon a time. Of the four suits, that's the one that has most to do with power: air, the sound the sword makes in the air, the spoken word; the weapons held by the Power that faces down the Power That Fell..."

He picked up the ace and the three cut packs, shuffling them together again.

Nita looked at him.

"So," Mr. Millman said, putting the deck down on

the desk and doing a credible riffle…much too credible, now that Nita thought of it, for a man who claimed that he couldn't get the cards to stay up his sleeve. "Any last questions before we finish up here?"

She looked at him, thought for a moment, and found a question it would never before have occurred to her to ask him. The answer would have been in her manual, but she wasn't going to consult that right now. Considering the question, Nita first made sure that she had the wizardry she wanted ready in the back of her head. If you were going to remove someone's memory, the less time you spent dithering over it, the better.

"Are you on errantry?" Nita said.

He raised his eyebrows again in that expression she'd learned could mean almost anything but surprise.

"No," Mr. Millman said. "But I know some people who are."

Nita sat there, astonished, trying not to exhibit it. Millman sat there and kept shuffling.

"You don't have to be a wizard to know one," Millman said, "once you know what you're looking for. And when you're willing to *see* what you're looking at. Not many people are, but that's humans for you." He fanned out the cards for her. "Pick a card, any card."

Nita picked one, turned it over. It was the joker.

Mr. Millman grinned, folded the hand up, tapped the cards back into order, and pushed the deck back toward Nita, meanwhile glancing at the door. "You know where to find me if you need me," he said. "And I've had a word with your sister's counselor: She'll be introducing me to Dairine later in the week. Meanwhile, go well."

Nita got up and took back her pack of cards, grinning, too. She headed for the door.

There she paused as something occurred to her. "'Supposed to have *been* counseling'?" she said.

Mr. Millman shrugged.

Nita shook her head again. "*Dai stihó,*" she said, and left.

That night Nita had a dream. In the dream she stood at the edge of darkness, looking in. Out there in the dark was a spotlight, wobbling around and around, shining on something, while somewhere off in the near distance, a single drum held a drumroll.

What the spotlight was following was a clown act. The clown had purple hair, and a little derby hat, and baggy patched pants, and it was riding around and around in circles on a ridiculously small bicycle, the circles ever decreasing. Around and around and around went the clown, in jerky, wobbling movements. It had a painted black tear running down its face. The red-painted mouth was turned down. But the face under the white greasepaint mask was as immobile as a marble statue's, expressionless, plastered in place. Only the eyes were alive. They shouted, *I can't get off! I can't get off!*

The drumroll went on and on. Beyond the light, a heartless crowd laughed and clapped and cheered. But there was no sound of growling now, no tiger waiting to pounce. It had already pounced. Now the tiger had become part of the clown...and the clown was its cage.

Nita woke up to the bright daylight, reflected from snow onto the ceiling of her bedroom...and she grinned.

The doorbell rang. Kit glanced up as he was throwing books into his book bag. He would have gone to the door himself, but his sister plunged past him. "What?" Kit said, looking all around to try to understand why Carmela was suddenly so hot to answer the door.

No answer came back. Kit could do little but shrug and finish packing his book bag. He stood up from the sofa just in time to look out the window and see the UPS truck pull away.

His sister closed the front door and nearly danced past him into the kitchen. *"What?"* Kit said.

Carmela got a particularly large knife out of the knife rack and began slitting the packing tape on the large box she'd been carrying. Kit fastened his bag and wandered over.

"It has to be clothes," he said. After a childhood during which Carmela's major occupation had been ruining the OshKosh overalls that were all their parents dared buy her, Carmela had suddenly discovered clothing as something besides protection from the elements. Now all her pocket money went in this direction, either down at the mall or via various strange mail-order firms. "Nothing but clothes gets you this excited anymore," Kit said. "Except maybe Miguel."

And having said that, Kit prepared to protect himself from the explosion that was sure to follow. *I can't believe I said that to her while she was holding a knife!*

But the explosion didn't follow. Carmela, grinning all over her face and singing a little la-la song, put the knife aside, opened the top of the box, and started removing the contents. These seemed to be only Styrofoam peanuts for the first thirty seconds or so. But then Carmela reached in and lifted out something wrapped in foam.

"It's not clothes," Kit said, astonished.

"Nope," Carmela said. "Much better."

This statement left Kit completely confused. Carmela carefully started unwrapping the foam from around the object.

"It's some hair thing," Kit said. "One of those hot curlers."

Carmela just smiled and kept on unwrapping.

The last bit of wrapping fell away. Carmela held the object up delightedly, admiring it in the morning light, and then thrust it into Kit's hands.

"Let's see what the directions say," she said. She turned back to the box and started digging through the Styrofoam peanuts again.

Kit looked at what he was holding. It looked very much like an eggbeater, except that eggbeaters don't usually have pulse lasers built into them.

Neets? he said silently.

A moment later the answer came back. *What?*

Can I please move in with you?

There was a pause . . . and then laughter.

I'll be right over . . .